HER SECRET
New Haven Series (Book 5)

Samantha J. Ball

Copyright © 2024 Samantha J. Ball

All rights reserved.

ISBN-13: 9798878675383

For Tamlyn. Your friendship and unwavering support mean the world to me.

"My command is this: Love each other as I have loved you. Greater love has no one than this: to lay down one's life for one's friends."
John 15:12-13 NIV

The New Haven Series

Chapter One

NEW YORK, September

"I don't understand why we're here." Glaring at her dinner companion, Emily Quinn snatched the white linen napkin off the table and dumped it onto her lap.

Henry Palmer slowly shook out his own napkin, poured water into their crystal tumblers, and then brought his forest-green eyes to meet hers. "Is it really *so* terrible spending time alone with me?" His deep, low voice rumbled across the table.

She pursed her lips. Their reservation was originally for four. Henry's best friend and business partner, Adam Wilson, and Emily's boss, Charlotte Scott, were *supposed* to join them. Obviously, that hadn't happened.

Emily picked up the menu and looked at some of the prices. She balked. "Can you believe this?" she whispered, catching Henry's eye. "Twenty-two dollars for a salad!"

"If you're worried about who's going to pay the bill, Emily, don't. It's already taken care of."

If only that were her concern. It wasn't. Charlotte had no doubt provided her credit card details when she booked this exclusive New York restaurant.

Emily's forehead wrinkled—something she couldn't stop any more than she could help being in this fancy place with

Henry. A man who elicited all sorts of emotions in her. Most of which she did *not* want to be experiencing. At all.

Huffing out a breath, she dropped her chin and drummed her fingers on the starched white tablecloth. There could well be stains all over this by the end of the evening. They would make an interesting match for those on her heart.

"I'm not worried about the bill, Henry. No one could possibly expect me, a mere nanny, to pay for a meal here." She waved her hand about the place. Everyone knew Michelin-starred establishments charged extortionate prices. She cast him a fleeting look. "I bet I could only afford a glass of water."

"The water's free." He smirked.

"Precisely."

A wine server appeared at their table dressed in a black suit and white button-down shirt. Without looking at Emily, he delivered a leather-bound manual to Henry; one that matched their white leather chairs. "The wine menu, sir."

Emily scowled, her internal temperature rising a few degrees. Only a man would be able to choose a decent vintage. Certainly not a young woman.

Henry glanced up from the extensive list. "Are you happy with a Cabernet Sauvignon, or would you like to choose?" He offered her the book.

Well, well. Score one for Henry. No man, not even her father, had ever asked her opinion on wine.

She shook her head. "A Cabernet's good."

"Excellent choice, sir." The man gave a single nod. "Someone will be with you shortly to take your food order."

Henry smiled politely. "Thank you."

Scouring the food menu again made Emily's mouth water. In her peripheral, she noted Henry leafing through the pages more quickly, as if he were familiar.

Instead of pondering what that might mean, she concentrated on what she wanted to eat.

In the end, they ordered separate entrees but agreed to share a main, the thirty-six-ounce ribeye. It surprised her how easily Henry agreed. Most men she'd dated—not that this was a date, she reminded herself firmly—thought it wasn't manly to share.

Score two for Henry.

Settling back into his chair, Henry surveyed their surroundings before resting his full attention on her. "So, where do you think Adam and Charlotte ended up?"

"Probably down a side road at a family-run establishment, one with homemade dishes on the menu." Emily tried to keep the jealousy out of her voice but didn't quite succeed.

They'd been about to enter this restaurant for a pre-Jays' concert dinner when Charlotte suddenly insisted she wasn't dressed appropriately. The white satin top paired with a denim skirt seemed perfectly suitable in Emily's opinion. Yet Adam, the kind and caring boyfriend that he was, offered to take Charlotte someplace more casual. That left Emily stuck with Henry until after dinner.

Exactly what she hadn't wanted.

Perhaps Charlotte planned it so Emily and Henry would have dinner alone together.

"Is that where you'd rather be, Emily, at a mom-and-pop restaurant?"

She contemplated saying no, but it would be a lie.

"If I had a choice?"

Nodding, Henry remained tight-lipped, his eyes fixed on her.

"Yes," she replied.

"Because of me?"

She was surprised by the hurt lacing his voice and his wounded expression. He cared.

"Believe it or not, Henry, it's got nothing to do with you."

"O-kay." His frown deepened. "So why aren't you comfortable here?"

"Let's just say I have a problem with the type of person who regularly dines at places like this."

Dark bushy eyebrows rose to meet a matching hairline. "And you have experience with these people?" he asked. His eyes sparked with an unidentifiable emotion. "Do you mean the rich and entitled patrons or the famous ones?"

"The former, really. If they're famous like the Jays, hopefully, it's because they've worked hard for their money and fame and weren't born with silver spoons in their mouths. The ones I have a problem with are those who use Mommy and Daddy's trust fund money to make others think they're important and feel they don't have to work to show they're deserving of attention." Emily cringed as she ended her tirade—even she could hear the bitterness in her tone.

A strange look passed over Henry's face, so fleeting she couldn't tell whether it was rejection or irritation.

What was his story? How come he'd spoken with such ease to the waiters?

Once their wine was delivered and expertly poured, Emily raised her crystal glass. She swirled the liquid, sniffed it, and then took a leisurely sip of the fine wine. Wow, smooth and velvety, with hints of spice. Excellent. Henry sure knew how to pick a great vintage.

She tilted her head to the side. "So, you went to Harvard, right?"

"Mm-hmm."

"And grew up here, in Manhattan?"

"Yep."

"Not in the Bronx, I assume?"

Henry's genuine laughter, deep and rounded, caused a couple of heads to turn. "No, definitely not the Bronx." His eyes sparkled with amusement. "What about you?" he asked softly, his eyes piercing hers. "Where did you grow up?"

Emily's breath hitched. Great. She'd walked right into that one. Maybe he'd move on to a different subject if she kept it vague. "New York."

"Oh, I didn't know that." A slow, easy smile appeared on his handsome face. And just like it did every time he let it loose, it wreaked havoc on her insides.

She gulped more wine, then took a fortifying breath.

"Whereabouts? You and I could've been neighbors." Henry

sounded thrilled at the possibility.

Hah. Not likely, she thought, holding back an unladylike snort.

"Maybe our parents, Henry, but definitely not us. You probably moved out of home when I started elementary school."

"Hey!" His smile dipped into a scowl. "I'm not *that* much older than you."

She guffawed. "Come on, we're at least ten years apart. For me, that's practically a lifetime."

"Really?"

"Well, it's double my lifetime."

Rubbing his index finger across his cheek, Henry examined her face. "You're young, but... I reckon you're over twenty-two."

"Not much over. I'm—" A guest, who looked decidedly like Daniel Radcliffe, walked by with a stunning brunette on his arm. In six-inch heels, the woman towered above him. "Um..."

"Emily?"

"Sorry." Blinking, she focused on her date. No, not date. Companion. "I'm twenty-four," she admitted, finally remembering the conversation.

Eyes shining, he flopped back in his chair.

Why did he look relieved? It's not like he'd want to date her. He was probably around thirty-five, and anyway, she was too young.

"So, an eight-year age gap."

"You're thirty-two?" Her mouth gaped. "I thought..." She swallowed her words.

"What?"

"Nothing."

"Okay. I'll let it slide for now." Folding his arms, he winked. The deep blue shirt he wore showcased his ample muscles as it stretched across his chest and strained at his biceps.

What would it be like to have those strong arms wrapped

around her?

Flushing, Emily looked away. Thankfully, the arrival of artfully presented entrees shifted their focus. Considering she'd skipped lunch to ensure she enjoyed her night in New York, she was glad her stomach hadn't yet rumbled. The thought of being around Henry tonight hadn't affected her appetite. Nope. Not at all.

"Charlotte mentioned you're studying part-time to become a teacher."

He'd been talking to her boss about *her*. Interesting.

Nodding, she took a bite of calamari and stifled a moan of pleasure as it positively melted in her mouth.

"Is it because you look after children?"

Emily set her silverware down. How much did she want to reveal? Honestly, she should stick to surface level.

Oh, what the heck.

"I've always loved children," she began. "I loved being in school and looked up to my teachers. I admired how they shaped us into future adults."

"Sounds like the perfect career choice. Did you always want to be a teacher?"

She shrugged. "Pretty much."

"Then why didn't you go to college when you graduated high school? Was it a financial thing?"

He would assume that.

"My father had different ideas about what I should do when I left school. Teaching was not one of them."

"Surely he didn't expect a bright woman like you to only be a nanny? Please, tell me he's not the sort to expect a woman to be barefoot and in the kitchen?"

Picking up her silverware again, Emily gave Henry the side-eye. "What's wrong with being a nanny?"

"Nothing." He smiled apologetically; at least, she hoped it wasn't mocking. "It's an essential job for some families. I just think you could use your talents more. Teaching, for one thing."

Seriously! Who did he think he was, giving her career

advice?

"I have a Business Management degree," she blurted, not meeting his eye.

"You do?"

When Henry's hand touched her lower arm, her eyes rushed to meet his. She could've sworn she saw pride in them. Warmth even. "That's amazing," he gushed, then frowned as he removed his hand. "Why haven't you done something with it?"

She twirled the stem of her wine glass. "It would mean working for my father, and I absolutely refuse."

"I take it you and your father don't see eye to eye," he said, his tone gentle yet slightly probing.

She raised her chin, clenching her jaw involuntarily. "My father loves me. He does. He just expects me to conform to his idea of what his precious daughter should be doing, where she should be living, and with whom she should be partnered."

"Sounds a little controlling."

She nodded. "Precisely why I ran away."

"So, the nanny gig's a temporary stepping stone until you become a teacher?"

"Kind of."

Henry rubbed his forehead.

"Even when I eventually teach full-time, I'll continue working for Charlotte. She's been so good to me. I don't want to let her down."

"Commendable."

Wiping imaginary crumbs from her lap, Emily inhaled deeply. The annoying man had power. Power to make her feel good about herself, about her decisions. That was dangerous. The last time a good-looking man paid her such compliments, she ended up—

"Would you like to see the dessert menu, sir, ma'am?"

"Thank you." Grateful for the interruption of her near walk down memory lane, Emily collected the proffered card from the server. After scanning the content, she discarded it and eyeballed Henry. About time she left the hot seat.

His eyebrows scrunched together. "What?"

"Do you plan on running Daily Bread for the rest of your life?" she asked. "Or do you have other ambitions?"

Instead of the irritation she expected, Henry smirked, leaving her more confused than ever.

"Now isn't that a million-dollar question?"

Chapter Two

Henry couldn't help smirking at Emily's question, a loaded one, for sure. What she didn't know was that their fathers sounded like they'd been raised with the same mentality. She might not be expected to run a billion-dollar group of companies one day, but Henry's dad had plans for his life just like hers did. Hence the reason he'd also run away from his New York responsibilities. Unfortunately, his time for playing hooky was running out.

He gave a humorless laugh. "Daily Bread will be in my past, if my father has anything to say about it. His son running a nonprofit is not what he envisioned, ever."

"You have a controlling father, too?"

Henry motioned to the dessert card in her hand. "You going to order anything?"

Her nose twitched adorably. "Do we have time?"

"Well, we don't have to hang around to pay, so yes."

"I'll have to remember to thank Charlotte." Emily patted her stomach with a satisfied smile. "That steak was the best I've ever eaten."

The woman was super-cute, not to mention beautiful. He grinned. "I'll give your compliments to the chef."

"You know the chef?" Her pretty brown eyes went wide.

"We went to high school together."

"So he's as old as you?"

Her innocent tone didn't fool him.

"Yes, Emily." He glowered. "He's ancient like me."

Remorse filled her face briefly, making him feel guilty. He didn't really mind being called old. Not when their almost decade age difference was significant. But generally, he went for women much younger than him anyway.

Nothing to do with aggravating his father, of course.

If Dad had his way, Henry would be married to the 'perfect' thirty-year-old with their second child on the way.

Settling down?

Not on his agenda.

The minute he entered a more serious-looking relationship, his parents would have him engaged within three months. They'd insist he claim his full inheritance and allow his father to finally retire. Henry would become CEO of Palmer Enterprises and, until his dad passed on, wouldn't enjoy another day of freedom.

A terrible thought.

His answer: date younger women who were nowhere near ready to settle down, and keep his financial situation a secret. Therefore, no incentive for anyone to become serious.

A win-win situation.

But Emily was different. While only twenty-four, she came across as more mature in her attitude and behavior. Discovering she had a business degree while on her way to becoming a qualified teacher, well, that was incredible. His estimation and admiration of her had grown substantially with that knowledge.

Unlike his usual type though, Emily's mere presence set his heart racing. He desired nothing more than to take her in his arms and kiss her senseless, to feel her body pressed against his, and to drown in her mesmerizing eyes. She was gorgeous. Even more so as he got to know her better.

An unexplained need to protect her welled up in him.

"I'm sorry, Henry. It's wrong of me to call you an *old* man." Emily's soft voice interrupted his musings. "You're not. It's just my way of—" She bit her lower lip.

Trying hard not to focus on her kissable mouth, he lifted

his eyes a few inches. "Your way of?"

Pursing her lips, she crossed her arms. "Nothing."

Fine. He wouldn't press. "It's cool," he said nonchalantly. "I know you're kidding around. Otherwise, Adam would get it from you, too." He smiled wryly. "It's your way of making me think you don't like me, so I don't make any passes at you. Right?" he said cheekily.

The way her face dropped and her expression blanked, he figured he might've nailed the reason. Warmth swelled through him. Oh, this was good; Emily *did* like him.

He reached for his glass and finished off his wine. "Am I right?" he asked. "Do I detect a little spark of attraction?"

"No, definitely not," she responded rapid fire. Her head dipped, but not before he caught the betraying blush on her cheeks.

Suppressing a grin, he mentally cheered at his discovery.

"What can I get you, ma'am?" their server asked, appearing at Emily's side.

"Panna cotta and a black coffee, please."

"Same." Henry handed back his card.

The man left, and Emily shot Henry a surprised look. "I can't picture you eating panna cotta."

"You will in five minutes."

She shrugged.

"Is it not a 'manly' enough dessert?"

"I expected you to choose the chocolate fudge cake."

"I'm glad I can surprise you," he said, reaching out to cover her hand. A flare of electricity shocked his fingertips. Pulling back swiftly, he spotted Emily's wide eyes before she quickly reached for her phone. Seconds later, she looked at him, all trace that she'd been as affected as him gone from her expression.

"Charlotte asked if we're on track, time wise."

"Tell her we'll be there."

After typing a short message, Emily slipped her cell into her purse and crossed her arms. Clearly, she didn't want to risk him touching her again. But boy, he wanted to. If a simple action like touching her could affect him so strongly, what would it be like to hold her hand?

His eyes traveled to her face and lowered to her mouth; her very inviting mouth, perfectly shaped for kissing.

Bad idea.

Closing his eyes, he hoped to clear his mind. Except, nothing changed when he opened them. The attractive woman still made his body hum and his mind go where it shouldn't.

Later that evening, the group returned to their hotel lobby on a high after the Jays' concert.

"How about a nightcap?" Adam suggested to Henry and Emily while keeping his girlfriend tucked beside him.

"I'm in." Charlotte smiled adoringly at Adam, who pressed a kiss to her head.

Henry was happy for his best friend. The two were clearly smitten. But he wasn't sure whether having a drink with them right now was wise. Casting a surreptitious look at Emily, he tried to gauge her feelings. Throughout the concert, whenever he'd snuck a sideways glance at her, their gazes had connected. Attraction had pulsed between them. They'd managed to hide it from Adam and Charlotte, but keeping up the deception for much longer might be impossible.

Excuses swirled in Henry's head.

"I think I'll head to bed," Emily said, covering a yawn. She gave Charlotte an apologetic look.

Before he could lose his nerve, Henry spoke. "I'll walk Emily to her hotel room. It's on the same floor as mine anyway."

No one objected. Not even Emily. Instead, they all said goodnight, and Adam led Charlotte toward the hotel bar while Henry followed Emily to the elevator.

The ride up to the sixth floor went quickly and quietly, and they stepped off together with Emily leading the way. Two doors down from the elevator, she stopped.

"This is me." She pulled out a plastic key card and then struggled to open her door.

After wiping sweaty palms down his pants, Henry gently removed the item from her shaking hand, and within seconds, the door buzzed open.

He faced her, his hand on the handle of the open door. "There you go." He gave a little smile. "You can tell Charlotte I did my duty and ensured you were safely escorted to your room."

"Thanks for doing your duty," she said lightly, a teasing glint in her eyes. "Though, perhaps I need to remind you that I'm not a child who needs looking after by her father."

Henry was so close he could smell her citrusy perfume, and his body hummed with longing.

"You calling me an old man again?" His voice came out low and raspy.

"No, but—"

Unable to resist, Henry slid his hands around Emily's slim waist and leaned forward. She stiffened until his lips captured hers, then she melted into his embrace and kissed him back. The door clicking shut behind them barely registered, so focused was he on the soft warm mouth responding to his kiss.

Although he'd kissed more than his fair share of women, none had quite the same effect as Emily. Henry felt like he was on another planet or soaring above the earth, looking down on a little piece of heaven.

He pulled her closer, ensuring no gap remained between their bodies. Emily slipped her arms around his neck and ran her fingers through the hair at the nape of his neck. At the same time, their lips passionately explored, and their elicited sighs and moans said more than words could. The more Henry discovered, the more he liked what he found.

His heart raced. He'd have to end things soon.

The elevator pinged, and they flew apart, their gazes clinging as they fought to get their breathing under control.

When the occupants were out of earshot, Emily hissed, "That can't happen again."

"Why not?" He frowned. "You can't tell me that wasn't the

best kiss you've ever had because it was for me."

"It doesn't matter." She shook her head, her gaze fierce. "You and me?" she said, pointing between them. "We can't be. It's not happening. I'm not interested in a casual relationship."

"Who said anything about casual—?"

"Or any relationship for that matter. I need to focus on my studies. I don't have time to worry about how long this would or wouldn't last. I have responsibilities and goals, and they don't include a man. Never mind our terrible timing, our lives are on completely different paths."

He couldn't believe what he was hearing. The first woman he'd considered getting serious with was effectively shutting him down. And she viewed him as a player. He might seem like someone with little interest in a permanent relationship, but that was because he'd avoided getting serious and settling down. The repercussions of a decision like that were monumental, life-changing even.

"Are you serious? You won't even entertain the thought? Try?" he implored, his heart racing for another reason entirely now. He didn't want this to end before it even had a chance.

"No." The fierce determination on her beautiful face would've taken his breath away if the rejection hadn't physically hurt so much.

Henry stepped back and swiped his hand over his face, then gripped the back of his neck. Trying not to sound devastated, he spoke in an even tone. "So that's it? I have to accept that you want no part in exploring where things could go with us? You don't want to take some time to think things through? Reconsider?"

"I'm sorry, no. Just because you're the most incredible kisser ever doesn't mean I'll change my mind."

The compliment might've bolstered his ego, but her outright rejection destroyed it.

When her second attempt to open the door worked, she stepped over the threshold and spun around. "Forget any romantic interest you have in me, Henry. It's for the best. I'll see you at breakfast."

The door swung shut, leaving him staring at the dark wood. She made it sound so easy. What were the chances he'd be able to forget anything about her? It's not like he could disappear to the other end of the country and never lay eyes on her again. They went to the same church, had mutual friends, and lived in the same city.

He was trapped.

Chapter Three

Five weeks later…

"So, Henry, have you found anyone special yet?"

Henry's eyes flitted from his mom, Denise, who'd asked the question he'd been skirting around for the past half hour, to his dad, Robert, seated beside her. The hope shining on his parents' faces almost did him in.

"Nope." He shoved a piece of meat into his mouth and chewed with gusto. The tender steak melted in seconds, annoyingly. Mom raised him to never talk with his mouth full.

"Well, that's a shame," Mom said, tucking a dark strand of hair behind her ear. The new pixie cut accentuated her cheekbones, making her appear edgy. It suited her.

"We hoped you'd be serious about someone by now." Dad's dark bushy eyebrows—almost identical to his son's—drew together.

Another forkful of meat bought time to think about how to respond. Frankly, the less time he spent in New York with his parents, the better. Not that he didn't love them. He did. He just preferred to stay out of their orbit. Then they'd forget about their plans for his future.

Sometimes, a visit to the city wasn't negotiable. Like this weekend. His sister Nicole deserved his presence at her daughter Isabella's fifth birthday party. Even if he would've preferred to lay low. Except, now he had to endure dinner with his parents in this Michelin-starred restaurant.

With no buffers.

Nicole had pulled out last minute, claiming a twenty-four-hour bug, while her husband, Travis, had opted to stay home and look after his girls.

Thankfully, dessert allowed Henry a further breather from probing questions. Mom surely would give up now.

"Well, I never!" Beaming, Dad shot to his feet, his dining chair luckily remaining upright.

"Never what?" Mom peered over Henry's shoulder. "Oh!" she said, grinning.

After swallowing the last bite of his chocolate mousse, Henry shifted for a better view. An unfamiliar couple approached, their smiles wide. Friends of his parents, no doubt. Curiosity satisfied, he shifted back to grab his water. The rich dessert had stuck in his throat.

"Denise, did you know the Quinns were dining here tonight?" Dad whisper-shouted to Mom.

Henry's eyes darted to his mother's. *Quinn?* Why did that name sound familiar?

"I didn't." Mom fiddled with her hair, suddenly looking flustered.

Dad stepped out from behind his chair, his hands outstretched. "Mark, Michelle! What a lovely surprise."

"Oh, this is perfect," Mom said, her eyes twinkling as she met Henry's eyes for a moment. She rose to join her husband.

What was perfect?

Why were his palms suddenly sweating?

Standing slowly, Henry turned and froze. Emily Quinn—the last person he ever expected to see here after their last conversation in New York City—stood in front of him. A smile tugged at his lips. About to lift his hand, he paused, confused by Emily's agitated gaze along with an almost imperceptible shake of her head.

His jaw clenched. Was he supposed to pretend he didn't know her?

Fine. He'd hunt her down when they returned home and find out why she'd been holding out on him for the past few months. Emily—a New York Quinn, living under the radar in New Haven.

Why?

Weren't her parents billionaires? Meaning she'd have a trust fund to rival his. So, why hide out in Connecticut?

The irony? He was doing the same thing. Except, his parents knew he was just biding time until they demanded he return to take over Palmer Enterprises.

Still, if Henry had anything to say about it, that wouldn't be for a very long time.

***

Emily's heart pounded. Could she make a run for the exit?

Probably not.

Of all the people on the planet, why Henry? A few deep breaths temporarily squashed the rising panic.

She really would have preferred to keep her secret—at least this one—for a lot longer. Maybe agreeing to visit her parents for their twenty-fifth wedding anniversary hadn't been such a great idea. Or perhaps the problem was allowing them to choose this particular restaurant.

"This is our daughter, Emily." Mom nudged her forward.

Fixing on a smile, she held out her hand. "Hello."

"Great to finally meet you, Emily. We've heard so much about you." Mr. Palmer gripped her hand, his smile warm and inviting like his son's. "You're even more beautiful than your parents led us to believe."

Wow, the man even oozed charm like his son.

Emily's eyes flicked to Henry. She caught the appreciative look on his way-too-handsome face, and her cheeks heated. She focused on his mom instead.

"I agree," Mrs. Palmer gushed, briefly touching Emily's arm. "You're exactly the kind of woman we'd love our Henry to get serious about." She glanced sideways at him. "I can't say I care for his usual bevy of ladies, though I do quite like that he knows Adam's sister, Brittany Wilson."

"You're very kind, Mrs. Palmer."

Since Emily wouldn't admit to knowing Henry, they bumbled through supposed 'first-time' introductions. She kept her expression blank, and he followed suit.

Mr. Palmer glanced between her parents. "Won't you join us for a nightcap? We haven't caught up in ages, and you'll agree, Henry and Emily should get acquainted." He shared a conspiratorial look with Emily's dad. "Not sure about you, Mark, but I hope to retire soon. That won't happen if my son insists on staying in New Haven and playing the Good Samaritan."

"Tell me about it." Dad's forehead crinkled. "This is the first time Emily's visited since she escaped the city five years ago. Her Yale business degree is wasted looking after children."

"Dad," Emily growled, her fingers digging into her palms.

"Hey, why don't we grab some fresh air on the balcony?" Henry held out his arm, his smile placating. "We can enjoy the view while our parents bemoan their non-conforming children."

"Excellent idea." Smiling tightly, she took his arm.

As Henry led her through the restaurant toward the doors at the far end, Mrs. Palmer's comment, "Don't they just make the perfect couple?" rang loud and clear in Emily's ears.

Once on the deserted balcony, she broke free and stalked to the barrier wall to look out over the city. Lights from the buildings dotted around them sparkled like tiny stars in the sky. Far below, cars, cabs, and pedestrians appeared like pieces on a monopoly board.

"You have some explaining to do, Miss Quinn." The scent of Henry's deliciously spicy aftershave invaded her nostrils as he stood beside her. "Why did you pretend you didn't know me?"

She turned her head to gawk at him. "Seriously?"

He shrugged. "Humor me."

"If my father had even an inkling we knew each other, attended the same church, and moved in the same circles, he'd have us married off in seconds. To him, you're the perfect man for me."

"I guess my mom and him are on the same page."

A cool breeze playing with their hair caused a stray strand to tickle Emily's face. She swept it away with a huff. "Just great."

"But it would be, wouldn't it, Emily? A match made in heaven."

"Your heaven, maybe. Not mine. I ran away from New York to escape exactly your sort."

"My sort?"

"Yep." She pursed her lips. She'd already said too much.

"I don't suppose you'd care to explain?"

"Nope."

They stood silently for a minute. From within the restaurant came the sounds of classical music and the echo of people's laughter. Down below, a car honked.

"Emily?"

Her eyes jerked to his. "What?"

Henry exhaled loudly. "We won't get away with not spending time together with our families. Now that you're on my parents' radar, you'll be invited to every gathering they arrange. I'll be expected to charm you into dating me. My parents will likely exercise their considerable influence to get your parents to agree to a family merger. Meaning you and I will be engaged within six months, and planning the biggest wedding of the century."

She scowled. "Over my dead body."

"Wow," he said, placing a hand over his heart. "I knew you liked me, but not that much."

Sneaking a peek at his chiseled profile, Emily swallowed hard. Maybe it wouldn't be the worst thing in the world to go along with what the Palmers and her parents were for sure discussing right this moment.

Except that was asking to get her heart broken.

She faced him directly. "Why would you go along with what they want, Henry? I thought you were trying to avoid the responsibilities you'd be saddled with if you opted for a more serious relationship."

"Probably because I've been thinking lately... I might be ready to settle down. Start taking life a little more seriously."

"You're really ready to put away playboy Henry?"

"I am." His mouth twisted in such an adorable way that she had to look elsewhere. "For the right woman."

She brought her eyes back to his earnest expression. "Wow, I never thought I'd see the day." The warmth in his gaze stole her breath. She gulped in some much needed air. "In that case..."

A charming smile lifted his lips. "Are you finally going to take pity on me and agree to date me?" His hopeful gaze tore at her heart.

Biting her bottom lip, she wondered for the hundredth time if this could ever work between them. Because if he ever found out her other secret, he'd break things off quicker than the snap of a dry twig.

Her gut clenched with indecision. She'd resisted for this long. Could she throw caution to the wind?

"No," she said eventually, her voice firmer and sounding surer than she felt.

Then she almost changed her mind when his smile fell faster than the curtain drop at a theater. Almost.

"No?"

"I'm sorry, Henry, but I left New York for a reason: controlling parents." Even though her heart constricted with pain, Emily kept her tone nonchalant, as if dismissing his affections was as easy as solving a basic math equation. "Do you honestly think I'd risk the independence I've fought so hard for to play into their hands by dating you?" She sucked in a breath and let it out slowly. "You should date Brittany."

Unable to look into his crestfallen face or piercing green eyes any longer, she turned toward the uncomplicated view. "Your mom seems to like her."

Chapter Four

NEW HAVEN, CONNECTICUT, late November

Henry stood beside Adam on the marble steps of the Grand Hotel, waiting for their first guests to arrive. Tonight was an important event in Daily Bread's calendar—their Annual Auction and Fundraising Ball—which was why Henry needed to be in the right frame of mind as one of the co-founders and directors of the charity to feed the homeless. The year ahead would be rocky unless they reached their fundraising goal.

He inhaled deeply and shook out his hands.

Luckily for his business partner, Henry was blessed with 'all the charm and gentle persuasion needed' to achieve just that. He chuckled under his breath. At least, that's what his best friend had told him earlier.

Employing his game face as the first donor vehicle pulled up, Henry greeted the exiting occupants with a welcoming smile. Though a line soon formed, it didn't stop him from keeping an eye out for the one person who wasn't likely to show. Not considering her determined words in New York a month ago. It had been a long shot, but he'd still asked Emily to accompany him tonight.

She'd turned him down flat.

Afterward, he'd reached out via text messages, but when the tenth went unread and unanswered, he'd gotten the message: she wanted nothing to do with him. Well, his brain had. His heart kept begging to differ.

On Sundays at church, she slipped in after the morning service started and left before the last song finished. Initiating conversation had been impossible. The situation wasn't helped either by the fact that Charlotte had broken up with Adam over a building dispute. It meant Henry now had little chance of seeing Emily in social settings.

But, with any luck, Adam's new building plans would win back his girl tonight. Then Henry would once again have valid opportunities to see Emily.

Stuffing his hands into his pockets, he focused on the latest arrivals. A genuine smile rose to his lips when he spotted a familiar brunette-haired woman. Easily a supermodel, Brittany Wilson looked incredible in her off-the-shoulder, slate blue chiffon dress. Her tanned complexion, thick wavy hair, and slim figure were exactly what agencies sought. Not that she was actually a model.

If only he were more attracted to her. Instead, his heart remained steady as Britt glided up the stairs and reached his side. Their eyes met, and her smile brightened, yet his heart didn't miss a beat. Not like it did every time he saw Emily.

A sleek, black limo pulled up to the curb, causing a stir among the guests lingering around the hotel entrance. A magnificently dressed group climbed out. First Jack and his wife Julie, then Melanie and her husband Steven. Henry's heart skipped a beat—or three—as Emily appeared dressed in form-fitting cherry-red satin. His mouth went dry.

Had she brought a date? He glanced briefly behind her. A woman in a sleeveless long silver dress emerged—Charlotte.

Adam sucked in a breath on Henry's right side while Britt's hand tightened on his left arm. She leaned in. "Are you all right?" she whispered. "You look like you've seen a ghost."

"Nah." He rested a hand on hers. "I'm just a little hot, don't you think?" Too late, he registered what he'd said.

Britt shot him a cheeky smile. "You're such a flirt, Henry," she said playfully.

Emily obviously heard. Barely greeting him, she quickly followed Steven into the hotel. Henry clenched his fists. Britt's timing couldn't have been worse.

He got over the initial embarrassment, then remembered that Emily had told him to date Britt. So she couldn't be mad now, could she?

Ignoring his churning gut, he greeted Charlotte, who'd elicited a real smile from Adam. Henry was thrilled for him. As long as the rest of Adam's plan worked tonight, he'd have his woman back.

If only Henry could say the same.

Not that Emily was his in the first place.

Later, Henry gave a welcoming speech and invited everyone to enjoy the three-course meal prepared by top chefs. Murmurs of appreciation filled the grand hall, but he barely tasted the food.

Rising from his seat to announce the silent auction winners a short while later, Henry's eyes involuntarily moved to Emily's. She watched him politely for a second, maybe two, then stared at her wine glass. Disappointed, he took a fortifying breath and clinked his dessert spoon against his glass.

After the results, the excited crowd eventually settled down, and the music began. Knowing he had no choice, Henry offered Britt his hand and smiled. "Will you dance with me?"

"I'd love to." She slipped her hand into his, her smile dazzling. Pity it did nothing for him.

For the first dance, a waltz, Henry kept his eyes on Britt. Well, for the most part. On the couple occasions he made eye contact with Emily, it was fleeting. When she caught him looking at her, she averted her gaze. An ache formed in his chest at her reaction. Really, he shouldn't waste his time.

Drawing on his years of experience flirting and playing the field, he focused on Britt, then the next woman he danced with, and the next, and so on. Emily wasn't even a blip on his radar. However, he quickly tired of his game when Emily seemed unaffected by his shenanigans.

Giving up, he wandered over to the bar to get a drink.

Turned out Emily was thirsty too.

"You look incredible, Emily," he said with a smile as she spun from the bar counter with a drink in her hand.

"Thank you." Her dull, somewhat automatic response matched her neutral expression. When he searched her eyes for even an ounce of warmth, he found none.

For the hundredth time, he wished he'd never gone to New York at the beginning of the month. If he hadn't, his parents wouldn't have tried to set him up with Emily, or at least make it extremely clear they'd be ecstatic if the two did get together. Emily would still be talking to him, and their friendship might've been something more by now.

He could dream.

"What can I get you, Mr. Palmer?" The bartender's question dragged his attention away from the captivating woman.

"A Pepsi, please."

When he checked over his shoulder, Emily had stepped away from the bar. Reaching out, he grabbed her wrist. "Emily, wait." Where his fingers connected with her skin, they tingled and sparked. He let go.

She faced him. "What?"

"I'd love to dance with you."

She raised her eyebrows. "That's not a question."

"Dance with me, please?"

"No." She closed her eyes briefly and let out a deep breath. "Thank you." Then, as she walked away, she held up her hand and scoffed. "I'm sure you'll have no trouble finding someone else more willing. You haven't had a problem so far."

***

Emily groaned. Why had she felt the need to be so rude? Henry was Henry; he was going to do what he'd always done. She didn't need to punish him for it. Except she wanted him to feel a little pain, too. Watching him dance with numerous women, charming them with his witty comments and handsome face?

Torture.

She wanted to be the one he gave all his attention to, but that was never going to happen. He wanted to dance with her. So what? One dance wouldn't make any difference. All it would do was leave her yearning for more.

Every day, she relived their kiss. Time hadn't made the memory hazy; if anything, it'd made it clearer and more intense. Clenching her jaw, she snuck a peek over her shoulder. Sure enough, Henry was on his way to Britt again. Or maybe it was the gorgeous redhead to her right.

Whoever it was, good luck to them.

After witnessing Charlotte cozying up to Adam, Emily snuck out of the hotel's front entrance. Their friends' collective mission of reuniting the couple was a resounding success, and her part in accompanying Charlotte to the ball over. If Emily had to look at Britt hanging on Henry's arm for a minute longer, though, she would absolutely scream. So what if he'd asked Emily to be his date first? Nor did it matter that she'd essentially given him the green light to date Britt, either.

What she wanted was for him to keep fighting for her.

She clenched her jaw. No, she didn't. He was way too old and came from her world—the one place she needed to avoid. The reasons why were not going to change, so feeling the way she did about Henry was pointless. If only she could get her heart to cooperate.

Little puffs of breath escaped her mouth as she strode down the stairs clenching the belt of her coat around her waist. A few smokers hovered further along the sidewalk. Far enough away not to have to hold her breath.

Lifting her eyes to the night sky, Emily immediately spotted the waxing crescent moon. The biggest, brightest stars sparkled back at her. Filled with awe, she marveled at her God. Just like Him, His majestic creation was glorious and awesome.

Pity she didn't feel worthy of His time. Poor judgment in past relationships had cost her that.

Turning from the magnificent sight, she headed toward the garden. A sharp wind whipped around her neck, and she grimaced. It sure was chilly out.

Footsteps sounded behind her, and she paused. Shooting a glance over her shoulder made her traitorous heart skip a beat. Didn't Henry have a date to entertain?

She picked up her pace.

"Are you really going to ignore me?" Henry's deep, warm voice stopped Emily in her tracks. She'd been rude to him earlier. He hadn't deserved it; she'd just been taking out her frustration on him.

The irony was not lost on her.

She turned and met his hesitant look and pinched expression. For once, he didn't seem so sure of himself.

"Did you need something, Henry?" She used her kindest voice, the one she'd been practicing for talking with school children.

He halted a few steps from her, his facial features softening slightly. "I wanted to make sure you're okay."

"I needed some fresh air and..." She inclined her head in the direction of the building they'd exited. "Charlotte deserves to be alone with Adam without me crowding them." Shrugging, she chuckled humorlessly. "She may be my date, but I have this feeling I won't be leaving with her."

"I think you're right." He smiled briefly. "Do you need a lift home? I'd be happy to take you."

Her heart stuttered at his hopeful expression. Shaking her head, she gave him a pointed look. "I think you're forgetting you brought a date."

Confusion knit his brow, and he scratched his nose. "Oh, you mean Britt?" He shoved his hands in his pockets. "My driver left with her just now. She needed to get back to Hartford tonight."

"I see." Emily tilted her head and gave him a quizzical

look. She didn't really know what to think. If that was how he treated his dates, she wasn't sure she knew him.

Henry must've realized her train of thought because he closed the distance between them and laid his hands on her shoulders. Despite her cashmere coat, she felt his warm touch. "Emily, I didn't send her home. Britt insisted. When I offered to go with the car, she straight-out shot me down. She can be very determined when she's made up her mind."

"I see." Now she sounded like a broken record. "I mean, okay, I understand," she corrected.

Henry's deep stare locked her in, making her knees go weak. When she managed to dip her gaze to his lips, her pulse skyrocketed. She swallowed hard, remembering the only time she'd enjoyed a taste.

"Emily?" At his husky-sounding voice, her head shot up, her cheeks burning. "All I want to do right now is kiss you." Her eyes widened, and he was quick to reassure her. "I won't, but you should know I'm exercising great restraint. Instead, I offer a compromise."

She opened her mouth to protest, but his fingers covered it, shocking her into submission.

"I won't kiss you," he said, the intensity in his smoky eyes belying his words, "*if* you promise we can be friends again."

Friends? "But—"

"No buts. Adam and Charlotte are back together. For the long haul, I reckon. So you and I are going to see a lot more of each other whether we like it or not. The last thing I want to do is to make things awkward or uncomfortable for anyone, least of all my best friend and your employer." His gaze flicked to her mouth, then back to her eyes. "So, do you agree to my proposition?"

She considered all sides. Hurting others just to protect her heart was selfish. There was only one answer. Not the one she wanted to give, but the one she had to give.

"Yes."

Chapter Five

"Merry Christmas, Emily."

Emily's head shot up, and she dropped the rented ice skate's slippery laces like hot lava. "What are you doing here, Henry?"

He wiggled a black Bauer skate bag and grinned. "What do you think?"

She stared at him. The dark scruff along his chiseled jawline was sexy as all get out, and he wore his brown hair longer than a month ago—the last time she'd said more than 'hello' to him.

Her gaze dipped to his black leather jacket. A blue-and-white plaid collar stuck out from under a fawn-colored cashmere sweater. Dark blue jeans hugged muscular legs.

Wow.

Jerking her eyes upward, she found him watching her intently, a slight smirk on his face. Warmth flooded her cheeks, and she looked away. Behind him, his parents greeted hers with hugs and laughter.

Now this unexpected outing—uh, set-up—made sense!

"Merry Christmas, Mr. and Mrs. Palmer," Emily said. "Lovely to see you." Hopefully they wouldn't detect the false cheer in her voice.

"You too, Emily." Mrs. Palmer smiled widely before eyeing

Emily's skates. Her lips thinned, and she gave her son a pointed look. "Henry, why don't you be a dear and help Emily with those? The laces can be tricky to tighten."

"Oh, that's alright." Emily frowned. "I can do it." Rockefeller Center skates might not be the best, but she could sort her own laces.

"Happy to help." Henry crouched down in front of her, but Emily swatted his hand away.

"I can manage perfectly well, thank you," she said in a low voice, keeping one eye on his mom. Thankfully Mrs. Palmer had moved out of earshot to chat with her mom.

"Suit yourself."

Plopping down on the bench beside her, Henry unzipped his bag and pulled out shiny black hockey skates—ones that probably cost more than the average family of four spent on groceries in a month. For someone who ran soup kitchens, it wasn't what she'd have expected from him.

"Why am I not surprised?" Annoyed that he flaunted his privilege, Emily tried not to sound judgmental.

"About what?"

She gestured to the fancy ice skate he had slipped on like butter sliding onto toast.

"A present from Dad," he said matter-of-factly.

"Oh."

Lord, forgive my judgment.

Gritting her teeth, Emily concentrated on the odious task of tightening her laces. With her heart rate no longer slow and steady like it had been ten minutes ago, and Henry's thigh pressed against hers on the short bench, it was a struggle. The occasional whiff of her favorite men's eau de cologne didn't help either.

"Yoo-hoo, Henry?" Mrs. Palmer called from just inside the rink. "You two coming or what?"

"Hold your horses, Mom! We're coming."

Emily tied the last bow then pushed to her feet, wobbling slightly.

Henry stuck out his hand. "Allow me?"

Pursing her lips, she slipped her now icy hand into his warm one. Tiny sparks fired through her palm to each fingertip, but she ignored them, permitting Henry to lead her to the rink entrance instead. Their eyes met, and for the longest moment, Emily forgot what she was doing. Henry's brows, pulling together to show his deep concern, just about melted her insides.

Blinking, Emily shook her head. This would *not* do. Not when the man was a known playboy. She'd have to keep reminding herself of that fact until she got it into her thick head.

To steel herself against his charms, she closed her eyes and set her jaw firmly. Then, lifting her lids, she faced the ice. "Right, let's do this."

Releasing her grasp on his hand, Emily stepped onto the slippery surface and pushed off slowly. It didn't take too long to get the hang of it. Sure, it'd been a while, but she'd been a confident speed skater before she'd had—

Shaking away the memory of the last time she'd skated, she focused on her surroundings. The lights of the beautifully decorated giant Christmas tree shone, but not as brightly as they would later when the natural light disappeared. From an elevated position and behind a low concrete wall, spectators chatted and laughed while poles bearing white and gold flags waved in the gentle breeze.

"Looking forward to the sunset?" Henry's low, sexy voice almost made her stumble.

She glared at him. "Someone should get you a bell."

Hurt flickered across his features, but he quickly covered it with a wide smile. "Next time I'll whistle so you don't get a fright."

Keeping her eyes in front of her, she continued to skate. "I've got a better idea," she retorted. "Why don't you stay away from me? That way there'll be no risk of me falling."

Literally or figuratively.

"No can do." A natural on the ice, Henry kept abreast of her easily. "First off," he said, "you agreed to be my friend, and frankly, I'm not finding you very friendly today. It's Christmas, remember? It's meant to be cheerful and festive."

"Humph."

"Secondly…" He swung around to face her, skating backward like a pro. "Our parents might not appear to be watching, but believe me, they're devouring every second. You really think this is what my parents do the day after Christmas?" he scoffed. "Never. They're usually entertaining a bunch of friends at home along with whichever of their children happen to be in the city for Christmas. I should've known they had an ulterior motive when they mentioned ice-skating."

Emily sighed heavily. "Well, you're not the only one. My parents are usually holed up in front of a movie right about now."

"So you understand why you not playing ball might look bad?"

"Where's your girlfriend, Henry?"

He looked at her quizzically. "Girlfriend?"

"You never mentioned a girlfriend, Henry." Mrs. Palmer appeared out of nowhere, her eyes laser-focused on her son. Clearly he'd learned the art of creeping up on people from his mother.

"I don't have—"

"It's Brittany. Adam's sister," Emily offered helpfully, not daring to look at Henry.

Mrs. Palmer clapped her hands. "You've been holding out on us, my boy. How marvelous!" Her sugary voice set Emily's teeth on edge. "Although we were hoping you and Emily…" She shook her head. "Never mind. When are you bringing Brittany to visit?"

"Mom, mind if I have a private word with Emily?" Henry kept his tone even, despite his tight jaw and firecracker eyes.

Yikes! What *had* she done?

"Oh, don't go, Mrs. Palmer." Reaching out to touch her arm, Emily smiled sweetly. "There are no secrets between me and Henry." A blatant lie, but hopefully, God would forgive her. She wasn't ready to incur Henry's wrath just yet, and his mom was just the sort of buffer she needed.

"Mom." Henry practically growled.

Mrs. Palmer slowed. "Fine. I'll leave."

***

Henry spun with his hands fisted on his hips. "What the heck, Emily?!"

The audacious woman shot him a demur look. "Oh sorry," she purred. "Is Brittany *not* your girlfriend?"

"You know very well she isn't," he said through gritted teeth.

"Then I guess you'll be disappointing your *very* happy mother when you explain that her beloved son is single. Still."

He narrowed his eyes. "I don't know why you're doing this, but it's my life you're playing with. Doesn't that mean anything to you?"

Guilt flickered briefly in Emily's eyes. She pursed her lips, then crossed her arms over her chest. "I'm sorry if you think I'm playing with your life, Henry." Her gaze shifted up to the people at street level looking down at them. "I feel exactly the same way."

What was the woman on about? It's not like she'd be forced to settle down and take over her father's billion-dollar company. Unless—

"Why do you think we're all here today?" she asked, breaking off his chain of thought. He opened his mouth to answer, but she cut him off. "So our parents can dictate our lives. My whole life, I've been told what to do. I finally managed to get away from it all. In New Haven. Now I'm being pushed again into something I don't want, by my parents. So I'm sorry if I said something rash, but I'd rather they think Brittany's your girlfriend than assume I'm yours."

Her bitter tone was hard to swallow. He clenched his jaw and fought down the words he wanted to say, 'Would it be so bad to be my girlfriend?'

She made it sound like it'd be awful.

"I guess I was naïve thinking you and I could be friends. Even though you promised," he said quietly, scowling when he remembered her previous agreement. "I get it. You don't *actually* like me, and you don't approve of my supposed lifestyle. I only wish I'd realized that before I—"

Clamping his mouth shut, Henry turned and pushed off on the ice.

Emily raced up next to him, her hand grasping his arm. "Before you what?"

"Nothing." The ache in his chest grew stronger. Telling Emily how he really felt when she clearly wasn't interested wasn't an option.

He brushed off her hand and accelerated forward on the ice. A desperate need to escape her enticing citrusy scent and her physical beauty spurred him on. Voluntarily torturing himself by staying close was a terrible idea.

Now, more than ever.

Overheated and thirsty from skating hard, he left the ice and aimed for the service area.

As he waited in line, Emily joined him, puffing hard. "Thanks for the workout." Her smile seemed tentative, her gaze guarded. "I may not be able to walk tomorrow, but hey," she said with a shrug, "that's my problem for trying to catch you."

"Sorry, not sorry." He gave her a tight half-smile but kept his tone soft. "Would you like a hot chocolate or some water?"

"Both, please."

After chugging down a bottle of water, they collected their hot drinks and gravitated to a table at the back of the glass enclosure. They sat in silence, sipping their drinks while peering out at the skaters still on the ice. Huddled in the center, their parents laughed while chatting.

At least they got on well.

Henry sighed and took another drink from his paper cup.

"I do like you." Emily's softly spoken words forced his eyes to hers. Tenderness blazed there for a fleeting moment before she schooled her expression. "But you must admit, no woman in their right mind would approve of a man who never dates a woman more than once. There's a term for that, you know. A playboy." He opened his mouth to object, but Emily raised a hand to stop him. "I know you're not one in a traditional sense, but equally, you're not the kind to settle into any kind of a committed relationship."

"Says who?"

She laughed, and he felt his indignation grow.

"Your actions speak for themselves."

His hand tightened on the table edge. "What if I had a good reason for my dating habits?"

"I find that hard to believe."

He looked at her for a long moment. Did she think he was *that* shallow?

"Forget it." Shifting back in his seat, Henry looked anywhere but at her. Only the coffee machine grinding its dark beans and conversations from other customers pierced the otherwise awkward silence between them. That is until boisterous laughter forced him from his apathy, and he caught Emily staring into space.

She gave a little sigh, flicked honey-blonde hair from her face, then tapped her fingers on the side of her paper cup. Sad eyes moved to meet his. "I am sorry, Henry. I agreed to be your friend, and I've been anything but."

A myriad of emotions crossed her face. None he could pinpoint for certain.

Honestly, he'd reached the point where he didn't think he wanted to keep trying, so he waited, watching her intently. Forcing her to be something she didn't want to be wasn't worth the aggravation. It was better to deal with the disappointment now than to let the feelings fester and grow until he either hated her or couldn't live without her.

He scrubbed his hand over his face. "It doesn't matter," he said, struggling to keep the hurt out of his voice. "I don't know why I've been pushing so hard when you're clearly not interested. It'll make the rest of this day hard, and once we get back home, I'll probably go back to my old church. I can't ditch my best friend all the time, though, so if you're around when I am, so be it. We'll have to make the best of the situation."

The more he spoke, the more her lips turned down, and her eyes started to fill. When the first tear dripped onto her cheek, alarm shot through him.

"Hey," he whispered, reaching out to gather her hands into his. "I didn't mean to make you cry. I thought…"

Had he been wrong?

He didn't think so. This past month, she'd avoided him at church and hadn't attended any events other than the fundraiser.

Hardly the behavior of a friend.

Emily ducked her head and shook it slowly. Her hands stayed in his for a few more seconds before she pulled one out and brought it up to press to her eyes. She heaved in a big breath, then looked up.

"You okay?"

Biting a trembling lip, she nodded.

Henry squeezed her hand and let go. Immediately, she set her hands in her lap. Fine. He got the message. Don't touch. Even when all he wanted to do was wrap her in his arms and tell her not to worry about a thing.

Finishing off his hot chocolate, he pushed back his chair. Time to leave.

"Henry?"

He steeled his heart.

"Can you forgive me for the way I've treated you?" The sincerity in her words tore at the walls he'd very recently erected around his heart. "Can we still be friends?" Emily's voice broke on the last word.

"Of course." How could he deny her anything? Even if he wanted so much more.

A tiny smile graced her lips. Those same lips he fought not to think about whenever he thought back to the Jays' concert. He jerked his gaze back to her now brighter brown eyes.

Time to lighten the mood.

"What do you say we start right now?" he asked, a smile tugging at his mouth. "Let's have some friendly fun. Race you on the ice?"

Her smile grew. "You're on."

Near the entrance to the ice, they were confronted by their parents, who all wore we've-won-the-lottery smiles.

"What's the bet they have a plan up their sleeves, and it involves you and me?" Henry said under his breath.

"No." She groaned. "That can't be good."

Mr. Quinn's gaze darted between them. "We're leaving, but don't let that stop you youngsters."

"We've got a joint New Year's Eve party to plan." Rubbing her hands together gleefully, Mom shared a conspiratorial look with Mrs. Quinn. "No point fighting for guests when we can pool our resources and throw the best party this city has ever seen. Right, Michelle?"

Henry chortled. "You think you can beat the ball drop, Mom?"

"No, but we can make sure everyone feels like they're right there." She winked.

"You two will be there, right?" Dad made it sound like a question. It wasn't.

Henry glanced at Emily, whose mouth had hardened into a thin line. "You in?"

"I wasn't planning on—" she started.

He bumped her shoulder with his. "Come on. It'll be dull without you." He leaned in so only she could hear. "Friends, remember? Friends do things together, help each other out."

She twisted her lips, and he wondered if she was about to renege on their most recent agreement.

"Um, I guess so. Okay."

Not quite the excited response he'd have liked, but he'd take it. The possibility of dancing with her in his arms and maybe even stealing a kiss at midnight?

Yes, please.

Chapter Six

Henry did a slow three-sixty. Where was she?

Oversized floral arrangements dotted the expansive, polished wood floor while contemporary wall art decorated spaces above the maroon velvet banquettes. All the women wore flawless makeup, glitzy jewelry, and snug designer gowns. But the one who caught his eye was nowhere to be found.

His eyes did another circuit. The Palmer-Quinn's New Year's Eve party would be the envy of every New Yorker. Daily Bread's annual event was like a child's tea party in comparison. Maybe next year he should insist on financing the fundraiser.

Except, Adam wouldn't be happy. When they'd started the nonprofit, he insisted Henry could match him in the initial investment, but he couldn't use personal funds to help the charity thereafter. Adam wanted to feel like they had earned the donations they received.

Henry hadn't pointed out that if wished, he could give generously to Daily Bread through a dummy foundation. Respecting Adam's request, though, he'd refrained. Of course, now that Adam was engaged to a wealthy woman, he'd probably be fighting with his wife about the very same thing.

Henry chuckled. Oh, the irony!

Noticing the Quinns on the other side of the hall and that

they would likely know their daughter's whereabouts, he headed in their direction.

Waiters, bearing silver trays of Bellinis and canapés, circled the room. Ignoring the alcohol—he hadn't eaten lunch—Henry paused to sample a deviled egg and a buffalo chicken wing. No point spoiling his appetite with a four-course Italian dinner still to come.

Every few steps, Henry groaned internally at the women who kept waylaying him by wanting to 'chat.'

When his mother suddenly blocked his path, he smiled in relief and greeted her with a kiss on each cheek. "You look incredible, Mom."

She beamed back at him. "You look rather dashing yourself."

"Thanks." He dusted some lint off his tux. "Rocking party, by the way."

"Yes," she murmured, her attention drifting. "I think Michelle and I did a good job."

Dad joined them, slipping an arm around Mom's waist. "Outstanding job, my darling," he said. His sharp eyes then fixed on Henry. "You alone, son? I thought you might've brought Emily."

Henry scratched his head, shooting another glance at the Quinns, who were entertaining a young man but no Emily. "I figured she'd come with her parents."

"You could've offered, you know." Mom gave him a disappointed look. "I know you have a girlfriend, but…"

Not wanting to get into *that* conversation, Henry shrugged. "Mind if I talk to you guys later?"

Before they could answer, he left.

After greeting Emily's parents and complimenting Mrs. Quinn on the decorations, he turned to the mystery man.

"Henry Palmer, hi." He plastered on a polite smile while holding out his hand.

The guy shook Henry's hand firmly. "Luke Bowman."

"So, how do you know the Quinns?"

"I dated their daughter."

What? Henry's heart lurched. Emily had never mentioned an ex. To be fair, when he'd asked about her prior dating life, she *had* answered vaguely.

"Luke also works for my father."

At the sound of the soft, sweet voice, Henry whipped his head around and found Emily. She wore a long, elegant, emerald-colored dress with a slit up one leg and thin spaghetti straps on her exposed shoulders.

Stunning.

His heart rate doubled, and swallowing did nothing for his now dry throat.

"Hello, Luke, I didn't know you were going to be here." There was a slight edge to her voice.

Or maybe that was just Henry projecting.

"Hey, Em." Luke stepped forward, resting one hand possessively on her shoulder, and planted a lingering kiss on her cheek. "Long time no see. You look ravishing."

The interloper spoke in dulcet tones, and Henry fought the urge to interrupt the reunion.

"Thank you." Emily blushed prettily, her eyes dancing with delight. "And you look as handsome as ever." She smiled demurely at the smooth-talking youngster.

Wanting to growl at the blatant flirting, Henry snatched up her hand and—accidentally, of course—knocked Luke's hand off her shoulder in the process.

Luke scowled at Henry, who ignored him. "Excuse us," he said before dragging Emily away.

Out of earshot, Henry swung her in front of him and immediately dropped her hand. Her eyes blazed like a lit-up forest. "What was that all about?" she fired at him.

"I was rescuing you from your *ex*." The word was a bitter sound to his own ears, and he prayed Emily didn't pick up on his jealousy.

She rolled her eyes. "I don't need rescuing."

Inhaling a calming breath, he gentled his tone. "What took you so long anyway?"

"Not that it's any of your business, but my dress got

caught in the car door on my way over." She gave an irritated huff. "Since I hadn't *planned* on attending any fancy New York party, I had to choose a replacement from my limited wardrobe." She peered down at her dress and frowned.

Lifting her chin with his thumb, he waited until she looked up. "No matter what you wear, you're beautiful." His gaze lowered to the floor then traveled to her face. "But this dress…" He brushed a finger over a strap. "It's incredible."

Pink bloomed on her cheeks, sending a thrill through him. He smirked. Good to know his compliments affected her, too.

"Would you like a drink?" he asked, glancing toward the not-too-busy bar.

"A white wine, please."

She made no move to follow him.

"You're not going to come with me?"

"Um." She angled her head over his shoulder. "Okay."

After ordering drinks at the counter, he shifted to face her. She stood so close that the sweet scent of her perfume washed over him, and his heart skipped a beat at her tender expression.

"Hi," she whispered, her lips lifting into a sensual smile.

Unable to think straight, Henry stared at her mouth while his insides went crazy.

"Goodness, Henry!" Emily gave a hearty laugh. "Perhaps you need lessons in social etiquette." Lowering her voice, she added in a flirty tone, "Usually, when someone says hi, you say 'hi' or 'hello' back."

"Sorry." He shook his head, still slightly dazed, then smiled softly. "Hello, Emily."

"One Chardonnay and one Corona." The bartender handed over their drinks, and Henry gently tapped his glass to Emily's.

"Cheers," they said together.

Her wide smile matched his for a moment, and he imagined them as a couple about to start the rest of their lives together.

"Here's to a new year with new beginnings. New

relationships." A guy could dream, right? But when her expression turned downcast, and disappointment tightened his gut, he added, "To friendship."

Emily, looking slightly less worried, nodded before taking a sip of her wine. Henry did the same. As cold, bubbly liquid slid down his throat, the first strains of Frank Sinatra's 'New York New York' sounded from the ten-piece band.

He looked over at the stage. He'd forgotten about the dancing. "I love this song."

"Me too." Emily's eyes found his. Something unmistakable sparked between them, tangible and powerful. He couldn't look away if he tried.

Selfishly praying that he wouldn't be rejected again, he opened his mouth to speak, but Luke appeared behind Emily, invading their personal space.

"I'd love to dance with you, Em."

"Actually, I was—" Henry began.

"If you'll let me?" Luke stretched out a hand to Emily, his puppy dog expression irking Henry big time.

"I'd love to." She slipped her hand into Luke's, and Henry's stomach sank.

***

"Thank you," Emily said, moving into Luke's arms.

"For asking you to dance or rescuing you from Henry?"

"Yes." She kept her answer vague on purpose.

Lately, all her parents talked about was how she and Henry were perfectly suited. If they could, they'd plan the engagement and wedding simultaneously. No matter how many times she insisted they were only friends, it didn't seem to register.

Luke, an ex-boyfriend from high school, would hopefully throw them off the idea. Ideal too, the fact he worked for her father and didn't know her secret either. Luke may be an executive, but it wasn't like he'd be running the company one day. Nope, that role was earmarked for her. Expected of her even.

Except, not happening. Not when it meant moving back to

New York. She needed to be in New Haven, where her heart was.

Memories flooded Emily as Luke steered her around the dance floor to Aerosmith's 'Don't Want to Miss a Thing'—the song they'd danced to after being crowned prom king and queen in their senior year of high school.

What a magical night. Until it ended in her worst nightmare. Actions had consequences, and she'd certainly paid the price. Luke, on the other hand, had no clue. His reaction then—and what it would be now—was not what she wanted to think about while dancing with him. Instead, she would picture an angelic face with eyes like—

"You're smiling."

Luke's voice brought her back to the party, and she noted his soft expression.

"Just thinking of the last time we danced," she said wistfully. It was the truth, just not the whole truth.

"Me too." His lips lifted into the heart-stopping smile she'd fallen for as a teenager. "Only, I never thought I'd be dancing with you ever again. Let alone to the same song."

"I know."

"I'm sorry, Em. I shouldn't have been such a jerk back then. I should've been more supportive after that night. I carry the guilt with me every day."

She sighed heavily but for a different reason. "Me too."

Luke hugged her for a long moment, then drew back, his tender gaze creating a swirl in her stomach.

"I'm glad I came tonight," he said in a low voice, swaying with her in time to the music. "I was nervous, knowing you'd be here."

"I deserve that." She reached up to touch his cheek, and his hand captured hers.

"It's okay. We're even, right?" Hope filled his voice.

She nodded. "I've missed you, Luke."

"I've missed you, too."

It was crazy, feeling so safe with someone she'd loved yet who'd totally torn her world apart. After five years, the emotional attachment should've long since been severed.

The song ended, and Luke led her off the dance floor, pausing in a quieter area. Hugging her midriff, Emily turned to meet his warm gaze.

What now?

"Will you save another dance for me, Em?"

"Of course."

"Your father wanted to introduce me to a few more people..." His attention strayed for a second, then returned. Twisting his lips, he gave a one-shouldered shrug. "Since he's the boss—"

"Go." She shooed him away with an encouraging smile. "I'll see you later."

Luke strolled off, his broad shoulders filling his tux way better than the boy she'd dated. Sexier. A flush heated her cheeks.

"So that's your ex?" A deep voice beside her made her jump.

"Do you *have* to creep up on me, Henry?"

He laughed, but it didn't sound happy. "Not my fault you're in another world, princess."

"Princess?"

Was he jealous? From under her lashes, Emily eyed his pinched expression and taut lips. Maybe he had a right to be jealous. From what she'd heard, Luke Bowman was a hard-working guy who typically was in relationships for the long haul. No one could accuse him of being a playboy.

Henry, on the other hand...

Sighing, she closed her eyes and counted to three.

"You two looked mighty cozy out there." Henry's undertone was hard to decipher.

She shrugged. "Yeah, well, we have a history."

More than she planned on telling him.

"High school or college?" he probed.

"Why the sudden interest? You looking for a new BFF?"

"No, just doing what friends do, you know. Getting to know you."

"Right. Getting to know me." She paused, narrowing her eyes at him. If that's all he truly wanted… "Well, okay. We dated senior year and broke up soon after graduation. Luke went to college and then got a job with my father. He lives in New York, and I live in New Haven." She raised her brows. "Anything else you want to know?"

"Will you dance with me?"

The question momentarily threw her. "Um…" she stalled.

Fine. With the current upbeat music, she could probably handle being in close proximity—well, maybe.

"Sure," she said.

Unfortunately, the dance floor was crowded. Therefore, every time her skin accidentally touched Henry's, it sparked —so not what she had in mind!

Only after she was able to loosen up and settle into the rhythm could she admire Henry's moves. A wonderfully rhythmic dancer, his antics and occasional poses made her laugh.

Too soon, the music slowed to a waltz. Henry stepped forward, his hand ready to take hers, his hopeful gaze asking permission.

Why not? It wasn't like dancing in his arms would change her mind. Henry was her friend.

Nothing more.

Except, being held close by him felt utterly delicious, like eating the smoothest piece of chocolate. Luke's embrace had been comfortable and familiar, Henry's irresistible and exhilarating.

Still, she slipped her hand into his and breathed in his intoxicating scent. The happy gleam in his eyes made her pulse jump and her stomach dip low.

Oh man! Any second now, her knees would buckle. Resisting the urge to trace his stubble, she planted her other hand on his back.

As Henry led her expertly around the dance floor with his eyes on her alone, a group of young ladies glared at Emily. Were any of them jealous exes of his?

Whatever. She didn't care. Not when she was the one dancing with the best-looking man in the room.

A slow, sexy smile grew on his handsome face, forcing Emily to look elsewhere. The problem was a number of curious couples now watched them.

"Henry," she hissed, "everyone's watching us!"

"Of course they are." He chuckled. "They're just envious because I've got the most beautiful woman in my arms. Don't you agree?" His eyebrows lifted in quick succession, and she giggled at his silliness.

"Henry," she admonished, smacking his arm playfully.

The music faded out a short while later, and she couldn't help but peer into his gorgeous eyes. All humor from before was gone, replaced by darkened depths she could almost drown in. When he dragged her flush against his body, Emily sucked in a breath.

"Thanks for dancing with me," he whispered in her ear. "You were the perfect dance partner."

Ripples of pleasure moved through her, and she stilled. He wasn't supposed to make her feel like this. But before she could object, Henry drew back and released her firmly. Then, without a backward glance, he strolled off.

Confused, Emily stood rooted to the spot.

A moment later, her heart stuttered as Henry—who she had to keep reminding herself was just a friend—now led another woman onto the dance floor, his arm snaked possessively around her waist.

She'd been replaced. Nothing less than she'd expected, really.

So why did that hurt way more than it should?

Chapter Seven

"You sound like the weight of the world's on your shoulders, Em."

Had she sighed *that* deeply?

She smiled weakly at Luke. "It's been a long day and an even longer week. I wasn't supposed to be in New York tonight."

A bald-headed server removed their dessert bowls and looked between them. "Coffee?"

"Please." Emily nodded, then stifled a yawn. After the superb four-course Italian dinner, an espresso sounded perfect. In less than an hour, they'd see the New Year in.

"I'm guessing you'd rather be in New Haven at some house party, shooting off sparklers at midnight and sipping Prosecco," Luke scoffed.

"Don't be a snob."

He held up his hands. "Just stating facts. To me, it's not about the venue or the decorations; it's about the company."

Another sigh pulled through her. "Well, I *do* miss the people in New Haven."

He shifted more fully in his seat, his big brown eyes alert and focused. "Tell me about your life there. Are you happy?"

"Why are you so interested in my dull life?" She searched his face for an answer but found none. Whatever the reason, he was holding it close.

"I never said it was dull, Em." Reaching forward, he

wrapped her hand in his and looked her straight in the eye. "Anywhere you are couldn't possibly be dull. You were always the life of the party, the most beautiful woman in the room."

Was he for real?

"Okay." She laughed without humor. "Who put you up to this?" She peered across and further down the long table at her parents, who smiled encouragingly before returning to their conversations.

Next, she glanced over at Henry, and her smile faded. He was sharing an animated conversation with a young woman on his right—clearly in his element and living up to his reputation.

Luke laughed, bringing her eyes back to him. "I'm just curious, Em. What has got you so attached to the place?"

"One…" She counted off on her fingers. "I love the family I work for. Charlotte's children are wonderful and challenging; they teach me new things daily. Two, I love my studies. It keeps me busy when I'm not babysitting or cooking the kids' dinner. And three, I love my church."

His eyebrows shot up. "I didn't realize you were religious."

Of course. He'd been out of the loop, and it wasn't something her parents—who were relatively private about their beliefs or lack thereof—would've mentioned. A smile rose to her lips, recalling that special day. She'd treasure it for the rest of her life.

Eternity actually.

"I left New York and became a Christian not long after. Guilt plagued me, and I realized I was a sinner in need of a savior." A lump formed in her throat, and her eyes watered. "The Lord Jesus was and is that for me."

Luke gave a slow nod, his intense scrutiny making her sit up straight. "I can see you're different, Em. You're more peaceful and mature, and even more beautiful than you were in high school."

"Stop with the charm already!" She giggled, nudging him.

Sobering, she eyed him suspiciously. "Why are you trying to butter me up? What do you want?"

"I want to visit you in New Haven, take you out. Would you let me?"

"You want to travel *all* that way for a date?"

"Yes."

Emily shook her head. "Well, if you're crazy enough to try that, then be my guest, but I won't hold you to it if you change your mind."

He leaned in real close, his voice low. "I have no intention of changing my mind."

"Oh."

Covering a heated face with her hands, Emily peeked through her fingers at Henry. Jaw clenched hard, his fierce gaze was on her. Did he think Luke had kissed her cheek or whispered sweet nothings in her ear?

Well, he could think what he liked. He shouldn't have left her side.

Dancing filled the remaining hour, and only the ones shared with Luke were enjoyable. The rest...not so much.

Henry stayed away. At least five gorgeous young socialites swooned in his arms during that time. Not that Emily kept count.

Bells sounded at the imminent approach of midnight.

"Quick, Em, come with me." Grasping her hand tightly, Luke led the rush toward the floor-to-ceiling windows, where a spectacular view of the glowing Empire State Building would enable them to witness the ball dropping from above.

While they waited, flutes of Moët champagne were hurriedly distributed to every guest.

As Emily took in the magnificent city lights, her senses became fully alert. Without turning her head, she knew when Henry arrived on her other side.

"A little different to New Year's Eve in New Haven." He spoke quietly but loud enough for her to hear over the gathered crowd.

'It is. But as someone told me recently, where you are is not so important. It's who you're with."

"I agree," he murmured, his warm breath hitting her cheek.

Feeling the weight of Henry's gaze, she met his eyes, then couldn't look away. The hazel flecks in his green eyes gleamed brightly, capturing her like fish in a net. Somehow, it made her feel powerless, though not in a bad way.

His eyes dipped to her mouth, and she licked her lips. Did he hope to kiss her at midnight? Or would he turn and press his lips to the gorgeous brunette standing to his right?

Her gaze slid to his mouth, and for a moment, she imagined they were alone. Her heartbeat sped up.

"Five, four, three—"

Emily swung her gaze from Henry. She couldn't miss the famous ball drop. Not when her family had watched it every year together until she'd left to live with her aunt.

Shouts and cheers abounded the second a fantastic firework display erupted.

"Happy New Year, Em." Luke's chaste kiss surprised her. The perfect gentleman, he didn't linger as other men might've.

By the time her eyes found Henry, his lips were fused to the brunette's. And that kiss was not chaste. Not at all.

After glaring briefly at the woman who had her *friend's* full attention, Emily ducked her head. Sudden nausea hit her stomach.

"Happy New Year, sweetheart!" Mom hugged her tight. "I'm so glad you're here."

She smiled faintly. "Me too, Mom."

"Happy New Year, my girl," Dad said, reaching for her next. "I hope it brings us both what we want." He shared a conspiratorial look with Luke, then shook his hand and wished him well.

"Um, I'll be back." Fighting a constricting throat and burning eyes, Emily pushed through the well-wishers.

Just outside the bathroom door, she heard her name. Turning, she frowned. A determined Henry marched toward her, the intensity in his eyes almost scary.

"I wanted to wish you a Happy New Year, but you'd gone." Strong hands cupped her upper arms, his electric touch searing her skin.

"I needed…I need the bathroom." She waved toward the door as if that would explain her actions.

When her gaze dropped involuntarily to his lips, she drew in a shaky breath. As much as she wanted him to kiss her, he'd said he wouldn't. But this was an exception, wasn't it? It's what one did on such occasions. With Henry's mouth inches away, Emily couldn't help herself. Closing the distance, she pressed her lips to his for a long second, then pulled back. "Happy New Year," she breathed before quickly escaping into the bathroom.

***

Fingers on his mouth, Henry stared at the closed bathroom door. That had been unexpected. Very welcome, but unexpected nonetheless.

A smile crept onto his face.

Should he wait?

The one person he'd begun to loathe moved toward him, and that made up Henry's mind. He wouldn't linger. Instead, he passed by a smug Luke, greeting him with a tight smile.

Why would Emily be interested in a guy like that? They may have been in school together, but she was much more mature. There was something about her, as if she'd been through some life-altering experience. Whatever it was, she'd grown up faster than the average woman.

One day he'd ask, but it was probably best if he didn't interfere for now. He'd finally gotten her to agree to be friends. He wasn't about to mess it up. Given Emily had spent the majority of the night in Luke's arms, well, clearly she meant what she said about not dating Henry.

Yet the way she'd kissed him screamed more than friends. However, her words said something else.

Henry searched for his parents while celebrations continued with champagne, indulgent black truffles, and caviar back in the main area. As much as he wanted to stay and spend more time with Emily, he couldn't bear to see her return with Luke. He'd be left to his own devices again, and he could only stomach so much conversation about the latest celebrities and the best places to eat.

"Henry! We thought you'd left."

"I'm about to. I'm exhausted." He sent his parents a closed-mouth smile. "It's been a fantastic evening, but Adam will appreciate a hand with the soup kitchen lunches tomorrow. I'm gonna head back to yours so I can get up in—" He glanced at his watch and groaned. "Five hours."

"Don't tell me you're leaving, Henry?" Mark Quinn's brow wrinkled as he and his wife joined the small group.

"I am. I assume Emily has a ride home?"

Michelle Quinn nodded. "Luke said he'd bring her home."

Of course Luke had.

Maybe he should text Emily and offer to share his ride back to New Haven tomorrow? It made sense, and friends did that, right?

"Okay, great. Well, wonderful party, everyone." Henry focused on the Quinns. "I'm sure I'll see you again soon."

"Yes," Mom piped up. "And next time, we hope you'll bring Brittany."

"Brittany?" Michelle seemed surprised, but there was something off about her expression.

"We mentioned her earlier. Henry's girlfriend—Adam Wilson's sister?"

"Oh, that's right." Michelle bobbed her platinum-blonde head.

Mom patted Henry's shoulder. "I'm thrilled my only son's ready to settle down. He's made us wait long enough. We had hoped he'd choose Emily..." She gave the Quinns a regretful smile. "But Brittany's an amazing woman, beautiful, mature—"

"Mom!" Feeling exasperated, Henry gave her a warning look.

"Sorry, but I'm just so happy for you."

So typical of his mother—showing zero remorse for discussing his private life in public.

"And so you should be, Denise." Michelle smiled warmly at her friend. "It's what we all want for our children. For them to be settled with the right man and happily married."

The right man?

Henry suppressed a huff. Luke Bowman might check all the right boxes on the outside, but there was no way he was the 'right man' for Emily. There was a reason they broke up in high school. A second-chance relationship hardly ever worked. Unless a child was involved, like Melanie and Steven.

Thank goodness that wasn't the case here.

Stuffing his hands in his pockets, Henry plastered on his most charming smile. "Goodnight, everyone. Mom, Dad, see you later."

In the town car organized by his parents, he tossed his jacket onto the seat beside him and stared at his phone. Emily would still be at the party, so it wasn't too late to text. What he didn't want was for her to read it in front of Luke. After Henry's parents made it clear he was unavailable, the Quinns, if they were as controlling as his parents, would be pushing Luke in Emily's direction even more.

Why, though, he had no idea.

From their previous conversations, Henry was surprised Emily would even entertain the notion of being with the guy, but Luke did have the boyfriend-from-school thing going for him. If she'd dated him, she must've liked him, maybe even loved him. Why did that idea sour his stomach and stab at his heart?

His reasoning was all over the place.

Clicking on her number, he brought the handset to his ear and held his breath. For all he knew, she was back on the dance floor and wouldn't even hear it ringing.

"Where are you, Henry? I came out of the bathroom, and you'd disappeared." In the background, the band still played.

"Luke showed up."

"I suppose that might've been a little awkward." A few seconds passed. "You sound like you're somewhere quiet."

"On my way home. To my parents' place."

"Oh."

"Daily Bread's soup kitchen stays open, even on New Year's Day. I want to get an early start, to help Adam."

"That's very kind of you. Though, I'm sure he'd have understood if you decided not to go back tomorrow."

"No doubt. Anyway, I'll let you get back to the party…and Luke."

He was about to hang up when she said, "Wait. Why did you call?"

He squashed a sigh. "It doesn't matter."

"Henry," she said in a stern voice.

Imagining her practicing that exact voice, he stifled a chuckle. She'd make a great teacher.

"I was going to suggest we share a ride back to New Haven, but I'm planning on leaving early, so—"

"What time?" she interrupted.

"Around seven?"

"I'll be ready."

He grinned. Alright then. Luke may be keeping Emily company for the next few minutes, but Henry would be taking her home tomorrow.

Not to his home, sure, but home. Far away from New York and Luke.

Chapter Eight

The following morning, Emily opened the main gates to her parents' property for Henry's town car, then quietly closed the heavy wooden door behind her. Security lights lit the surroundings, their brightness contrasting directly with the pitch-black sky. Shouldering her purse, she picked up her suitcase and descended the steps to the stone driveway. A cool wind whipped through the tall trees lining the drive, and she shivered involuntarily. Maybe choosing not to wear a knit cap or gloves was a mistake.

The back passenger door swung open, and Henry climbed out. His wide, warm smile made her forget she'd ever been cold.

"Good morning." He leaned in, looking like he was about to greet her with a kiss, and Emily's heartbeat sped up uncomfortably. Instead, his arm brushed hers as he retrieved her luggage. "You ready to go home?"

She swallowed, chasing down her ridiculous pulse.

"More than ready," she managed before climbing inside the vehicle and setting her purse at her feet.

Henry slid in beside her on the backseat and gestured to the driver that they were ready to leave.

"Thanks for letting me share your ride," she said as the car pulled forward.

"I didn't want you catching the train home."

She shot him a surprised look. She'd never told him her

travel plans.

Reaching forward, he pulled two aluminum travel mugs from the cup holders.

"Peppermint Mocha?" She grinned at the man who knew her morning coffee choice.

"What else?" Henry winked.

"Mmm, this is perfect," she said after taking a sip and meeting his smug gaze. "Thank you."

"You're welcome."

"Why'd you think I'd be taking a train home?" she asked.

He cocked a brow. "I saw you coming out of Grand Central the day we arrived."

Heat rushed to her cheeks. "Oh."

"Why didn't you tell me you were seeing your parents for Christmas? I'd have picked you up and brought you home."

She shook her head. "I didn't want to impose."

His hand came to rest on hers, creating sparks she had an urge to shake out. "That's not the reason, is it?" His intense gaze penetrated, questioned.

He was so close. The musky scent he wore, most pleasant. Too enticing. She glanced away.

"It doesn't matter," he said. "In the future, if you're coming to New York, let me know. I have a feeling I'll be visiting too."

Her gaze darted back to him. "Why?"

"I'd have thought that was obvious," Henry said, his voice husky.

Before he shifted away, he squeezed her hand. A wave of awareness shot through her, and she absentmindedly rubbed the spot where his hand had been.

Soft classical music played through the speakers, and Henry remained quiet. She liked that every second didn't need to be filled with conversation. What she didn't like was how her heart always beat slightly faster when she was with him.

Eventually, she snuck a peek at the cause of her erratic heartbeat. Henry had set his flask down and now leaned against the headrest with his eyes closed.

Finishing off her drink, she did the same.

Later, Emily startled awake, her head on Henry's shoulder and her arm resting across his stomach. She dared not move. How long had she been sleeping, and where were they?

Gingerly, she lifted her head and arm away from Henry's body. Thankfully, he didn't stir. However, he chuckled—low and throaty.

Her gaze snapped to his. Merriment danced there, and he wore a knowing look. Or was it desire?

"You have a good nap?" he asked.

She swallowed, ducked her head. "Mm-hmm."

Oh, for a mirror. Smoothing her hands over her long hair, Emily identified and untangled a few knots. Hopefully she hadn't drooled on Henry's sweater.

"Are you thirsty? Would you like some water, or do you fancy another coffee?"

Mouth agape, she stared at him. "When did they start putting coffee machines in town cars?"

"No, silly." He laughed. "We can stop. In fact, I'm starving. Why don't we grab some breakfast?"

Tapping her jean-clad thigh, she considered his invitation. He was just being a concerned friend, right? It wasn't a breakfast date. Because if it was, then…

"Emily," he admonished, "if you're as hungry as me, it makes sense to stop and eat."

"Okay." She let out a nervous laugh. "I could probably eat a whole stack of pancakes, and I could definitely use another coffee."

He gave her a lop-sided grin. "So, pancakes for breakfast, huh?"

"And waffles and bacon and eggs and—"

He held up his hands, laughing. She really liked the sound. Liked the way his eyes shone and the fine lines that crinkled around them. "I get the picture. I like that you're not a poached egg on a cracker kind of girl."

"Nope. Not yet. Give me a few years, old man," she teased.

"Then I'll be joining you with the poached egg."

With a mock-hurt look, he puffed out his chest and folded his arms across it. "Are you saying I need to run more than six miles a day?"

"No." Honing in on his muscular physique, she blushed. "You're perfect."

The minute the breathless comment was out, she wished to retract it. Feeding Henry's ego so wasn't a good idea.

Encouraging him? Also no.

"Well, that's a relief," he said, joy filling his expression.

Once he'd given the driver an instruction to stop at the nearest restaurant, Henry peered back at her. Their gazes met, tangled. The air between them became charged, and she attempted to look away but lost.

"Emily?" he said softly, hesitantly.

Her heart thundered in her chest. "Yes?"

He shook his head. "Never mind."

***

Henry watched as Emily peered out the tinted car window, her lips pressed tight. Gentle daylight offered a glimpse of I-95 concrete barriers and bare-branched trees, nothing else.

He sighed. Not exactly riveting viewing. Asking Emily to spend the day with him wasn't a good idea, no matter how easy it was to be with her. He should be grateful for this time together. If he started getting greedy, she'd back off, then their newly cultivated friendship would disappear. And he couldn't bear that thought, not when he wanted so much more.

Emily didn't.

He understood why. Sort of. She considered him a playboy. That image—one he'd purposefully portrayed—had gotten him off the hook in the past when a woman desired a serious relationship. It had also kept his father off his back. But now Henry wanted rid of it.

What he needed was to come up with a game plan. Show Emily he could commit to a serious relationship. That he was the trustworthy, reliable man who'd make a good husband

and father one day. Sure, he had his faith and his wealth, but without the love of the right woman? He didn't want to consider that option.

In order to man up and be in the position to take on his father's empire, he desired a life partner who would complement, support, and love him. The way he would her.

But who would be willing to effectively fake date him so he could prove his worth?

Britt?

Mom and Dad already thought they were a couple. And Adam? What would he think if Henry dated his sister?

He recalled Adam's warning: "I think Britt has a thing for you, so be careful. Don't hurt her." Henry had laughed off the ridiculous idea. Ever since Adam had introduced her in college, he and Britt had been good friends. Sure, they bantered a lot, and sometimes Britt appeared to barely tolerate him, but deep down Henry knew she was just teasing.

Honestly, spending time with Britt was almost as easy as being with Emily. Not quite, though. Britt hardly made his heart beat faster, as gorgeous as she was, but she'd make a great fake girlfriend.

Could he persuade her?

Adam had mentioned some persistent men were pursuing her, ones who wouldn't take no for an answer. Maybe they could help each other out, as friends, with a mutually beneficial relationship?

The car slowed down, bringing his scheming to an end.

"We're here," he said unnecessarily.

Emily turned to look at him just as a loud rumbling came from his stomach. She giggled prettily. "Right on time, too, by the sounds of it."

He pretended to glower.

"Don't worry," she said, holding up her hands as the back door swung open. "Any minute now, mine will join yours in the choir." Despite their laughter, they still managed to scramble out of the vehicle.

Henry gestured to the restaurant. "What do you think? Is it suitable?"

The Milford restaurant—The Corner—built with large gray bricks, had a bottle-green canopy over the storefront. He imagined, come spring, they'd have outdoor seating and maybe even some brightly colored umbrellas.

"It's perfect." Emily's smile lit her pretty brown eyes, and his heart skipped a beat.

Inside, gentle, creamy-colored walls flanked a bright red wall. Dark wood tables and chairs occupied most of the floor space. The mismatched bookcases, filled with an eclectic collection of scattered books, gave it a homey feel. Not to mention the generous fire crackling over in the fireplace. The buzz of customer conversation added to the coziness, while the smells of sizzling bacon and strong coffee wafted from the service area.

After grabbing a couple menus from the entrance, Henry guided Emily to a free table.

A rosy-faced woman with a white apron spread across her pregnant belly walked over, a pen poised above a pad of paper. "What can I get you, folks?"

"Buttermilk pancakes with a side of fruit and an Americano, please," Emily said.

"Make that two Americanos," Henry added. "And I'd like the sausage breakfast burrito."

"Coming up." The woman shoved the stationery into her pouch and waddled away.

"So…" Henry leaned back against the padded wooden chair and crossed his arms. "Any plans for the rest of the day?"

"Um." Dragging the bowl of sugar sachets toward her, Emily started pulling them out one by one.

"You aren't going home to study, are you?"

"No." She concentrated on separating the white and brown packets. "I'm not sure. Technically, I'm on holiday until tomorrow." Shoving the whole lot back into the bowl, she raised her eyes to his. "What about you? You heading straight to the soup kitchen?"

He nodded. "After I drop you off. There's always a lot of prep before we serve a meal, and most staff are off for the holiday. I know Adam will appreciate as much help as possible."

"Would you...?" Emily chewed her bottom lip.

Stifling a groan, Henry quickly lowered his eyes and paused the wayward thoughts trying to take over his mind.

"Could I come help you out?" Emily asked.

He grinned. "Absolutely." And to think he'd chickened out of asking her the same thing. "Are you sure? It can be a real eye-opener if you know what I mean."

"You think I'll be put off by the sort of people who frequent the kitchen?" Huffing, she grabbed the pepper shaker and spun it between her hands.

"No, I—"

"I'm not a snob, Henry. I do understand that not everyone is born into a life of luxury like me. And in case you didn't notice, I'm very comfortable riding the train with the masses and wearing thrift store clothing." She pointed to her silky-looking floral wrap dress. "This may be a Diane Von Furstenberg vintage, but I picked it up for fifty dollars in New Haven. A steal, believe me."

"Hey, take it easy," he said, raising his hands. "I only meant, besides peeling and cutting vegetables, you could end up sweeping and mopping floors or washing dishes by hand."

Surreptitiously, he checked out her fingernails, relieved to find they weren't the falsely manicured kind he'd seen on all the single women at the party last night.

Emily scowled. "You *do* know I cook for Charlotte and the kids, right? I may not have to mop floors, but I've watched it being done. It's not rocket science." She gave him a long, searching look. "Unless you're trying to change my mind?"

"On the contrary, I'm looking forward to your company. Besides"—he shot her a cheeky smile—"you're awfully cute when you get riled up."

"Hey." She mock glared at him. "Be nice."

"Here you go, folks. Your food'll be out in a minute." Their server set down their drinks and left.

Henry tasted his coffee. "Wow! The flavor is fantastic."

"You sound surprised." Emily chuckled, lifting her cup. "Mmm, you're right."

"See?" He gave her a pointed look.

Ignoring him, she ran a finger around the mug's rim. "The real test is the food. Although, I'm so hungry they could probably serve me rubbery pancakes and week-old fruit and I wouldn't notice." A teasing smile diluted her serious tone.

"Really?" He smirked. "I think you'd notice."

Their meals arrived, and they dug in immediately, eating like ravenous newborn puppies. The food *was* incredible.

"You seemed to enjoy Mr. Bowman's company a fair bit last night," Henry commented after taking a breather from his meal. "I assume you plan on seeing him again."

"In ten days."

She was counting the days?

He scowled. "So, the *ex* part doesn't matter?"

She sighed deeply. "It's complicated."

"How so?"

"We broke up because of a difference of opinion." Her gaze dropped to her twiddling thumbs. "It's been a long time, and I guess I'm finally ready to forgive him." She blinked, bringing her attention back to him, and shrugged. "We're older and wiser now, and he's changed. He wants to try again, and I'd like to."

"Well, your parents clearly approve of him. Though, I'm surprised you aren't running in the opposite direction. I thought you didn't want them controlling you."

"I'm not being forced into anything here, Henry," she said defensively. "I loved Luke long before they even knew about him. The fact that he's ended up working for my father is complete coincidence. I can't see how they'd be pulling the strings in this situation. Luke would never fall for that."

"I'm sorry. I never meant to imply you were a puppet."

Covering her hand to reassure her caused his pulse to spike, so he snatched his hand away.

He waited for his pulse to normalize before saying, "I have one more question," to which she raised her eyebrows. "Please don't be mad. I kinda like having you as my friend." He took her tight smile as permission. "Luke's not after your money, is he?"

Her snort was most unladylike. "Hardly. I guess you've never heard of the Bowman's because they're English."

He shook his head.

"I'd wager Luke's trust fund would rival yours."

Great. The one good reason Henry had for Emily to steer clear of the man, discounting the title of ex, was toast.

Evidently, Luke Bowman was a perfect match for Emily Quinn.

That made him feel *so* much better.

Chapter Nine

"Hey, Emily!" Adam said, a broad, inviting smile replacing his initial shock. "Great to see you here."

"Thanks, Adam. Happy New Year." She smiled back before sweeping her eyes around Daily Bread soup kitchen's decently sized main hall.

Adam shifted his attention to Henry. "Hey there, bud. Glad you decided to make it."

"I said I would." Henry smirked.

"And you brought a...friend?" Adam glanced briefly at Emily, curiosity shining in his eyes.

"Yep."

A strange look passed between the men.

What was *that* about?

Henry strolled over to a large chest of drawers and began collecting paper plates and napkins. Meantime, Adam asked Emily about her Christmas.

"It was different."

Adam's brow quirked.

"In a good way," Emily quickly reassured him. In turn, she asked if Charlotte had managed the kids on her own.

He waved off her concern. "Oh, don't worry, she wasn't alone. My folks have been staying with her, so she's had plenty of help."

A sigh of relief slipped out. "I bet the kids loved all the attention."

Setting bottles of sauce and eating utensils onto the tables, Adam chuckled. "They sure did."

After a minute of watching the men work, Emily blurted to Adam, "How can I help?"

He examined her, his expression skeptical. "You sure you want to get those clothes dirty?"

She glanced at her thrift store designer T-shirt, jeans, and boots, glad she'd changed out of her dress before leaving the restaurant. "I don't mind at all."

"Well, okay then. The kitchen staff could likely use your help with food prep. Henry can introduce you to Linda." He winked. "She's in charge."

Sidling up to Emily, Henry spoke in a stage whisper, "I'm glad he's finally realized it."

They all laughed, Henry's delightfully low chuckle bringing goosebumps to Emily's arms.

She ignored them.

The kitchen was a hive of activity. A buxom older woman turned from the oven, a tray of roasted vegetables in her hands. She grinned. "Mr. Henry, aren't you a sight for sore eyes? I can't remember the last time you were in my kitchen."

After sliding the tray onto a counter, she opened her arms to him.

"Happy New Year, Linda," he said, embracing her. "It's good to see you."

Linda stepped back, regarding Emily with interest. "And who do we have here? Another beautiful young lady. It's quite the day for those."

"This is my friend, Emily Quinn." Nudging her gently forward, Henry's hand heated her lower back. "She's also Adam's girlfriend's nanny."

"Anyone who's a friend of Henry's is welcome here," Linda said, wrapping strong arms around Emily and briefly pulling her close.

She sucked in a breath.

Linda chuckled, releasing her. "Mind if I call you Emily? Adam's girlfriend's nanny is rather a mouthful."

Laughter burst from Emily. She liked this woman.

"Emily is fine."

Henry glanced around the kitchen. "Is there anything Emily can help you with, Linda?"

"Does she know how to chop onions?"

"I do," Emily answered.

With a nod of approval, Linda shepherded Henry toward the kitchen exit. "Away with you, young man. I'm sure Adam needs you."

"You hear that, Emily?" Henry grinned, looking over his shoulder. "She called me a *young* man."

"If you say so," she responded, trying to keep a straight face.

Pausing at the exit, he shot Emily a questioning look, but she waved him away. "Go. I'll be fine."

"Okay, I'll check on you in a bit." A twinkle appeared in his eyes. "You'd better not be crying when I do. I'm not good with crybabies."

"Ha ha."

She'd just started slicing carrots after finishing the onions when a glamorous brunette breezed in, carrying boxes of tin foil.

"Here we go." The woman's inquisitive gaze caught Emily's for half a second before it swung back to Linda. "Where shall I put these?"

"Next to the ovens, please. You're an absolute lifesaver, Britt." Linda smiled gratefully. "Thank you."

So *that* was Adam's sister—a petite woman with a figure most models would envy. Glossy brunette hair fell in waves over her shoulders, and her beautiful pale green eyes sparkled with confidence. This was the woman Henry's parents 'approved' of. And no wonder because she was gorgeous.

Emily clenched her teeth.

Britt dumped her load onto the counter and turned, her

gaze assessing. "I don't believe we've met. Do you usually volunteer here?"

"First time, actually." She kept her tone polite. Sort of.

"Well, thank you. I know Adam appreciates any help, especially on a holiday."

"My pleasure."

Britt spun on her heels, took a step, then swung back around. "I didn't get your name."

"Emily."

"Emily...hmm." She tapped her lip. "Wait a minute. Not Charlotte's kids' nanny?"

"The very same."

"Oh, I'm so sorry. I didn't realize."

The sudden look of admiration on Britt's face confused Emily.

"Charlotte's been raving about you this past week. Apparently, you don't only take care of her kids, but you're also studying to be a teacher. That's incredible."

"Thanks."

Britt frowned. "Weren't you in New York for the holidays?"

"I was. I came back with—"

"There you are, Britt." Henry strolled into the kitchen. "Adam's asking for you." His eyes traveled between the two women. "I see you've met Emily."

"Yep. We were just chatting, but I'd better report to my brother before he fires me." She winked at Emily, then laid a hand on Henry's arm and fluttered her eyelashes at him. "See you in a bit?"

"Uh-huh."

Fighting a burning sensation in her chest, Emily lowered her head and focused on her job. She had no desire to watch the perfect couple.

"How's it going?" A deep voice startled her.

Silly. Of course Henry hadn't left yet!

She swallowed. "Good."

"Listen, Charlotte's bringing the kids over. Adam and I are

taking them out for a milkshake before we serve lunch. Will you join us?"

She shook her head. "Thanks, but I'm happy here and still full from breakfast."

A flicker of disappointment crossed his face. Or maybe she just imagined it.

"You sure?"

"Britt will no doubt happily keep you company while Adam and Charlotte act all mushy. So yes, I'm sure."

***

Though his heart protested, Henry's head agreed it was probably better that Emily didn't come along. This way, he'd get a chance to talk to Britt. The problem was, when the holiday was over and everything went back to normal, he'd be lucky if he saw Emily once a week—at church on Sunday.

Sighing, he re-entered the main hall. The lovebirds—Charlotte and Adam—were in each other's arms, whispering who knows what. A jolt of jealousy hit. Not that he had any interest in Charlotte. He did, however, have a growing desire to settle down with the right woman and start a family.

"Henry! Come join us." Britt waved him over from across the room. "These kids are running me ragged."

He laughed. They were playing a game of tag.

"I'd love to."

The kids were fast. After five minutes, he started to feel dizzy from darting here and there. Charlotte's eldest son, Peter, had just made him 'it.' All Henry had to do was run faster than Britt—pretty easy—catch her, and he'd win.

The second he grabbed her arm from behind, she spun fast toward him, taking him by surprise. Worried she'd fall backward, he snaked his other hand around her waist and brought her to him. With her body molded to his, he could see right into her lovely green eyes.

"I thought I was going to fall!" She gave him a lop-sided grin, then pretended to swoon. "My hero."

Over her shoulder, he caught Emily staring. Judging from her guarded expression and taut lips, she wasn't thrilled about her view.

Immediately releasing Britt, Henry headed in Emily's direction. But she had other ideas. Bypassing him, she hightailed it over to Adam and Charlotte. "Hey, Charlie," she said.

"Hey, Em." After a quick embrace, they drew apart. "I heard you were here."

Emily looked between the couple. "You two look positively radiant. I assume you had a good Christmas?"

Charlotte gazed adoringly at her boyfriend and sighed happily. "It was perfect."

"Wait a minute." Henry scrutinized his best friend's face, then his girlfriend's. "Adam's wearing the same smug look he has whenever he beats me in a race or thinks of an idea before me."

"You're engaged!" Emily beamed as she pointed at Charlotte's left hand. "Congratulations! Oh, I'm so happy for you two."

"Awesome news, bud!" Henry pumped Adam's hand. "But why am I only hearing about this now? I was in New York, not some remote place in the jungle or deepest, darkest Africa." He feigned hurt. "You could've called."

"Sorry. I—" Adam shared a knowing smile with his fiancée. "We wanted to tell our friends in person. Right, darling?"

"Yep." Charlotte's smile stretched so wide Henry wondered if her mouth would ache later.

The truth hit him: even his best friend, who'd hardly ever dated in the last few years, was going to get married. None of Henry's many girlfriends over the years had been serious.

Watching Emily gushing over Charlotte's stunning ring, he sighed heavily. Pity the only woman he would consider a lifetime with wasn't interested in dating him.

"We should probably head out," he said when things quietened. He motioned toward the kids. "They're all gonna be real thirsty soon."

"You're right." Adam clapped his hands loudly. "Britt.

Kids. Milkshakes are calling. Time to go."

"Woohoo," Peter shouted, immediately echoed by his younger brother, Daniel.

Their older sister, Amy, rushed up to Emily and flung her arms around her waist. "Miss Emily! Are you coming with us?"

Looking apologetic, she shook her head. "Sorry, Amy. Miss Linda needs me in the kitchen."

"Mom, *please* can I stay and help Miss Emily?" Amy half-whined, her hands joined as if she were praying. "I can have a milkshake another time."

"It's great that you want to help, sweetheart," Adam answered for Charlotte, "but the kitchen's a strictly child-free zone."

Brushing her hand lovingly over Amy's head, Emily smiled brightly. "I'll see you later. You'll be back to help serve the food, right?"

"Yep." Amy's chin lifted. "Mr. Adam said we could help dish out vegetables."

Always ready with a kind word, Emily clearly cared for her charges. Henry loved that about her.

Britt linked her arm with his and smiled expectantly. "Time to go?"

He nodded, vaguely aware of Emily quietly disappearing into the kitchen. His posture sagged. At least she'd be staying to help serve the food.

The milkshake place was thankfully quiet. They collected their orders then filled two booths; the kids sat together in one, the adults opposite. Unsurprisingly, the topic of conversation revolved around weddings and the best time to have one.

"I love winter weddings," Britt said dreamily.

Charlotte groaned, rubbing her arms. "No way. Too cold. I'd much rather a summer wedding. Then the kids won't be in school, and either Adam's parents can watch them while we're on honeymoon, or they can stay with Mel and Steven. My brother and Julie would have them, but with the Jays' schedule, I never know whether they'll be in the country." She sipped her shake, looking thoughtful for a moment, then smacked her forehead. "I just realized Mel can't look after the kids then."

"You sound very certain of that," Henry commented.

"I'm not sure if Mel's telling everyone yet or not…" Charlotte bit her thumbnail. "But since she's past the tricky stage—"

"She's pregnant," Henry guessed.

"Yes, and I'm pretty sure the baby's due around then."

Britt gave a nervous laugh. "Definitely not a good idea to ask Mel then."

Was she worried Adam would ask her to look after the kids? Because she seemed to have no problem entertaining them earlier in the hall. Either way, Charlotte hadn't mentioned the obvious choice.

"Why isn't Emily looking after them?" Henry asked, thinking he'd missed an important piece of information.

"She won't be here in the summer," Charlotte answered. "Well, I'm not entirely sure about her dates yet, but it's safest not to plan our wedding around her."

"Where's she going to be?"

"Honestly, I never asked." Charlotte frowned. "She requested the time off just before she left for Christmas break."

"Really?"

Adam shot him a look, then changed the subject. "What about a spring wedding?"

"You'd rather get married sooner than later, wouldn't you, brother dear?" Britt teased.

Adam's answer was lost on Henry. He was too busy trying to figure out Emily's plans for the summer. By then, her teaching course would be finished. Perhaps she was going away with her parents?

He made a mental note to ask.

Later, on the way back to the soup kitchen, Henry realized he still hadn't spoken with Britt. He waited until the car pulled up, then grabbed her hand before she climbed out. "Mind if we have a word before going inside?"

"Sure."

Henry led Britt to just outside the steel door used for kitchen deliveries. Thankfully, it was still light, otherwise it wouldn't have been the wisest place to hang out. He gathered her hands in his and looked her in the eye. While his heart thumped a little harder than normal, his stomach felt like a band of hopping insects had settled in it.

"Would you have dinner with me tonight?" he asked, his voice tight. "I have a proposition for you."

"Sounds intriguing." Britt smiled beguilingly. "I'm in."

"Great." Squeezing her hands, he puffed out a long breath of air.

The door behind them swung open, and Emily appeared. "Oh, sorry! I didn't mean to interrupt. I-I was just throwing out the trash."

Henry groaned. Talk about timing! What were the chances Emily wouldn't take the scene the wrong way?

With his luck? Zero.

Chapter Ten

"Thanks, miss." A weather-beaten old man with one lazy eye held his soup bowl out to Emily. "This is my favorite," he said, his grin revealing missing front teeth.

"It does smell delicious." Offering a brief smile, Emily ladled out three full-to-the-brim spoons of carrot and coriander soup. She nodded toward the other side of the soup tureen. "Don't forget to take some French loaf."

He tipped a hat that had more holes in it than material. "I will, though my wife always used to say, 'Johnny, don't fill up on the bread. You'll regret it when you reach the main course.'"

She chuckled. "A wise woman."

Sadness filled his expression until his lips lifted into another toothless smile. "That she was. She died three years ago, and I miss her. But I'll be joining her in heaven soon enough."

"It's lovely that you have that assurance, Johnny. God bless you."

The next gentleman in line wore a permanent scowl. After issuing a curt nod and a mumbled thanks, he stomped off toward one of the long trestle tables set up for eating. A tiny Christmas tree, festively decorated, stood at the center of each table. Colorful streamers and bowls of candy dotted the table's length, adding to the festive atmosphere. Christmas carols played softly in the background.

Serving alone at the soup station, Emily kept her gaze forward, tuning out her surroundings. She definitely hadn't seen Henry and Britt come inside nor noticed them standing side by side serving the pre-carved meat and sauces.

Shoving down feelings of envy and jealousy, she glanced at the line zig-zagging to the main entrance and outside. Linda had warned her it would be busy. After Christmas, folks seemed to have even less disposable income than normal, while the cold also brought in more visitors.

Grateful for the excuse to concentrate on others, Emily chatted with the colorful characters showing up with empty bowls. She held her breath several times until the stench became more bearable as they moved on. Their dirty, limp hair—often in desperate need of trimming—and their third or fourth-hand clothing helped her understand why Adam and Henry had such a heart for these people. The need was great.

Although she wore thrift store-bought clothes too, she'd purchased them from shops where these folk likely couldn't afford a birthday card, let alone a pair of shoes. And truth be told, she could access her savings account anytime. Her parents' generous monthly allowance, given throughout her childhood, had never been touched. They'd paid for everything.

At twenty-five—less than a year away—she'd gain access to a trust fund of ten million dollars. Nothing compared to what she'd inherit eventually. Just thinking about it made her feel incredibly guilty. She'd never need that much money and couldn't even imagine spending it. She needed to find something worthwhile to invest the money in.

Maybe she'd talk to Adam and Charlotte. Charlotte's generous inheritance funded her Widows and Orphans foundation, which in turn would support the orphanage-come-homeless shelter she and Adam would be opening soon.

Slight issue, though. So far, Emily had kept her true identity hidden, and she intended to keep it that way.

She could ask Henry's advice. He was a friend and had

been sworn to secrecy after they'd bumped into each other in New York. A sideways glance at him revealed his warm gaze glued to her. Her heart stuttered. Seconds passed, and she couldn't move. Only Britt, elbowing Henry, broke the eye contact, enabling Emily to look away.

The line soon disappeared, and Linda turned up, her smile lighting her round face. "You're done?"

Emily nodded.

"Splendid." Linda motioned to the leftovers. "Please, help yourself."

"Thanks, but I had a big breakfast." She patted her midriff. In reality, it had been hours ago. Still, given the giant ball in the pit of her stomach, the idea of eating was nauseating.

Linda tilted her head. "Alright, well, a bunch of dishes are waiting to be hand-washed in the kitchen. If you're game?"

"I am."

Emily snuck a peek at Britt and Henry, seated at one of the far tables, deep in conversation. Stifling a groan, she left the dining hall.

Later, Henry approached with a broad, appreciative smile. "Don't you think you've done enough?"

She dried the last serving bowl and placed it in the cupboard. After folding the damp tea towel, she faced him. "Is everything cleared up in the hall?"

"Almost," Henry replied, laying a hand on her shoulder. Her eyes darted to his hand, and he quickly removed it and stepped back. "Adam's supervising the last of it. But you've been a tremendous help. Thank you."

"My pleasure." She gave a close-mouthed smile. "Besides, I enjoyed talking to everyone. No matter their level of appreciation." She shrugged. "I only wish I could do more."

"Volunteers are always needed."

"I'm sure." She frowned. "Except, I barely have time to myself during term time. Also, I need to be available for Charlotte."

"Fair enough." He crossed his arms and glanced around the kitchen. Although staff bustled about, they looked about done.

Emily's gaze settled on Henry's handsome profile. "Maybe…" she began. Was this a good idea? Probably not. "Maybe you and I could talk about other ways I could get involved."

He studied her. "Anytime."

"How about tonight? We could order pizza and—"

"I'm sorry." He cut her off, his smile apologetic. "I already have plans. Britt's leaving tomorrow," he mumbled.

"Of course! Sorry."

His eyes met hers boldly. "But after that, I am all yours."

Emily's heart raced. If only he meant those last four words literally.

"I mean—" a scarlet-faced Henry blustered.

Smiling, she waved him away. "I know what you meant. I'll text you when I'm free."

Henry's back pocket buzzed with a message. He pulled out his phone, and after scanning the screen, he looked at her. "My dad's driver is due any minute, and I promised you a lift home," he said softly.

"Don't worry about me. Charlotte's going the same direction, so I'll catch a ride with her."

Unidentifiable emotions crossed his face while he stared at her. "All right. I guess that makes sense. So I'll see you soon?"

"Yep." Silence echoed in Emily's ears. The kitchen staff must've left without her realizing.

Henry suddenly held out his arms and shot her one of his charming a-girl-could-die smiles. "Friends hug, right?"

Without overthinking, she stepped into those strong arms, and when he tightened the embrace, she melted into him. His familiar musky scent quickly enveloped her, bringing with it a sense of belonging. A happy sigh escaped. Then, all too soon, he released her, taking her breath and his warmth with him. Without a backward glance, he strode away.

Note for future self-preservation: avoid Mr. Palmer's hugs if at all possible.

**

"Here's to the new year." Henry held up his wine glass and smiled at Britt, grateful the restaurant had managed to squeeze them in despite his late booking.

"To the new year." Smiling brightly, she tapped her glass to his, then took a dainty sip.

Fortunately, their two-seater table was in a quieter area, away from the rowdy, jam-packed family tables. Henry scratched his brow. It was now or never. Time to state his case.

"Don't be mad at Adam," he said, trying not to grimace, "but he filled me in on your recent situation."

Britt's smile all but disappeared, and there was an edge to her voice. "What *exactly* has he been telling you?"

"About the unsuitable men hitting on you," he said gently.

Leaning back against her chair, Britt crossed her arms and glared at him. "I told Adam he doesn't need to worry about me. I've been handling myself just fine, thank you very much."

"You should be happy you have a brother who cares."

"I am. I just don't want him treating me like a little girl who needs protection. I can look after myself."

He gave her a pointed look, and she jutted out her chin.

"I can."

"I'm sure you're right, Britt," he said softly, not wanting to aggravate her further.

After savoring a few sips of his wine, he changed tactics. "Adam mentioned you have a six-month contract in New Haven."

"I start Monday."

He grinned. "Congrats, that's great news."

"Thanks." She leaned forward again, her eyes lighting up. "Can you believe I get to stay in a fully furnished luxury apartment downtown?" He opened his mouth to comment, but she hadn't finished. "There's an on-site fitness center, a pool"—her voice rose in pitch as she waved her arms animatedly—"*and* a rooftop sun-terrace with billiards and table tennis. I don't have to cook either if I don't want to, and

I'll be walking distance from plenty of bars, cafés, and restaurants."

"It sounds amazing," he said, laughing as he rescued a wine glass and a salt shaker. "I'm really happy for you."

Britt beamed at him.

"So…" Schooling his expression, he took a deep breath. "Since we're going to be in the same city, it got me thinking."

She waggled her eyebrows. "I didn't know you did that."

"Ha ha." He smirked. "You're in a new city with different challenges and a whole lot of single men—this is a college town, after all. I reckon you could do with someone to ward off their advances. Enable you to concentrate solely on your job."

"I assume you're putting yourself forward?" Mirth danced in her eyes.

"I am."

"Why?"

Henry swallowed. "Honestly, Christmas with my parents offered a different perspective."

"I don't follow."

"My sister, her husband, and their nine-year-old joined us, and we had so much fun. My niece is truly a treasure. Everyone adores her. The point is, sharing the holiday showed me what it could be like. You know, if I had my own family one day."

Closing his eyes, he rubbed the back of his neck. He should stop talking and shelve this mad idea. Apart from, when he glanced at Britt and her open expression, it felt like an invitation to keep talking.

"My father's anxious to step aside," Henry continued. "He'd like me to settle down and start with my CEO training at Palmer Enterprises so I can take up my rightful place."

Britt's jaw went slack. "CEO. Wow."

"Crazy, right?"

She nodded, looking slightly shell-shocked.

Good to know Adam didn't share everything with his sister.

"I'll admit I'm not quite ready for all that, Britt. But if I start slow, I'll get there. Eventually."

"What does this have to do with me?"

"Well…" Henry played with the cuff of his long-sleeved shirt. Adam was adamant about his sister not getting hurt. That wouldn't happen, right? Not if this wasn't for real. He conveniently shifted his slight concerns to the back of his mind. "I'd love to get my parents off my back. A steady girlfriend—one they approved of—would help immensely."

Britt blinked.

"Someone like you."

"So, you're proposing we date?" She sounded uncertain. At least she wasn't horrified at the thought.

"Effectively, yes." He nodded. "Exclusively."

"I see." Slowly, understanding filled her features. "Then I can tell anyone who shows me more than a passing interest that I'm taken, and you can tell your parents you have a girlfriend. That you aren't just playing the field like usual."

"Exactly," he said, pleased she got it so easily.

A minute later, a server delivered their steaks and topped up their drinks. Henry blessed the food, and they dug in.

"Mmm, this is so good," Britt mumbled around a mouthful of food. "Tasty and tender."

"I knew you'd like it."

While they ate, catchy pop music drowned out other noises from the bustling restaurant. Eventually, Britt lowered her silverware.

"Okay, I'm up for it."

As he processed her words, his heart skipped a beat. A smile crept onto his face. "Thank you."

She angled her head. "It's a good thing I actually like you, Henry. Otherwise, this proposal of yours would be a moot point."

Grinning, he pointed his fork at her chest. "Ditto."

Her happy smile brought a measure of relief. He'd met his objective for tonight—getting Britt to agree to be his pretend girlfriend. Now, he had to make it work. He needed Emily to see him as a serious prospect. Not as someone who had no desire to settle down.

Was Emily alone tonight? Maybe eating pizza like she'd suggested? Or had she cooked instead. He'd tasted her food at Charlotte's, so he knew the woman had skills.

Considering all her amazing talents, Emily would make an incredible wife and mother. Charlotte's kids certainly loved her. The way she'd stepped up at the soup kitchen lunch today? Awesome. If he didn't already like her—well, more than like—that would be the cake topper.

"You look like you're a thousand miles away." Britt's soft feminine voice cut into his thoughts.

"Sorry." Dragged from his musings, Henry focused on the stunning woman before him. The one who was now his girlfriend, for all intents and purposes.

"This *is* delicious," he said, stabbing a bit of the juicy steak and popping it into his mouth. He followed it with a sip of wine, then waved his hand around. "I vote we come back here another time."

"I like the sound of that."

He did too.

Except deep down, wasn't he just kidding himself? There was only one person he wanted to bring here on a date, and she would never go for it.

Chapter Eleven

"Emily!" Henry exclaimed, striding through the church foyer toward her. "There you are."

Busted.

Where did he *think* she'd be anyway? Others might make New Year's resolutions to attend more regularly—like taking up a gym membership to assuage their guilt—but not Emily. Nope, her faith was important. Fellowshipping was never a bind or a chore. Instead, it encouraged and rejuvenated her.

Emily focused on the cup warming her hands as Henry's boots pounded the wood floor. Of course, she'd rather *he* held her hand to keep it warm, but that wasn't going to happen.

"You okay?" A finger lifted her chin, forcing her eyes to the person she would prefer to avoid.

"Yep."

Grr, that aftershave! She needed distance from its enticing scent. It had the power to reel her in and make her want to kiss him. She took a small step back, and his hand fell away.

"What about you, Henry?" She pinned him with a teasing smirk. "Are you happy to be back at work instead of lazing about? With no more servants at your beck and call?"

"If I didn't know you were a Quinn,"—he spoke so softly, Emily had to lean in to hear him—"I'd be hurt by your insinuations."

Smiling cheekily, she offered a half-hearted shrug before sipping her coffee.

Henry's low, throaty chuckle sent goosebumps over her skin. "I *am* happy to be running with Adam again every morning," he said. "Holiday overindulging always messes with my physique." He patted his mid-section, drawing attention to where his fitted white button-down molded his flat stomach.

Emily sucked in a breath—the man hadn't gained an ounce! She'd stake her life on it.

"I also have a lot to focus on, like fundraising for the year ahead, never mind the building project."

"Glad to hear it." Why did her mouth feel like sandpaper?

She raised her paper cup for another sip, scowling when Henry put a hand out to stop her. "You said you'd be in touch to rearrange that pizza and discuss some ideas."

"I've been busy," she offered, hoping he'd buy it.

A muscle in his jaw twitched. "Fine. Let me know when things settle down and you find a few hours to spare."

"Sure."

A long moment passed, the lines across his forehead deepening as he scrutinized her. She nearly shifted but managed to stay still.

"Why do I get the feeling you're agreeing just to stop me pestering you?"

"I'm not—" Emily spotted Charlotte beckoning her over, and she stifled a relieved sigh. "Sorry," she said, briefly meeting Henry's eyes, "I'm being summoned. See you inside?"

He grasped her arm when she tried to sidestep him, causing heat to ricochet along her sleeve. "Will you save me a seat?" he asked.

"I'll try." She stared at the hand still holding her arm. As if it suddenly burned him, he let go, and the warmth from his touch dissipated like a puddle on a hot day. "But if there aren't any..." she trailed off, her heart racing.

Avoiding his questioning gaze, she hurried toward the auditorium. With any luck, there'd be no free seat within two rows of her.

Either luck was not on her side, or the Lord had another agenda because Adam and Charlotte had conveniently left the two seats nearest the aisle unoccupied.

"Hey, Emily."

"Hey, Adam." She flopped down beside him, almost spilling her coffee in the process.

The music began, and everyone stood.

Henry slipped in beside her. "Thanks," he whispered, leaning in so his breath tickled her cheek. A glance in his direction revealed a grateful and slightly triumphant smile.

Finding him too close for comfort, Emily quickly faced forward. She'd come to praise and worship her savior, Jesus, and that's what she'd do. Easier said than done, though. Henry's familiar scent filled her nostrils and his arm occasionally brushed hers. Still, she refused to look at him. She certainly paid no mind to his smooth, deep voice, singing perfectly in tune.

Finally, they were instructed to take a seat, and Emily wondered if sitting next to the man would be any easier.

It wasn't. Henry hadn't bothered picking up a program, so he wanted to share hers. Since he chose not to take a Bible, he read hers over her shoulder instead—his warm breath on her neck sending tingles down her arm. Thankfully, the passage was short. When she snapped the Bible closed before prayers, he snickered.

"My command is this," Pastor Tim said. "Love each other as I have loved you. John fifteen verse twelve." His eyes, full of acceptance and love, traversed the whole congregation. "Whenever we feel inclined to ignore someone or desire to snap at them because they're annoying us or we don't want to forgive someone who's hurt us, we need to remember that we are called, as followers of Christ, to treat others the way He did. To love them the way He did. The way He does. Unconditionally."

After that preamble, Emily couldn't concentrate. The pastor's opening words tossed about in her mind. Mulling it over, she examined her treatment of Henry in light of the passage. She may have agreed to be his friend, yet she hadn't acted like one. On the other hand, Henry seemed genuinely interested in being her friend. He'd gone out of his way to be the kind of person one could call a friend, and she'd done nothing to deserve it.

Forgive me, Lord, she prayed. *Help me to love Henry the way you love him. To put him first, not my feelings or my desires. Forgive me for my thoughts of jealousy and envy toward Britt and help me to love her the way you love her, too.*

When the sermon ended and the band struck up the final song, she rose and turned to Henry. Laying a hand on his arm, she waited for him to look at her.

"I'm sorry," she murmured.

His eyebrows shot up. "For what?"

She'd been behaving badly. Surely, he knew that?

"Everything."

***

Henry didn't usually wish for the service to end, but as they sang the final song, Emily's cryptic apology rang in his ears. He'd noticed her contemplative expression during the sermon. Knowing she'd been thinking about him bolstered his ego.

After the final amen, he grabbed her hand. "Come with me."

Leading her down the aisle to the exit, Henry tried not to enjoy the feel of her soft, warm hand fitting perfectly in his. For a second his heart stopped, then began to race. How was he going to tell her?

If she truly was his friend—a bit of a stretch lately, honestly —she'd be happy for him.

A small room at the back end of the theater housed cleaning materials. Henry pushed open the door, switched on the light, and nudged Emily inside. He followed, shutting the door behind them. The place smelt a bit musty and contained a hint of chemicals. It didn't matter; they wouldn't be there long.

"Why'd you drag me into this *delightful*-smelling room?"

Her teasing smile—a refreshing change from the scowl of late —belied the slight annoyance in her tone.

"I wanted to talk to you without any interruptions."

"So talk." Her light chuckle took the sting out of the clipped instruction.

Gulping in a breath, he squared his shoulders. "What did you mean when you said you were sorry for everything?"

"In case you hadn't noticed," she answered immediately, "I haven't been a very good friend."

"I noticed." He tried to keep the bitterness out of his voice but wasn't sure he succeeded.

"Pastor Tim's opener convicted me. I'm so sorry, Henry."

"You're forgiven."

Her mouth gaped. "As easy as that?"

The surprise on her pretty face made him want to laugh. He stifled it, nodding instead. "Now that we have that sorted, will you promise to give me a date and time to share ideas, like we discussed?"

"I promise," she said solemnly.

"Thank you."

He shifted from foot to foot, then swallowed.

Her eyebrows shot up. "Was there something else?"

Before he lost the nerve, he mustered up as much confidence as a grown man could in the presence of the woman he liked a lot.

"I wanted you to hear this from me firsthand," he blurted.

"O-kay." She bit her bottom lip, and he had to blink away the distraction of her kissable mouth.

Meeting her concerned gaze, he brushed his thumb across her upper arm. "It's not bad," he said. "It's only that Britt and I are dating. Officially."

"Oh." A myriad of emotions crossed Emily's face—shock, resignation, and possibly disappointment.

Maybe the last was just him being hopeful.

"That's wonderful, Henry!" The enthusiasm in her voice sounded forced, and when she did smile, it didn't quite reach her eyes. "Your parents will be thrilled."

Not the response he desired. Not at all. He wanted Emily to say it was a mistake, that he should be dating her instead.

Remember, Henry, he told himself, *friends. That's all Emily wants.*

"I'm glad you're okay with it." He chuckled awkwardly. "I'd hate to have our first fight over who I'm dating."

"It wouldn't be a great start to a friendship, no."

Unable to look away, Henry stood gazing into her soulful brown eyes. Eyes he could easily lose himself in. Eyes that—

"We should get out of here before someone sends out a search party."

He blinked. "Right. Yes, of course."

They exited the room carefully so as not to hit anyone behind the door. Thankfully, it was clear.

"There you are!" Charlotte rushed forward, her worried gaze flicking between them. "I've been looking all over for you, Em. Where did you two disappear to?"

"I'm here." Emily joined Charlotte, then turned briefly to Henry. "I'll text you later."

"You'd better, or else—"

"Don't worry," she said. "I will."

After a cute wave of her fingers, she and Charlotte headed toward the children's church classrooms. He'd have offered to accompany them, but Emily probably needed time to process his bombshell. She might've been the one to suggest it, but a gut feeling told him it wasn't what she really wanted.

What was done, was done. And Emily was right: his parents would be thrilled. Likely as much as her parents were about Emily and Luke reuniting.

He, on the other hand, was not thrilled at all.

Chapter Twelve

"Em, don't say you're calling to cancel." Luke sounded agitated. "I'm halfway to New Haven already!"

"Relax. I only wanted to warn you that Charlotte's insisting on meeting you at the door."

"Why?"

"Well, I don't exactly date—not normally—so something about a random stranger whisking me away tonight." Emily chuckled nervously.

"We'll talk about why you don't date later, but I'm *not* some random stranger," he said indignantly.

"I know, but Charlotte hadn't heard of you until today."

"You wound me, Em."

She pictured Luke with a hand over his heart and a pretend tortured look on his handsome face and smiled. "Hey, just because I haven't spoken about you doesn't mean I didn't think about you…occasionally." She may be stretching the truth a little—Luke was never far from her mind, though likely not for the reason he'd think.

"I feel a *whole* lot better now," he said sarcastically.

"Come on. That's not fair."

"I know." He huffed. "Sorry."

She waited for a beat and inhaled deeply. "I need you to promise me something."

"Anything."

"Don't mention that I'm a New York Quinn, please. No one

here knows, other than Henry, and I want it to stay that way."

"Why?"

"Luke," she said sternly.

He was quiet for a bit. "What if Charlotte asks how we met? Do I say at your parents' party?"

"No," she squeaked, then cleared her throat. "Stick to the truth but keep to the bare minimum—we dated in high school, had no contact afterward, and now you work for my father."

Those truths were all anyone needed to know—even him.

"All right. I promise."

"Thank you." The breath she hadn't realized she'd been holding finally released.

"I'll see you in about half an hour. I hope you're hungry."

Laughter loosened the last trace of tension in her body. "Starving."

Later, when the doorbell rang, Emily's butterflies returned full force. Grabbing her coat and purse, she rushed to the front door entryway but came to an abrupt halt. Too late to intercept Charlotte, she caught the tail end of Luke's greeting. "I look forward to getting to know you and your family better," he said in a charming voice.

He planned on visiting often? That made her smile.

Peeking around the corner, she noted Luke's designer blue jeans, white T-shirt and sneakers, and dark gray cashmere peacoat.

Casually dressed, like she'd asked? Check.

Subtle about his bank account? No.

Handsome as heck? Yes.

After getting her swoon under control, she stepped into sight. Luke's eyes widened in appreciation, and his lips lifted into that gorgeous smile she'd always loved.

"Em, you look amazing!"

"Thanks." She blushed. The loose-fitting, long-sleeved peach floral blouse was new, and her dark-wash jeans offset it perfectly.

He held out a dozen pink roses—her favorites.

Another plus for Mr. Bowman.

"They're beautiful, Luke. Thank you." She brought the flowers to her nose and inhaled their sweet scent.

Charlotte's assessing gaze cut briefly to Luke, her expression wary. She held out her hands to Emily. "Here, let me."

"Thanks, Charlie." Emily smiled gratefully. They couldn't miss their Saturday dinner reservation at the trendy bar-come-restaurant-come-nightclub. Everyone in her college class raved about the incredible pizza. Just thinking about it made her mouth water.

A short while later, a college student—dressed all in black —led them to an area below the restaurant's main floor. A low ceiling covered cozy-looking wood-paneled booths on one side of the huge space. The level above held more tables. A glass-sectioned garage door filled an entire wall and looked out onto a primarily dark sidewalk. Only a couple of streetlights illuminated the ground.

After ordering a bottle of white wine and a large pizza with a side salad to share, Luke crossed his arms on the table and leaned forward. "Tell me everything you've been up to since high school."

The dread from earlier crept back into her stomach.

One of the main reasons she'd avoided New York for so long was so she wouldn't have to explain anything. Yet if Luke was serious about inserting himself into her life, she'd have to tell him the whole truth. Besides, ever since she'd run into him in New York, the Holy Spirit—some might call it the voice of an angel on her shoulder—had continued to convict Emily of her deceit.

Luke deserved to know her secret, but gathering enough courage to tell him? An entirely different story.

She gulped some water, clasped her hands in her lap, then took a fortifying breath. "After graduation, I took a gap year."

"To travel?"

"Sort of. I stayed out west with my dad's sister in a little bed and breakfast, which I helped run. I also learned to cook and clean, and wash my own clothes. Quite a change, considering I thought everything went to the dry cleaners." She gave a self-deprecating laugh. "If I'd traveled, I'd probably have stayed in five-star hotels and had everything done for me like I was used to."

"I bet your aunt missed having your help when you moved here."

She nodded. "I felt bad abandoning her, but I had to go." *Please don't ask why*, she silently begged.

"Did you visit your folks during that time?"

"No."

His eyebrows rose in surprise. "You didn't want to?"

Emily shifted uncomfortably in her seat. Why was this starting to feel like an interrogation?

"If you *must* know," she began, not bothering to hide the edge to her voice, "I needed to grow up. If I'd returned to New York, even for a long weekend, I'd have wanted to stay and be pampered."

His expression softened. "I understand."

"It was hard, but I decided to suck it up. At least my parents knew what I was up to, because I kept in contact."

"Well, I'm glad you had the opportunity. Especially after..." He trailed off.

Frowning, she glanced behind her. Where was that wine?

Thankfully, their server approached with a bottle in his hand, apologizing for the wait. After pouring the wine, he left, and Luke lifted his glass, an unidentifiable gleam in his eye. "To us and our future."

"To us," Emily echoed as they clinked glasses. She studied him over the rim of her glass. "You do know I reserve the right to stop this getting-to-know-each-other thing again, right?"

He smiled confidently. "I know, Em. Chemistry was never our problem. If I'm being honest, I think I fell in love with you the first moment I saw you."

Laughing, she almost choked on her wine. "In second grade?"

"Yep." His eyebrows wiggled in a flirty gesture. "You always were, and still are, the most naturally beautiful girl—" He winced. "—woman, in the room."

Her hand flew to her chest. "Such a charmer."

Emily's attention drifted to their server as a strong smell of pepperoni and garlic permeated the air.

"This had better be good." Luke stared at the mashed potato pizza placed in front of them. "Otherwise, I'll be leaving on an empty stomach." Next, he shook his head at the large salad bowl filled with mixed greens, pears, gorgonzola, and nuts. "That's not going to fill me up, either."

"Oh, you of little faith." Chuckling at his pinched expression, Emily shared the salad while he sorted the pizza.

After giving thanks, she took a bite. "Oh, wow."

Luke eyed her skeptically.

"I dare you," she urged. "I promise it's amazing."

He sank his teeth into the first slice and murmured a few seconds later, "Okay, I'm a believer."

She smirked.

Pausing in between mouthfuls, Luke looked at her curiously. "So, why don't you date?"

"Well, studying while working as a nanny is pretty full-time. Plus, I haven't been that interested."

"Fair enough." Luke tilted his head. "Why a nanny?" he asked without a hint of censure.

"I honestly didn't know what to do after finishing my business degree. And since returning to New York wasn't an option, I searched for an income stream. Our church newsletter had an advertisement for a live-in nanny, so I applied." She sighed happily. "I'm so glad I did. Charlotte Scott's amazing, and a wonderful employer. The minute I met her and her adorable children, I was hooked."

"Will you keep nannying once you're a qualified teacher?"

"That was my plan." She twisted some hair around a finger. "Except, Charlotte's engagement to Adam might change things."

He quirked a brow. "How so?"

She shrugged. "Not sure. We haven't discussed it yet. They haven't even set a wedding date."

"If Charlotte doesn't need you anymore, will you find a teaching position here or back home?"

"This is home," she said firmly.

A look of alarm crossed his face. "You don't plan on coming back to New York? Ever?"

"I wouldn't say not ever, but right now, I don't have any intention of living there."

His penetrating gaze bore into hers. "Why?"

"Why?" Wiping her mouth, she avoided looking at him directly. "Because I love my life here, my church, my friends. New Haven is where I want to be. Why would I go back to New York, where I'm expected to behave a certain way, take on a responsibility I'm not interested in, and be told whom to date and eventually marry? No, thank you." She couldn't hide the bitterness in her voice.

Luke let out a long breath like he was exhaling his disappointment. "I see." A few seconds passed until he grinned cockily. "Then I guess I'll have to convince your father to open an office here."

Emily glowered at him. "Why would you do that?" The idea of her father inserting himself into her life here? Super unappealing. This was her safe haven. She couldn't have him intruding.

"Because I now have a vested interest in New Haven." He winked.

"I think you're assuming way too much here." An occasional visit to New Haven was risky enough. To have him here permanently? Bad idea. "We broke up for a reason, remember?"

Luke's face fell.

"I do." Twisting his fingers together, he spoke with a slight tremor. "Em, I'm so sorry. I was wrong, and I regret my decision every single day." Tears swam in his eyes. "I have for years."

Impossible. He'd been adamant about not being saddled

with the responsibility.

When their night together resulted in a pregnancy, it caused their relationship to unravel faster than Emily could say New York. She could still remember Luke's response when she'd told him her news, "I won't have our lives ruined by this, Em. We're too young to get married. Just get rid of it." His harsh tone had brooked no argument.

Devastated, she broke up with him and refused to take his calls. When she eventually picked up the phone after his relentless calling, she told him she'd taken care of it.

Things could've been so different if he'd offered to marry her. They may have had the support of their parents. Instead, days later, she'd fled to her dad's sister in another state, knowing she'd never be accepted as an unwed mother in New York's high society. Her aunt was easily sworn to secrecy since the siblings weren't on speaking terms.

Then, immediately after giving birth, Emily released her beautiful baby boy for adoption and sobbed in her aunt's arms.

Lately, she'd been regretting that decision more and more. Given it had been an open adoption—and knowing they would allow her contact—Emily was able to move to New Haven, where her son's adoptive family lived. She'd stayed away while pursuing her business degree, but now she saw her son more often. But it still wasn't enough.

"If I could go back and speak some sense into my younger self, I promise you, Em, I would."

Luke's voice jerked her back to the present, to the sorrow etched on his forehead. It stabbed at her chest.

"What would you tell yourself?" she asked softly.

"I'd say, 'Luke, you've been given a precious gift from God. No matter how young you are, the only right choice is to support your girlfriend. Help her make an informed decision, not dictate what she should do with her body.'" He swallowed hard, his voice husky as he added, "By asking you to take care of it, I avoided responsibility. I never should've done that. It was wrong."

Glancing away, he shoved his fingers through his hair. "If only…"

Emily brushed her hand over Luke's arm, willing him to continue.

"If only I hadn't told you to abort our child. But it's too late now, isn't it?" His strange, almost questioning gaze skittered to hers, then left.

Did he somehow know the truth?

She shook her head. He couldn't.

Tell him. Tell him, her mind screamed, yet her tumbling stomach affected her ability to speak. Fighting down nerves and tears that threatened to fall, she pushed out the words. "I didn't do it."

"Do what?"

"I-I didn't have the abortion."

At his wide-eyed stare, she crumpled. Guilt from the past five years reared its ugly head as tears flooded out. She grabbed her napkin to stem the flow.

"Hey, it's okay," Luke said, handing her another one to blow her nose on.

"T-thanks." Sniffing, she somehow regained control.

How could he be so kind when she'd willfully gone against his wishes? Expecting him to be livid, she almost started crying again.

Luke captured her hands with his and stroked her knuckles with his thumbs. His gentle touch and soft gaze eased the tightness in her chest. "I can't tell you how many nights I wondered what being a father would've been like. To know whether we would've had a son or a daughter."

She offered a shaky smile. "Our son looks a lot like you when we first met."

"Looks?" A deep frown replaced Luke's smile. "You *know* him? Where is he?" he asked angrily. "Your father never said —" He closed his eyes, then continued less aggressively. "He never mentioned a child."

"I never told anyone." Emily kept her voice low. "Only my aunt and his adoptive parents."

"You gave up our son for adoption?" Luke's harsh, accusing tone pierced her fragile heart.

Surely he realized she couldn't keep their child? What did he think had happened?

"All these years, Em, I thought…" He shook his head with a look of disbelief. "I thought you had killed our baby because of me. I lived with that guilt and now discover it was unnecessary." Narrowing his eyes, he growled, "You could've saved me all that heartache and those recriminations, don't you think?"

Once more, tears burned at the back of her eyes. "I'm so sorry, Luke. I should've told you." She blinked rapidly. "But I didn't want to give you the chance to change my mind. After I gave him up—the worst day of my life, by the way—I had no contact with the adoptive parents. I went to college and got my degree." She grimaced. "Leaving my baby to be raised by strangers was the hardest thing I've ever done."

Luke, his expression contemplative and tight, said nothing as a busboy removed their empty dishes and deposited two dessert menus in the center of the table.

"So you know our son."

It wasn't a question, but she gave a whispered answer anyway. "Yes."

"When did you contact the adoptive parents?"

"A year ago."

"What's his name? Where does he live? Does he have decent parents? Is he aware you're his birth moth—?"

"Hey, slow down, Luke. His name's Noah, and he lives here."

His expression immediately softened. "The reason you don't want to leave."

She nodded. "His parents are wonderful. They love him like their own flesh and blood."

"Do they have any other children?"

"No, Lisa couldn't have children, so she and Sean decided to adopt one child—our son."

"You always talked about having a few children. Do you

remember?" he murmured, his smile gentle but fleeting.

"It's still my plan for when I settle down eventually."

Time moved on with Luke seemingly lost in thought. Eventually Emily drew in a fortifying breath.

"Luke?" she said, then waited until his unfocused gaze met hers. "Noah has everything he needs. As far as he's concerned, I'm Aunt Emily—a close family friend. That's how Sean and Lisa introduced me. It hurt initially, but seeing Noah this past year and getting to know him has eased the pain."

"Maybe I could—" Luke pursed his lips, then raised imploring eyes to her. "Could I be Uncle Luke? Another family friend?"

Emily's heart soared and sank simultaneously. He wanted to know his son!

But now her perfect bubble had a crack in it, and it was only a matter of time before it burst. And like an explosion, its effects would be far-reaching.

Chapter Thirteen

Henry sighed. Making Adam wait outside Lighthouse Church with him was ridiculous. For all he knew, Emily was spending the day with her ex-boyfriend. His chest constricted at the thought. If only Britt had been willing to come this morning. When he invited her, she'd declined with a guilty smile.

"I might come another time, Henry. But it's all been a little overwhelming with a new job and home. I need some time alone."

"Will you at least join us for lunch after church?"

"Yes, of course."

"You know, bud," Adam said, looking toward the entrance and rubbing his hands briskly. "If we stay out here much longer, my fingers are gonna fall off."

"Fine, we can go in," Henry relented.

Inside the foyer, he scanned the faces of those either drinking coffee or enjoying cream cheese bagels. Emily wasn't one of them.

Last Sunday, true to her word, she'd texted, and they'd arranged to meet during the week. At the last minute, she'd chickened out and asked for a raincheck. He'd graciously allowed it, making it clear it was her only 'get-out-of-meeting-with-Henry-free' card. He hadn't heard from her since.

Hopefully they weren't back to square one.

Catching movement to his right, Henry's heart skipped a beat. "I didn't think you were coming," he said, his tone more brusque than intended.

Emily scowled. "Hello to you too, and why would you think that?" She peered at her watch, then huffed. "I'm here plenty early. I even have time to grab a coffee." Strolling toward the refreshments counter, she glanced over her shoulder. "Would you like one?"

He followed like a puppy dog. "Yes, please."

"I'm surprised you don't already have one." Frowning, she stuck a cup under the coffee machine.

He shoved his hands into his pockets. "I've been pre-occupied."

She handed him a steaming paper cup, then eyed him thoughtfully after pressing the button for a second cup.

"I thought Britt would be with you. Didn't she start her job this week?"

"Yes, but it's been a hectic week. She'll be at the lunch later."

"Lunch?" Emily gave him a blank look before starting in the direction of the auditorium.

"Charlotte invited us all. I assumed you'd be there." Lengthening his stride to catch up, he breathed in her sweet perfume. Why did the woman have to smell so good?

She shook her head. "Nope."

"You have other plans?"

"Something like that." Blinking, she looked away.

He frowned. Why was she being cagey?

They crossed the aisle to join Charlotte and Adam in their usual row. After saying hello, Henry sank into the seat beside Emily and accidentally touched her arm. The spark shouldn't have shocked him, but it did. He yanked back his hand, his eyes flying to hers. Other than quirking a brow, she seemed unaffected.

"How was your date last night?" he asked.

A wide, beautiful smile broke out, one that reached her eyes. "Great, thanks. We had mashed potato pizza and ended up dancing until midnight."

Emily's not your girlfriend, Henry reminded himself as he clenched his teeth. Instead, he kept his tone casual. "Sounds like fun. Luke must've driven back to New York in the early hours."

She narrowed her eyes at him. "Actually, he stayed overnight at a hotel, and we had breakfast together before he left."

"Oh."

The band started up, and Henry pushed to his feet. Since he was here to worship his Father and Creator and not think about a woman, he made a concerted effort to push images of Luke and Emily dancing closely to the back of his mind.

Ignoring the actual woman next to him was much harder. Her pretty laugh when Pastor Tim joked about his kids wanting pizza when they discovered he'd cooked the dinner, and her hand accidentally brushing against his when she removed her coat, were timely reminders of her very real presence.

He should've sat in the back. Except, he'd have focused on the back of her head and still watched her every movement.

He released a pent-up breath. *Lord, help me fix my eyes on you.*

When the sermon began, he pulled out his phone and made notes, which helped. Before long, it was time for the final song—"This is Amazing Grace"—one of his favorites. Afterward, he slid his gaze to Emily to find her staring openly at him.

"What?"

Pink tinged her cheeks. "It's just—" She bit her thumb nail. "You immersed in the Spirit…it's an attractive look on you."

Turning from him, Emily slung her purse over her shoulder and touched Charlotte's arm. "Enjoy your lunch, Charlie. I'll see you at home later."

"Wait, what? You aren't coming?"

"Uh, no."

"Please come. I've booked a table at Tre Scalini." Charlotte narrowed her eyes. "You weren't planning on studying today, and Luke's left, right?"

"Yes."

"Then join us."

"You have to come," Adam added. "My sister's going to be there."

"It won't be the same if you don't." Henry couldn't help putting in his two cents worth.

"Okay." Resignation filled Emily's voice, but Henry couldn't help but grin.

Lunch suddenly became a whole lot more appealing.

***

While everyone else entered the Italian Restaurant's main dining room, Emily hung back with the children. Avoiding Henry wasn't the reason. No, rather, it allowed Charlotte to focus on her fiancé.

After a waiter directed them to the reserved twelve-seater table, Emily situated the boys at one end. She then took the last seat, catty-corner to them—in between Adam and Amy. Britt and Henry sat opposite. Two other couples from church sat to their right.

Conscious of Henry's eyes tracking her every movement, Emily inspected the large room's period furnishings. They were beautiful and well-chosen, and the chandelier lighting added to the elegant and warm atmosphere.

But what about the food?

Snatching up a menu, she cursed the tingles of awareness that told her Henry hadn't redirected his attention. She swiftly decided on her meal, then assisted the children while others chatted about the service.

Britt soon became the subject of interrogation, what with her new job and living situation. Smiling brightly, the woman talked about how great her co-workers were and went on to describe her wonderful new accommodation. Clearly, Britt enjoyed the attention.

Emily pulled paper and coloring pencils from her purse and handed them to Amy and the boys.

"Will you play Tic-tac-toe with me, please, Miss Emily?" Amy asked.

She smiled softly at the sweet child. "Of course."

"Do you know what you're eating?" Henry asked, looking at her expectantly.

Why did he want to know? It wasn't like they were going to share this time.

"Grilled salmon," she replied before focusing back on Amy. "Would you like to start?"

Amy nodded, then proceeded to win three games in a row. When Emily suggested they play Snowman, the child gave her a knowing look.

"I'm still gonna beat you, Miss Emily."

A burst of laughter escaped her, and Emily quickly covered her mouth while shooting a glance at Henry. Eyes sparkling with amusement trapped hers. The connection only broke when the tantalizing aroma of caramelized onions hit her nostrils and a plate of succulent-looking meat appeared on the table.

He grinned at Emily. "It smells good, right?"

"It does. Maybe I'll try the veal next time."

"Mmm, that smells incredible." Britt leaned over Henry's shoulder and batted her eyelashes. "You won't mind sharing, will you?"

"Any time, Britt."

Emily gritted her teeth at the woman's blatant flirting. Of course, Britt had every right to be overly friendly—she was dating the man, just like Emily had suggested.

If only she hadn't.

Too late.

Once the rest of the food arrived, Adam gave thanks, and everyone dug in. Emily kept her head down throughout the meal as conversation buzzed around her. After enjoying every morsel of the tender fish, she finished her drink and packed away the children's things.

"Bathroom break, anyone?" she asked, peering between the kids.

They all shook their heads, but Britt perked up. "I'll come."

Her stomach sank. Just what she wanted: Henry's girlfriend playing escort.

While the women washed their hands in the bathroom afterward, Britt's eyes met Emily's in the mirror.

"I'm surprised you're here. You don't mind?" Britt asked.

"Why would I?"

Britt dried her hands on the cloth towel, keeping her eyes on Emily. "Do you normally work Sundays?"

"I work whenever Charlotte needs me." Oops, had that sounded defensive? She toned down her annoyance. "She's a pretty easy-going boss."

A slow smile spread over Britt's face. "She's fortunate to have you."

"I'm the lucky one."

She dried her hands and reached for the door handle, but Britt reached out to stop her. "Before you go, I wanted to make sure you're aware."

Emily tamped down a sigh. "Of what?"

"Henry's my boyfriend."

A chuckle escaped. "Oh, I'm aware. I'm the one who suggested he date you."

Britt's look of surprise was priceless.

At the table, Peter asked Henry if he'd take them to the park. "There are so many cool places to play there," the boy declared.

"Why don't you ask Miss Emily, Peter?" Britt peered over at her with a sugary sweet smile. "It's her job, isn't it?"

"But it's Miss Emily's day—" Amy began, but Emily shushed her.

"I don't mind, Peter. Let me tell your mom." She stood and moved to where Charlotte was discussing wedding venues with the other couples. "Charlie?"

"Yes?"

"I'm taking the kids to the park."

"You don't have to do that. You're supposed to—"

"I don't mind." She cut her off.

Her boss eyed her for a long moment. "Fine. But we'll talk about this later."

Despite the brisk breeze, the sun shone. A few birds tweeted in the treetops. The boys immediately raced off to the spring riders in the playground. Amy followed more sedately and joined them. After a while, they grew bored of the activity and moved on to the swings. With three in a row, Emily took turns pushing the boys. Thankfully, Amy could swing herself.

A few minutes later, a deep voice beside her made her jump. "Let me help."

"Henry! What are you doing here?" She kept her eyes on the swings.

"Keeping you company."

She gave him a sideways glance. "And Britt?"

"She's on a work call." He chuckled. "Can you believe it?"

Pushing Daniel higher, Emily laughed too. "Well, she thinks I'm working, so…"

His eyes narrowed. "Why would she think that?"

"Your girlfriend has no clue who I am, so please don't say anything. As far as she's concerned, I'm the nanny, not the friend."

His features softened. "I'm sorry."

"It doesn't matter." She waved him off. "I don't care. If only she understood that this is more than a job for me. I love these kids."

"I can see that, and I admire your dedication and devotion."

Judging from his earnest expression, he meant it. Her heart constricted briefly. "Thanks."

They pushed the boys in amicable silence until they'd had enough and the brothers rushed off to play tag with their sister. Emily shoved the toe of her boot into the sand. "There's something else you should know."

"What?"

"Britt's a little insecure. In the bathroom, she made a point of telling me that you're her boyfriend. As if she felt threatened by me." She shook her head, then met his intense gaze. "Which is silly because we both know that's ridiculous, right?"

Henry eased closer, causing her pulse to quicken. When he pushed a strand of hair behind her ear, Emily sucked in a breath at the intimate gesture.

"Is it, though?"

Chapter Fourteen

"So, how are things at Daily Bread?" Rose-scented perfume sweetened the air as Emily unwound the multicolored scarf from around her neck. Shifting slightly, she added it to the black cashmere coat draped over her chair and turned to face Henry.

He blinked. Alright then, straight to the point of their date.

"Busy." Clasping his hands on the red plastic-covered table, he leaned forward. "Linda asked after you. Said she misses her pretty volunteer."

Chuckling, Emily eased back, lengthening the distance between them. "You sure *she* said pretty?"

"I may have embellished, but not because she wouldn't agree."

"Well, tell Linda I'd love to help out again, but it'll have to be during mid-winter break."

"We're open Saturdays too, you know." He smirked.

She gave a cute one-shouldered shrug. "Sorry. I keep Saturdays free for Luke."

Henry pursed his lips. Like he needed reminding of her new priority.

"I guess Daily Bread will take what it can get." He pointed to his chest. "Me? I'm not sure I can wait until the next school break."

"You see me every week at church, Henry."

"Hardly the same." He folded his arms across his chest. "I

thought friends were supposed to hang out more than once a week. Besides, there's always a bunch of people at the service. It's not like we're alone."

A teasing glint entered her eyes. "Such a needy friend."

Feigning a hurt look, he waited as a server delivered their drinks, then took their burger orders and left.

Henry stirred his soda with a straw while casting his eyes over her. No visible signs of strain. No dark rings under the eyes. Even so.

"Are you settled back in at college?" he asked. "Has your workload stepped up?"

"Yes to both."

"Are you coping?"

"For the moment." She sighed. "I'll need to spend more evenings writing up notes soon."

"I hope you're not planning on burning the candle at both ends." His voice came out gruff sounding. Coughing, he cleared his throat. "You know... You could always give up your day job."

"Henry!" Her forehead scrunched up adorably, but he resisted the urge to reach out and smooth it. "I'd never let Charlotte down like that."

"Surely she and Adam won't need your help as much when she's married?" Maybe Emily hadn't thought it through much, but wasn't it obvious?

"I don't know." Her expression turned thoughtful. "We haven't talked about it yet. I guess Charlotte's avoiding it."

"Why?"

"My guess? She probably thinks I rely on the income and the accommodation she provides."

He tapped his fingers on the table, then gulped down more soda. "Makes sense, I suppose. So, when *do* you plan on telling them your real financial situation?"

Panic quickly replaced Emily's neutral expression.

"What is it?" he asked, reaching across the table and squeezing her fingers. A brief, heated spark appeared in her eyes before her gaze dropped to their hands. He swiftly removed his.

"Nothing."

"You can tell me anything. Trust me, I promise not to repeat it."

Should he push? Because he meant every word. Their friendship may be relatively new, but he'd never given her any reason not to trust him. Although, if she knew his girlfriend was a cover to convince her that he could be serious with a woman, well then, that would blow any trust out of the water.

A sobering thought.

His shoulders slumped. Maybe he needed to rethink the whole Britt-as-his-girlfriend thing. Except, he'd given Britt his word and made the arrangement so he could protect his best friend's sister from predators. Surely that stood for something?

"I got pregnant in high school."

Though the whispered words shook him, he managed to keep any judgment from his voice, but not the surprise. "You had a *child*?"

Emily nodded, her eyes glassy.

"You were so young," he said gently, itching to grab her hand again. "That must've been really difficult."

When she swallowed a strangled cry, he quickly handed over a spare napkin. A shaky smile accompanied her murmured thanks.

"Can I assume the child was adopted? You've never spoken..." He left the sentence hanging, unwilling to consider the alternative and how that might've impacted her emotionally.

"He was adopted."

A measure of relief flowed through him as he exhaled quietly. "That's good, right?"

"Yes," she said with conviction, her eyes lighting up. "He lives in New Haven."

Huh? He hadn't been expecting that. How had she kept this secret from everyone?

"So you know him?"

"I do."

Henry let it all sink in. Emily had a child out of wedlock from before she went to college, and now she was living in the same town as her son. Where was the father? Who was the father?

Suddenly, he stilled. "Luke's the father."

Her eyes went wide. "H-how'd you guess?"

"It doesn't take a genius. You dated in high school and got pregnant. So, unless you were unfaithful..." He trailed off. That thought wasn't one he wanted to contemplate either.

"Never! It was only the once."

"All it takes." He offered an empathetic smile.

"I know." She hung her head. "And I've regretted it for a long time."

"Hey," he said, stretching out a finger, intending to lift her chin. The arrival of their entrées stopped him. He scooped up Emily's hand instead. "Shall I give thanks?"

"Please."

"Heavenly Father, thank you for this food and our friendship. Please bless our time together. Amen." He briefly tightened his hold on her hand, then let go and opened his eyes.

Emily's glistened.

"You okay?"

"I will be." Worried eyes accompanied her closed-mouth smile. "I appreciate you taking this bombshell in your stride, Henry. For being a good friend."

His fist tensed. "That's what friends do, right?" Slowly, he loosened his fingers.

"Right."

Henry munched on a couple fries as he mulled over what he'd learned. How did Emily feel as an unwed mother dating her child's father?

After being sexually assaulted at sixteen, Henry's sister, Nicole, had fallen pregnant. Miraculously, she'd kept Isabella. Years later, she met Travis and fell in love. Despite not being

Bella's biological father, Travis had wholeheartedly accepted the child.

A shudder went through him. Had Luke forced himself on Emily?

No. She wouldn't be dating him now if that were the case. Of that he was sure.

Did Luke know about his son? Likely not. But why keep him a secret?

"You're frowning." Emily's soft voice interrupted Henry's scattered thoughts. When he looked at her through unfocused eyes, she shot him a lopsided smile. "I imagine you have a hundred different questions. Why not just ask me? I'll tell you whatever you want to know. As long as I have your word that you won't tell anyone else."

He shook his head. "It's none of my business."

"Fine." Ducking her head, she concentrated on her food, and he did the same until unanswered questions caused him indigestion.

"Why weren't you and Luke together before now?" he blurted.

"Because..." Blinking, she swallowed her mouthful. Her voice trembled when she answered him. "He found out I was pregnant and told me to take care of it."

Sweeping a hand through his hair, Henry swore under his breath. "Well, I guess that answers my next question."

"Which was?"

"Why the two of you aren't married."

Her lips twisted.

"Does he know he has a son?"

"I told him last weekend."

He stared at her. "How did he react?"

A tiny smile settled on her lips. "Rather well, considering he'd been living with tremendous guilt thinking I'd gone through with the abortion. When he discovered I hadn't, well, you can imagine."

"But your date still ended amicably?" At least, that's what he thought she'd told him.

"Yes. Luke realized the awkward position he'd put me in, especially when he started working for my father. After that, things became a lot more complicated."

"I take it your parents are unaware of their grandson."

"Yes." Her lips pressed together. "And it's going to stay that way."

"I see." He shoved another piece of meat into his mouth, chewed for a bit, then swallowed. "How do you plan on keeping your secret, exactly?"

"Easy. By never letting my parents get involved in my life here and never returning to New York permanently."

Henry's stomach sank. And so did his dream of Emily being the woman God had destined for him. What was the point of holding out hope with Luke and son in the picture? Never mind that he *had* to move back to New York. Eventually.

There was no *if* about it.

***

Noticing Henry's sudden grim expression, Emily wished she knew what was going through his mind. Did he think Luke wouldn't move here to be with her?

"Assuming things get serious between you and Luke..." Henry spoke slowly, as if worried he'd offend her otherwise. "Will he give up his high-powered job in the city and move to New Haven?"

How had he guessed her thoughts?

"Say Luke moves here," he continued a little brusquely. "How long do you think you'll be able to keep your secret then?"

Her chest tightened. Perhaps she hadn't thought through all the implications. Living a lie? It was deceitful, and the truth would come out.

Henry shrugged offhandedly, but his eyes pierced hers. "I suppose it's too soon to know what will happen after only one date."

She blinked away a stray tear.

"I will say this, Emily." His tone softened, along with his

gaze. "If I found out I had a son, and his mother was anything like you, I'd want to marry her."

Yeah, right. Like Henry would ever get married! The man avoided serious relationships. That he was suddenly dating Britt, even if Emily was the one to suggest it, was beyond her. She might not like Britt too much, but she *was* Adam's sister.

That had to count for something.

Britt, being closer to Henry in age, wasn't his usual type. So why had he changed his modus operandi?

Her thoughts shifted to Luke. Their attraction from high school remained, and they were still compatible. They also had a lot in common: wealthy families, a son, and a desire to be married one day.

Was that enough?

She had no idea if Luke would ever leave New York or not. Or whether he'd be happy living in New Haven and keeping their son a secret from her parents. The more she thought about it, the more unreasonable it sounded.

Pushing her plate away, she folded her arms on the table and finally met Henry's penetrating gaze. "You know what? Tonight was meant to be about charitable work, not my personal life. How about we concentrate on that?"

A server cleared their plates and handed over dessert menus. "Let me know if you'd like anything."

Emily managed a smile. "A latte, please."

"Same, thanks." Henry waited until they were alone, then said, "I have a few ideas." Sparkling eyes matched his excited tone, and some of her irritation melted away. "They depend on how much you're prepared to donate and whether or not you'd continue giving or if this would be a once-off donation."

"I haven't decided yet."

"Okay, well, with a one-time donation, you could give funds to a selection of charities in the city. We'd do some research first—find those you're willing to support and determine any deficits in their fundraising targets."

She nodded. "I like that idea."

"But"—he held up his hand—"*if* you choose an ongoing donation, you could buy either an apartment block or a few abandoned, possibly condemned houses and renovate them. Afterward, you could rent them out at reduced rates to working folk who can't afford normal rentals. The properties would require continuous upkeep, so you would have to carry on contributing toward the costs."

She grinned. Both sounded like wonderful ideas that could make a massive difference to people's lives.

"Could we investigate both options?" she asked, tapping her hands together while trying not to sound overexcited. "Until I know the figures, I have no idea what I'd like to spend."

"Sure. I can do that for you."

"Thank you." She held his intense gaze for a long moment, then dragged her attention to her hands. Rubbing her thumbs over one another, she wondered if he really could spare the time. "I know I'm asking a lot, and I don't want to take advantage," she said. "You've got so much going on with Daily Bread, as well as The Scott Wilson Home; those should be your priorities." She sighed. "I'm happy to help, though."

He waved away her concerns. "It would be my pleasure. And having your company while I do it? Even better."

His eyes, the color of emeralds sparkling in the sun, captured hers. Her pulse raced, time standing still as she sank deeper. Those beautiful orbs seemed to say, "Hey, I see all of you, and I appreciate everything about you."

If she didn't say or do something, she was pretty sure her insides would melt from the intensity of his gaze. Moments before their coffees appeared, Emily managed to squeak out an "Okay," and the staring contest ended.

Stirring frothy liquid gave her an excuse to consider Henry's character. Not only generous, the man was also thoughtful, kind, and considerate. On top of his GQ model good looks.

Pity he was also a playboy.

Stir, stir, stir.

"I could have some initial proposals for you to review by the weekend." Henry's smooth voice forced her chin up.

"That quickly?"

"It won't take long to get a list of charities in the area and find some properties perfectly priced to sell fast."

"Wow. Okay. Well, I'm free after church." She held her breath, suddenly wondering if she was doing the right thing forcing more alone time with him. "If that works for you?"

Indecision flickered across his face, but he nodded. "I'll make a plan."

"Henry." She waved her hand dismissively. "Don't change your plans. Rather, tell me when it suits you."

"Right after church."

"Henry." She reiterated her warning, and he exhaled loudly.

"It's fine, Emily. Besides work, helping you is my priority."

"Britt won't be happy to hear that." She frowned at him. "Especially if you had plans with her. I wouldn't be thrilled to find out my boyfriend was willing to blow me off to spend time with a friend."

"You're right." Hanging his head, he scratched his forehead. After another deep sigh, he glanced up again. "Can you do a late afternoon coffee instead?"

Emily was right—he *was* supposed to see Britt after church. Knowing he wanted to see her instead messed with her heart. On the other hand, it made her wonder about his loyalties.

How committed *was* he to Britt? Because from what she'd seen recently, the answer was clear: not very.

Chapter Fifteen

So, this was Luke's surprise.

Emily zipped up her down coat and glanced again at the Ivy Mountain State Park sign. At least she knew where they were now and what to expect on this date. Luckily, the wind had settled down, and though the clouds hung low and dark, neither rain nor snow was expected until later in the evening. Not too unpleasant for a hike, then.

Luke set a grueling pace. Not that she was complaining. The brisk walk along the asphalt raised her internal temperature faster than the hand warmer he'd given her when they arrived. Thankfully, Luke's stride eased off when they reached the dirt trail.

"We need to be careful," he said, holding out his hand. "After the first mile, the footing's a little rocky in places with some steep inclines."

She slipped her gloved hand into his. "Okay."

During the next fifteen minutes, she admired the beautiful winter wonderland. Peaceful and pristine; every tree, shrub, and surface covered in white. Finally, they slowed enough for her to catch her breath.

"This place is amazing, Luke. How did you hear about it?"

His lips lifted in a satisfied smile. "I researched the area, and this trail came up highly recommended."

"I see." The man was certainly resourceful.

For the next few steps, they concentrated on the uneven

path.

"We should see some frozen water soon." He shot her a mock stern look. "Don't get any ideas about gliding across it."

Emily laughed, remembering them sliding over frozen water patches in Central Park one year. Her boot had dropped under the ice, and she'd screamed. The water had only been a few inches deep, and Luke had teased her mercilessly for ages.

"We'll also pass through woodlands." Luke's expression softened. "If we're lucky, we'll see some birds."

"I shall keep a look out then," she responded with a grin, loving that he remembered her love of feathered creatures. He beamed back at her. "So, how was your week?" she asked. "Is my father keeping you busy?"

Luke stopped in his tracks, the muscles in his arms tightening. Dropping her hand, he picked up the pace again. "I'd rather not talk about it."

"O-kay."

Don't ask about work. Noted.

A few minutes of silence passed before he slowed slightly and gave her a pointed look. "Did you speak to Sean and Lisa about me meeting Noah?"

She frowned at Luke's demanding tone. "No, they're out of town."

"Any idea when they'll be back?"

"I don't exactly have access to their social calendar, Luke."

He let out a deep sigh.

"I know this is hard, but you *will* meet him. Have a little patience."

He ran a hand over his cheek—a gesture of frustration she remembered from high school. "Easy for you to say, Em. You can visit whenever you want. I'm desperate to do some catch-up."

"I get that, but it's not like I can see him whenever I want to, either. I have to book my visits long in advance."

He stopped for a second, his eyes narrowing. "You're

telling me I may have to wait longer, even once you've talked to them? I won't be able to just see him?"

She grimaced. "Yes."

Huffing, Luke clenched his jaw, and she shook her head at his exasperation. Nothing she could do about it; he'd have to deal with it.

A small mound of snow caused Emily to almost stumble, and she let out a squeak of surprise. Luke immediately steadied her, then grabbed her hand. "Thanks," she said.

A curt nod was his only response.

No matter. She liked that he took care of her. Even as a teenager he'd been kind, thinking of others first. One time, they'd been eating lunch in the school cafeteria when a girl carrying a tray of hot food slipped on the floor. Liquid splattered everywhere. Hot meat sauce and spaghetti tipped onto the ground and all over the girl's open-toed shoes. No one else bothered to move except Luke, who'd rushed over with napkins. He helped the poor girl clean herself and assisted her back onto her feet.

Emily had collected the remaining items from the tray and then retreated to the kitchen to find replacements. When she returned, Luke's arm was wrapped around the teary-eyed girl while he quietly comforted her.

Smiling at the memory, Emily snuck a peek at his handsome profile. The hard line of his mouth indicated continued heavy thought.

She sighed. Guess he still needed more time.

They reached the wooded area, where she occasionally heard a bird chirp. Her gaze rose to the tree branches, searching for the source. A sudden sweet whistle had her heart beating faster. Scanning the area, she spotted the vibrant red bird. It sat on an overhead branch around twenty-five yards away and bore a distinctive crest and a black mask on its face.

"Luke, look! A male cardinal!" she whispered, tugging on his hand as she pointed ahead.

He grinned at her. "Well spotted! It may be small, but its

red feathers are hard to miss."

The bird, ready to take flight the second they got too close, eyeballed them as they approached with soft steps.

Emily kept her voice low. "Do you know that they fluff up their feathers to create air pockets for insulation? It's how they survive the cold since they don't migrate like other birds."

"You sound just like a kindergarten teacher, Em." Luke's mocking tone caught her by surprise. "Oh, I know why, because that's what you want to be."

Her body tensed, and she glared at him. "What's wrong with being a teacher?" He opened his mouth to answer, but she cut him off. "I happen to think it's an important profession," she muttered, clenching her free hand into a fist. "Our son needs good teachers, Luke. I hope others like me, who are passionate about teaching, won't shy away from becoming teachers because some think it's a job for those who can't make it in the business world." She gave him a pointed look.

"I'm sorry." He sighed. "You're right. I just don't understand why you wouldn't want to work for your father. You're a shoo-in. While I have to slog to climb the corporate ladder, you'd be able to glide to the top."

"Let me get this straight. You're mad because I won't take what's rightfully mine, even though I don't want it?"

"You don't mean that. You'll eventually give up this teaching idea and come back to New York. It's where you belong."

Luke obviously believed the nonsense he was spouting. But he had no idea. How could he?

She turned back to the reason they stopped in the first place. "I imagine he's hoping to forage for some tree sap," she said. "Insects seem a little scarce at the moment."

A few seconds later, the bird fluttered off to a higher branch and out of sight.

Luke pulled out his phone, frowned, then stuffed it into his coat pocket. "We need to get going."

"You on some kind of deadline?" she asked tightly as they began traipsing over the uneven ground again. There was less snow in this area, given the extensive tree cover. "I thought we had the whole day."

"We do." He smiled, like they hadn't just argued. "But your hot chocolate, beautiful lady, won't stay hot forever."

"I don't understand."

"You don't need to." He winked.

They saw a few more birds, yet Luke refused to linger. Apparently, whatever he had planned wouldn't wait. The man had arrived in a helicopter, for goodness' sake! He clearly wasn't above making a grand gesture of some sort. She racked her brain for ideas of what but came up empty.

Butterflies swirled in her stomach.

"I wish you would tell me what you're up to," she moaned when Luke's expression brightened, and he quickened his pace. "I'm not sure I love surprises."

"You'll love this. You asked for it, after all." He squeezed her hand, his excitement palpable.

"I did?"

"Hot chocolate," he said, his face a picture of innocence.

How could she stay mad at him when he was so adorably handsome and charming?

Mostly.

As they emerged from the heavily wooded area, the snow's glare made it hard to distinguish anything unusual. Emily shielded her eyes.

"There it is. Right on time." Luke sounded pleased.

She squinted harder. Was that…? It couldn't be.

"I can't believe you organized a sleigh ride!" Letting go of his hand, she clapped hers. "You remembered." She turned to hug him. "Thank you!"

Extracting herself from his arms, Emily strode toward the horses. Their shiny black coats contrasted sharply with the pristine white surroundings, while the maroon sleigh brought a pop of color.

Drawing closer, she slowed to remove her right glove.

"Hey, boy," she cooed, brushing her hand up and down his smooth neck. "You ready for this?"

The horse gave a little snort.

Laughing, she jumped back and glanced at the silver-haired driver. He wore a black top hat and matching overcoat and trousers. "They're gorgeous!" she gushed, causing the wrinkles around the man's eyes and mouth to grow more pronounced.

"Much appreciated, ma'am." He tipped his hat. "I'm quite fond of them myself."

Luke motioned towards the sleigh. "Shall we?"

She giggled happily. "Yes."

Once they were on the bench seat with a warm fleecy blanket stretched over their legs, Luke asked, "Our drinks, Martin?"

"Here you go, sir." Martin pulled two labeled stainless steel flasks from a box at his feet. He passed Emily the hot chocolate and gave Luke the hot mulled cider.

Worrying she might burn her tongue, Emily took a tentative sip. "Mmm, so good." She moaned in delight.

As the horses began to walk forward, an icy breeze blew on Emily's cheeks, sending a shiver down her spine. Fortunately, Luke's body heat warmed her one side. Her hands, wrapped around the hot flask, helped too.

Riding in an open sleigh over fields of snow in the company of a handsome man was one of the most romantic experiences she could think of. No one had ever done anything like this for her before.

"This is so beautiful, Luke," she whispered, leaning in close. "Thank you."

His gloved fingers brushed her cheek, his eyes staring deeply into hers. "I want to make this date—all our dates—memorable, Em."

"Well, you're doing a good job. So far."

"I guess the day isn't over yet."

"No." She chuckled. "No, it isn't."

Settling into the rhythm of the sleigh bouncing over the

uneven ground, Emily listened for the cardinal's call. Instead, she heard the jingle of the horses' bells and thought of the Christmas just passed and her time in New York. She recalled ice-skating with Henry; how much fun it had been.

What was he doing today?

Something with Britt, no doubt.

Emily's good mood dissipated faster than a finger snap.

She couldn't imagine Henry riding in a sleigh over a snow-covered mountain. Dinners in fancy restaurants—like the one they'd shared the night they'd seen the Jays with Charlotte and Adam—were more his style. The way that night had ended, well, her face heated at the memory. Henry's incredible kiss had made her toes curl and taken her completely by surprise.

Despite her insisting it could never happen again and shutting down any hint of a relationship other than friendship, Henry kept asking her out again and again. Turning him down was the right thing. They would never work as anything but friends.

She just had to keep telling herself that.

"You okay?" Luke's deep voice brought her back to the present. Concern dotted his brow. "You look a little flushed, Em. Is something wrong?"

"Of course not," she murmured, covering her cheeks. Funny how easily the lie slid off her tongue. If Luke knew she'd been reliving a memorable moment involving another man, he'd have every right to be more than a little perturbed. Luckily for her, he had no clue.

She needed to keep it that way and stop letting Henry push his way into her thoughts and dreams.

Easier said than done.

Chapter Sixteen

Emily stifled a giggle. Sitting next to Henry in church earlier had been fun, especially watching him squirm—in a good way—whenever their hands accidentally touched.

And Britt's dirty looks had been so worth it.

She wasn't sure why he was dating the woman, other than the fact she'd encouraged it, and so had Henry's parents. Honestly, he didn't seem that into Britt.

All the more reason to keep her attraction in check and not allow these growing feelings. Of course, it would be so much easier if she weren't about to see him alone.

Butterflies flared in her stomach and held it hostage.

Refusing to think of this as a date—because it wasn't— Emily remained in her deep blue jeans and peach long-sleeved T-shirt. She grabbed a different scarf; the wool one had given her neck an angry rash.

In the bathroom, she squirted on a little extra perfume, touched up her mascara and lipstick, and brushed her hair. She stared at her reflection in the mirror. Ready.

Weirdly, she pictured Britt's flawlessly tanned face framed by stunning brunette locks. The woman could easily be a hair model or a model, period. She was incredibly beautiful, sexy and—

Blinking hard, Emily forced Henry's girlfriend from her mind. It would do no good to compare. In God's eyes, she was beautiful and loved by Him. That was all that mattered.

The doorbell rang as she collected her phone and purse from her nightstand. An overwhelming urge to run her hands down her jeans hit.

Not a date, she reminded herself.

Since Charlotte and the kids were out with Adam, Emily quickly shrugged into her coat and set the alarm. Opening the door, she smiled at Henry.

"Hey, Emily." The masculine scent of his aftershave wafted over. Man, he smelled good. "You look amazing."

Briefly examining her casual outfit, Emily laughed. "Gosh, Henry, if this is amazing, you need to up your standards!"

Sincerity blazed in his gorgeous eyes, and a genuine smile tugged at his lips. "Sometimes it's not about what we see when we look at someone, but what we know about them."

Time stood still, sparks zapping between them. Emily's breath caught as emotions, painful and warm, swirled in her chest. If she stood there much longer, she'd move closer and hope Henry kissed her. Daylight would fade soon, making this feel even more like a date than it already did. She needed to break the spell.

Stepping to the side, she forced a casual tone. "Okay, Mr. Maturity, that's a little too deep for me. I need coffee."

After navigating a couple of the stairs, she peered over her shoulder. He hadn't moved.

"Can we go, please?"

"Sure, Miss Bossy. Or is it Miss Impatient?" he teased, finally coming to life.

"More like Miss Thirsty."

She couldn't help comparing Henry's practical, electric, and much less flashy car to Luke's rides—a helicopter and a high-end sports car.

That spoke to their characters. Didn't it?

"You warm enough?" Henry asked, fiddling with the heating.

"Toasty and parched."

He grinned. "Okay, okay. I get the hint." Pointing the car toward downtown, he pulled out onto the street and then glanced at her. "How was your day with Luke?"

She couldn't help but smile. "Great, actually. We went on a sleigh ride. Something I've dreamed of since I was a little girl."

"Sounds like a lot of fun. And cold." Henry's small smile didn't reach his eyes.

"Well, with Luke, a fleecy blanket, and a hot chocolate to keep me warm, I couldn't complain."

"Neither did he, I bet," Henry muttered without looking at her.

"Do you have a problem with Luke?"

He shook his head. "Of course not."

Crossing her arms, Emily stared out the side window at the snow piles on the sidewalks. They weren't as high as they could be, but still—

"What else did you do? Did Luke fly you to New York for lunch?"

She turned to stare at Henry. Why was he being ridiculous? Sure, they could've done that, but the point was for Luke to visit New Haven.

"No." She sighed heavily. "We had brunch at a small hometown place, which, by the way, was delicious." Remembering their lovely waitress, she smiled.

"What are you smiling about?" Henry asked, his brow furrowed.

"Just that when Luke tipped twenty dollars, the waitress looked like she might kiss him."

"Twenty doesn't sound like much."

She clenched her jaw at his disparaging tone. "Well, it was, considering the check wasn't much more than that!"

"Flashy."

Fighting her irritation, she blew out a frustrated breath. "How about you keep your snarky comments to yourself."

"I'm only telling the truth." Henry gave a one-armed shrug. "That's what friends do."

"Friends are also supportive and don't make digs about their friend's boyfriend."

Stopping a little more abruptly than normal at a stop sign, Henry's narrowed gaze shot to hers. "He's your boyfriend now?"

"He is."

"Kinda fast, don't you think?"

"It's not like we just met. And, in case you'd forgotten, we have a son."

Expecting another cutting remark, Henry surprised her by keeping his lips zipped.

During the rest of the short drive, his jaw muscles twitched every now and then, but he remained quiet. Instead, his eyes stayed on the road, which was fine with her.

Pulling into an available space in the Grove Street parking lot, Henry cut the engine and released his seat belt. He shifted to face her, his expression relaxed. "I thought we'd go to Koffee? I know it's after three, but I'm sure they'll still do coffee if we don't want wine or beer."

"Koffee?" she said with a closed-mouth smile. "Exactly what I'm dying for."

Henry laughed, and Emily joined in. Maybe this non-date would be okay after all.

***

With red-painted brick walls, beat-up leather couches, wingback armchairs, and a counter with bar stools, Koffee felt more like someone's cozy living room than a coffeehouse.

Emily ordered a regular latte, but the charming barista—sporting a goatee and black-rimmed glasses—persuaded her to have an Irish Coffee. Henry asked for a Moka Tan.

After the man fixed their drinks, they carried them over to an area containing two cozy armchairs facing one another. Henry sat down and checked out the space. The far wall was littered with photos, creating a lovely homey feel. It wasn't ultra modern, like some spots in New Haven, but this place suited him since he wasn't a college kid anymore.

While he sipped his coffee, Henry observed the other customers and almost choked on a snort. He quickly set his mug on the low table so it didn't spill.

Emily's eyebrows scrunched together. "What's wrong?"

"Nothing. I was thinking this place is a good fit for me, you know, more age appropriate. But then I realized how many college students there are here and…"

"And don't forget," she said, a smirk on her pretty face, "I'm not exactly old either."

"No, you're not."

Raising her cocktail glass, Emily took a tiny sip of her drink. "Wow, this is really good!" She chuckled. "Whiskey and coffee—who'd have thought?"

"I'm older and wiser than you," Henry said, deepening his voice, "And I happen to have tasted an Irish Coffee before, so I knew it was good. I'm happy to be the reason you're experiencing something new and being educated in the process."

"Ha ha, old man," she teased. Sobering, she peered at his glass. "How's yours? What's in it, exactly?"

"I believe an espresso shot with spicy rum, Irish cream, and Ghirardelli chocolate. I know it sounds weird, but you should try it." Smiling encouragingly, he offered her his mug. "It's creamy and delicious."

"I'm not sure I'm old enough." She kept a straight face, but she had to be joking.

"Ha ha," he mimicked. "You're over twenty-one…unless you lied to me?"

A bunch of youngsters entered the establishment, chatting and laughing loudly together.

"They look like a fun group," he commented when her attention wandered to them.

"Yeah." Emily sighed, a faraway look in her eyes.

Did she miss having friends like that? She'd never mentioned a best friend, or any friends for that matter, other than Charlotte. Except, Charlotte was also her employer, so that was different.

"Did you ever stay in contact with any friends from school?" he asked, curious.

Flattening her lips, Emily shook her head. "Honestly, I was

too afraid of what they might think of me."

Momentarily confused, he frowned.

"Being pregnant, you know?" she whispered.

"Surely at least one friend wouldn't have judged you?"

The mug in her hands became her sole focus.

"I'm sorry, Emily." Sad eyes lifted to him. "I can't imagine what it must've been like going through that alone."

"It wasn't too bad, really." She smiled weakly. "My aunt's a wonderful Christian. I came to know Jesus because of her. If it weren't for my faith, I wouldn't have coped as well as I did. His strength enabled me to carry my baby to term and give him up for adoption."

"Your faith keeps you going now, too, doesn't it? When you don't have your son with you every day."

"Hundred percent. It's tough, and I shouldn't complain. Not since I decided to give up my son and not tell my parents. But,"—her eyes brightened—"Noah's adoptive parents are wonderful, Henry. They let me see him, although technically, they're not obligated to."

He smiled gently. "You're fortunate. Many wouldn't want any interference from a birth parent."

"I know. It's the reason New York's out. At least not while my son is here. I want to see him as much as possible."

"I understand. I'm happy here, too, but ultimately, I don't have a choice; I have to move back. Thankfully, my parents aren't pushing me to return. Yet." He smiled ruefully. "They're always hinting."

"So, what charities should I support?" Emily's sudden subject change gave Henry whiplash. It also reminded him why they were there: to focus on Emily's wish to invest in other's lives.

Not on a date.

He had to admire her tenacity and determination; it reminded him of himself at that age. Wow, she really was still young, he realized. Yet, she'd already had a child, and if she were serious about Luke, they'd likely settle down and have more.

A knife-like pain stabbed at his chest.

He took a deep breath and dug out his phone and a piece of paper. "The list isn't exhaustive, but it's a good start."

Emily scanned the sheet he held out and chewed on her bottom lip. Henry couldn't help his eyes dipping to her mouth.

Talk about torture! Ever since their kiss after the Jays' concert, he'd imagined pressing his lips to hers countless times. Instead, he had to be content with being her friend because that's what she wanted. She obviously had no problem denying their attraction, but really, he should be encouraging her relationship with Luke. As her son's father, it made sense.

And Mr. Quinn liked the young man enough to allow him to date his daughter. That, in itself, spoke volumes.

"Would it sound crazy if I said I wanted to help every one of these charities?" Emily asked, sounding hesitant.

Henry matched her shy smile with an encouraging one of his own. "Not at all. I love that idea. It speaks to the kindness in your generous heart and would be a great use of your resources."

She ducked her head. "Thanks."

"Assuming you have enough left of your trust fund to live on afterward."

When her gaze shot to his, he winked.

"Funny." She didn't laugh. "I don't *need* my trust fund, Henry. Next year, I get another huge lump sum and eventually, I'll inherit my father's estate. It's ridiculous. How much money *does* one person need?"

He bit back a laugh at her outrage. "Not much, depending on how you choose to live. I mean, if you want to fly around in a helicopter, eat at Michelin-starred restaurants, and own a few homes around the world, then you'd need quite a bit more."

She swatted his arm. "You just described our parents!"

"True." He grinned. "But that's not you or me."

"No." Shaking her head, she grinned too. "I still can't

believe you're *the* Henry Palmer." She tapped a finger on her cheek. "You sure you're not his doppelgänger?" she asked, her eyes twinkling. "Because I picture the real Henry living in a Fifth Avenue penthouse overlooking Central Park, flying on his private jet to exotic destinations, and parading around a stunning woman every chance he gets." She wrinkled her brow. "Oh, wait, Britt fits the bill exactly."

She was jealous?

He chuckled at the thought. A man could dream.

"Nope, I'm the one and only Henry Palmer. Sorry. You're stuck with me."

"It might sound cheesy, but I'm happy to be stuck with you." A light blush settled on Emily's cheeks, and his pulse sped up at the insinuation until she added, "As friends."

Not knowing how to respond, he finished his coffee and crossed his arms. Emily stared at his sheet of paper.

"What's up?" he asked when the silence had gone on for too long.

Her head jerked up, a sheen of liquid showing in her eyes. "Noah's been out of town, and I miss him. Hopefully, I'll get to see him next weekend. Unless his parents have other plans, then I don't know what I'll tell Luke."

"Why?"

"He's pressuring me to arrange a meeting with them and Noah."

"I understand his impatience, Emily," Henry said, touching her hand. As tingles sped up his arm, he pulled his hand away. Feeling angry that Luke had caused her current distress, Henry somehow managed to keep his tone neutral. "He wants to get to know his son. Make up for lost time. It's what I'd want to do."

"I know. The situation's delicate, though. Luke may not feel an instant connection to Noah like I did." She covered her face with her hands and groaned. "How can I introduce Luke to his son if he then becomes a nonentity in his life? Noah's so little."

Henry gave her a gentle smile. "I'd say pray about the

situation, then leave it in God's hands." He waited for her to meet his eyes. "His timing and purposes are perfect, Emily. Unlike us mere mortals, He never makes a mistake."

"You're a wise man, Henry." Her appreciative smile made his stomach flip and his heart raced. "And a good friend."

Great. That word again—friend—equivalent to dumping a jug of water over him. Also, a timely reminder that they weren't in a romantic relationship.

"I take it you still don't want to tell your parents about their grandson?"

"No." Emily's swift answer brooked no argument.

Time to change the subject.

"What else is on your list of dreams?"

She blinked. "What?"

Goodness, how he wanted to smooth the lines between her eyes. Or kiss her taut mouth until it relaxed and kissed him back.

He smacked himself mentally. A *friend*, remember?

"You mentioned riding a sleigh. What else have you always wanted to do?"

Emily's eyes lit up, and she laughed lightly. "Oh...I don't know," she said, twisting her lips.

Once more, his eyes honed in on her mouth. He forced his eyes elsewhere.

"I'd love to go up in a hot air balloon," she said, then shrugged. "Not sure I'd have the courage, though."

"Would it help if I held your hand?" He held his breath, his eyes locked on hers.

"Yes." Her breathless response caused his stomach to tighten.

"Then maybe I'll take you sometime...if I get the courage."

"I'd also like to go sledding."

He stared at her. "You've never sledded?"

"Nope." His face must've shown his surprise because she giggled. "Hello? Only child with busy parents. It wasn't exactly top priority."

"Okay, now that's just sad." Jumping to his feet, Henry

held out his hand. "This needs rectifying immediately."

Laughing, she waved away his hand and pointed to the exit. "I think you've forgotten it's dark outside."

Like a balloon pricked with a pin, his excitement deflated. "In that case, we have a tobogganing date for..." He scratched his head. "Maybe after church next Sunday? Unless you're busy with Luke?"

"I'd love that, and no, I won't be seeing Luke." She beamed at him momentarily, then her expression turned somber, and his stomach dropped. "But Henry?"

"Yes?"

"It's not a date."

Chapter Seventeen

Emily tugged thick woolen socks on under black ski trousers, then rose from the bed. Her lips felt dry, so she scanned the bathroom cabinet shelves for lip balm. Spotting sunscreen first, she pulled it out and smiled. Henry was taking her to East Rock Park to, in his words, 'embrace the snowy adventure of sledding.'

When the doorbell rang, she stuffed black mittens and a beanie into her purse, then scooped up the hot pink, black, and white ski jacket she'd borrowed from Charlotte.

At the front door, she ignored the sudden tightness gripping her chest. Sure, hurtling down a slippery slope on a piece of plastic with no brakes was a little terrifying, but that wasn't why she felt a momentary panic. Nor was it a result of being half-excited or half-apprehensive about going out with Henry.

Nope, not the reason at all.

After bundling Emily into his heated car, Henry sank into the driver's seat and glanced at her. "You excited or nervous?"

"Why?"

Chuckling, he pointed at her bouncing knee. She held her hand on it and smiled guiltily. "I guess."

"You know it's totally safe, right? If we fall off, we'll land in the snow, not on rocks."

"Hey!" She pointed an accusing finger at him. "You

promised you'd make sure there was no falling involved."

A mischievous smile appeared on his stubbled face. "I said I'd do my best."

"Same thing. Your best is to keep me on the sled."

"You'll be fine." He chuckled again, the low, throaty sound sending shivers up her spine.

"I'd better be." She patted her jacket. "Charlotte'll kill me if I get this stained."

"I doubt that. She needs you."

Emily quirked a brow. "You're saying I'm indispensable?"

"Yep, and irreplaceable."

"Ha ha. I'm not so sure about that."

Emily peered out the window as they wound their way up the hill towards the Soldiers and Sailors' monument. She still hadn't spoken to Charlotte about what would happen when she and Adam married. So far, it looked like the wedding would be at the beginning of Spring Break, so on the second Saturday in April.

Would her nannying role continue as is?

Adam would presumably move in with Charlotte since he lived in a one-bed apartment. What would it be like then, with an adult male in the house?

"Hey, where'd you go?" Henry asked, breaking into her thoughts.

"Just thinking about how things are going to change."

"You mean after the wedding?"

She nodded.

"I'm sure nothing will," he assured her, "other than Adam's sleeping arrangements."

"Ew, Henry."

He shrugged. "What? I'm sure I don't have to explain about—"

Sticking her fingers in her ears, she sang, "la, la, la," until he laughed.

For a while after that, the only sound in the car was the whirr of the warm air blasting out the vents.

Henry cleared his throat. "Can I ask you something?"

"Go ahead."

"Why doesn't Luke come to church with you?" Avoiding eye contact, Henry rubbed the back of his neck. "I know he stays the night."

How could Henry even think…?

She gave him a pointed look. "I hope you know he doesn't stay with me."

"I didn't want to assume."

"Frankly, Luke would love nothing more, but I've made it clear that's not happening until I have a ring on my finger."

His mouth fell open. "You've talked about getting married?"

"Not in the way you're thinking." She laughed softly. "But you must realize, I don't date anyone I can't imagine a future with. I may be young, but I'm not interested in wasting time with a guy I've no intention of marrying."

"Good to know." He said it so quietly she wondered if she'd heard him correctly.

"Luke doesn't go to church, Henry. He's not a believer."

Stopping at the lights, he stared at her. "So you won't sleep with a guy before you're married, but you'll date a non-believer?"

Feeling her face heat, she ducked her head.

He had a good point.

"I don't mean to sound judgmental, Emily," he said softly, "but the Bible talks about being unequally yoked."

She sighed. "I hadn't thought about that, only that our situation isn't typical." Facing him, she noted his kind, concerned expression. "We may not be married, but we're already family."

Clearly not a fan, Henry's lips morphed into a tight line.

Well, there was nothing she could do about the facts.

Once they'd parked, Henry grabbed a sled from the trunk and led Emily to the top of the hill and the breathtaking view of New Haven. Kids of all ages screeched as they sped down the snow-filled slopes on their sleds. Others dragged their sleds behind them as they trekked up from the bottom, wearing huge, satisfied smiles.

Beside Henry and Emily were groups of friends and families building snowmen or enjoying snowball fights. Everyone looked to be having a ton of fun.

"Shall we join them?" Henry pointed to the sledders. "Or would you prefer to do the snowman thing first?" His gaze swung to the more sedate activities on their left.

"Sledding first, please."

His broad smile melted her insides like snowmen warmed by the rising sun.

Soon Henry's arms were wrapped around her waist, and Emily knew she was in for the experience of a lifetime.

"Ready?" he asked, his warm breath tickling her ear. She gave a single nod, and he pushed off with his feet. As they hurtled down the hill, the icy wind smacked her face. She screamed.

"Hey, I've got you." Henry tightened his hold, and she relaxed into him immediately, knowing that he'd protect her no matter what.

When they reached the bottom in record time, she turned to him, her hands clapping in delight. "Can we go again? Please?"

"So you liked it?" He laughed. "Because, honestly, I couldn't tell from that scream." He gave her a lopsided grin, then squeezed her waist gently before removing his hands from her body.

She faked a hurt look. "Isn't screaming part of the whole adventure?"

"Maybe." He rubbed his ear, grimacing. "As long as it doesn't have a detrimental effect on my eardrum."

"Ha ha."

Patting her mittened hands together, they began the long trek up the hill. Twice, Henry had to pull her out of the way of a rogue sledder, and one time, he yanked her in front of him to prevent a head-on accident. Breathless at the near miss, she spun in his arms. Henry's eyes squinted in concern, and her heart beat erratically.

"Phew! That was close." She briefly lowered her eyes to his mouth before they flew back up. "Thank you."

"I told you I'd take care of you," Henry said gruffly.

Electricity coursed between them, and Emily dared not move. If she only stretched a couple of inches, then she'd be able to taste his lips and relive the kiss that had blown her mind and left her reeling.

She swallowed hard.

"We should move." Henry's comment broke the spell, shattering the illusion. It brought her back to the present and, with it, her good sense.

Since the man hadn't moved, Emily shifted out of his arms and continued in the direction they'd been going—uphill.

"You did pack a thermos, right?" she asked. Somehow, she kept her tone even, in direct contrast to her pulse, because that hadn't settled at all.

***

Not long after the sun had set, Henry rang Charlotte's doorbell for the second time that day. He couldn't believe he'd agreed to this just so he could spend more time with Emily. Britt had invited him for dinner, but he'd asked for a raincheck. She might be free most weeknights, but Emily wasn't. School took up her weekday evenings, and now she had a boyfriend, Henry couldn't be picky about when he saw her. He'd take what he could get, even if it meant helping babysit three kids.

Amy swung the door open. "Mr. Henry, you'd better come quick! Miss Emily's in the kitchen." She marched off, leaving him to shut the door.

What on earth?

Striding behind Amy, Henry smelled onions as he rounded the corner into the enormous open-plan kitchen. No fire or smoke. Instead, Emily stood with tears running down her face.

Alarmed, he crossed over to the island and grabbed her wrist. "Hey. Are you okay? What happened?"

Looking up, she burst out laughing.

Huh? Was this some kind of prank?

"I'm fine," she spluttered, motioning to the chopping board. "It's the onion, silly."

Relief flooded him, and he let her go. "Right." He turned to mock glare at Amy, who stood near the fridge. "Amy had me there for a second."

The child smirked. "Gotcha."

Emily laughed as she pushed the diced onions off the board and into a small bowl. "Amy, how about you weigh out the spaghetti," she instructed. The child scampered off, and Emily faced Henry. "You ready to be put to work?"

"Ready and willing."

"Okay, first off…" Bending over, she pulled a large saucepan from a cupboard and handed it over. "Fill this with four quarts water and leave it on the stovetop."

He finished the task quickly, then watched while she fried the onion.

"Shall I set the table, Miss Emily?" Amy wiggled the silverware in her hands. Emily nodded, then blinked at Henry as if she wasn't sure why he was there.

Nudging her shoulder, he smiled. "What's next?"

"Um." She glanced around the kitchen. "Could you grab a bottle of Prego from the pantry cupboard, please? Third shelf down."

"Yep."

When he brought her the sauce, she was breaking up ground beef. He frowned. "That's not mac and cheese."

Chuckling, she nodded in Amy's direction. "My plan got vetoed in favor of pasta with meat sauce. I hope you don't mind?"

Her adorable pout made him want to lean down and kiss her perfectly shaped lips. Controlling the desire, he opened the bottle of sauce and slid it over to her. "Luckily for you, it's my second favorite meal."

"You mean lucky for you." She waved the spatula at him. "You'd be eating toast for dinner otherwise."

His hand flew to his chest. "You wouldn't!"

"Since you're crashing my babysitting gig, I *so* would." Her smug smile had him focusing on her mouth. His heartbeat picked up, remembering what it tasted like, how soft and warm her lips were when he—

Thank goodness Emily shifted away from him, halting his walk down memory lane. In a vain attempt to distract himself from the pretty woman, he leaned back against the counter and checked on Amy's progress. She was almost done.

"What are the boys up to, Amy?" he asked.

"They're building a Lego city in the playroom."

"Awesome! I can't remember the last time I played with Legos."

"You should go help them, Mr. Henry. They'd love that. I know because they asked me, but I wanted to watch my movie, and now I'm helping Miss Emily."

He peeked at Emily, who was watching him with an amused smile.

"Go join them, Henry. I know you want to."

"But I'm here to help you."

"Entertaining the boys while keeping an eye on them is helping."

"Okay. But holler if you need me to do anything else, alright?" *Like, kiss you.* He squashed the errant thought hard and fast, like popping bubble wrap.

"I will, don't worry." She turned back to her meat sauce.

After dinner, the kids showered and pulled on their pajamas. Emily read the boys a story in Daniel's room while Henry read a chapter of *The Lion, The Witch, and The Wardrobe* to Amy in hers. They said goodnight, then Emily took Henry back to the kitchen to brew coffee and find a snack-sized pack of Reese's.

In the basement, they occupied the sofa directly in front of the sixty-five-inch television—a fact Henry knew because Adam had asked Charlotte one evening how large the screen was just before a movie marathon.

Flicking through movies on the Hallmark Channel, Emily paused. "You sure you want to stay?" She shot him a skeptical look. "The kids are probably asleep."

"Why wouldn't I?"

She shrugged. "Your choice."

The movie she chose was based on a true-life story about a woman who needed a liver transplant and ended up falling in love with her donor. It wasn't his usual action-packed adventure movie, but Henry enjoyed it anyway. Maybe it was the company.

He kept his physical distance throughout the show, even when Emily decided to curl her legs under her body and subconsciously shifted closer.

Later, their gazes connected as the credits went up, and she stifled a yawn.

"I should go," he said, wishing he didn't have to work the next day. "You're tired."

"Stay a little longer? So we can talk?"

"Sure." Deny this woman anything? Impossible.

She stared down at her hands twisting in her lap. "The thing is, I don't know what to do."

"About?"

"Luke met Noah's adoptive parents yesterday."

"But not Noah?"

She shook her head. "That's been arranged for next weekend. They wanted time to introduce the idea of an 'uncle' to him."

"I see. Did they get on with Luke?"

"Luke's very charming when he wants to be." She gave him a coy look. "He reminds me of you."

A smile tugged at his lips. "Finally, I'm compared to a younger man." He winked. "It does wonders for my ego, you know."

Swatting him, she laughed. "Anyway…" She cleared her throat. "I'm supposed to have Noah for the weekend, and now Luke's insisting on taking us to New York."

He frowned. "Isn't that a little much, given it'll be Noah's first time meeting him?"

"Exactly." She looked pleased. "You get me. Never mind

the risk that we'll run into my parents." Her gaze shifted to the TV briefly. "I told Luke I didn't think it was a good idea, that it was too much for our son, but he dismissed my concerns."

"You need to put your foot down, Emily. Luke may be the boy's father, but he can't bully you into doing what he wants. I agree that he needs a chance to know his son, but at a pace you're comfortable with."

"I wish…" Her smile seemed sad.

"What?"

"Nothing." She shook her head vigorously. "It's silly."

"Try me."

"I wish you were meeting Noah, not Luke. You're so great with kids, especially little boys. I think he'd love you."

"If he's half as great as his mother, I think I'd love him too." He hadn't meant to admit that but couldn't take it back.

Blushing, Emily pushed to her feet and collected their mugs.

"Emily." Henry grasped her wrist and stood. When she met his eyes, he ambled closer. He brushed the back of his finger over her hot cheek. Her eyelids fluttered closed, and his pulse accelerated. All he had to do was lean in—

Her eyes flew open, and she stared at him with wide eyes. "Henry, don't," she said, her voice shaky.

"I won't." He swallowed hard. "It doesn't stop me from wanting to, though."

"I thought you were happy to be my friend?" The vulnerability in her voice and her use of that word he couldn't get away from made his heart ache.

"I was. I mean, I am."

She looked at him doubtfully.

"I *am* your friend, Emily."

A deep sigh lifted her chest. "Okay, because I'm with Luke now, and you're with Britt."

"I know."

It didn't mean he liked it one bit.

Chapter Eighteen

A few days later, Emily glanced at her phone and did a mental calculation. Charlotte wanted her in the formal dining room by eight.

Thirteen minutes was enough time, right?

Emily slid her palm down her jeans, took a deep breath, and pressed the call button. Sean and Lisa agreed that the sooner Luke knew he'd have to meet Noah here, not in New York, the better.

"Hi, Luke. We need to talk," she said when he answered.

A few minutes later, she sighed in relief, tucked her phone into her back pocket, and headed to the dining room. Britt's distinctive laugh awakened the butterflies in her stomach. Henry was bound to be one of the five guests. Charlotte hadn't mentioned who to expect, just to prepare dinner for seven, including Emily.

"There you are." Charlotte smiled as Emily entered the beautifully decorated room. A bunch of multicolored roses with baby's breath filled the middle of the twelve-seater table, while strings of fairy lights hung along the walls, giving the room a cozy atmosphere.

"We were just talking about you." Adam sat beside Charlotte, a smile on his face, too.

Squashing her slight irritation, Emily forced a smile and glanced at those gathered around the white cloth-covered table. Charlotte's brother Jack and his wife Julie were there, as well as Britt and, yes, Henry too—all dressed up.

Great, she must've missed the memo.

"Hey, everyone." She wiped her hands down the jeans stretched over her thighs. Again.

"Hey, Emily. It's been a while." As always, Julie's smile was kind and welcoming.

"It has. Good to see you." She looked at Charlotte. "Shall I bring in the food?"

"That would be lovely."

In the kitchen, Emily pulled the chicken and vegetable casserole, and the roast potatoes from the warm oven and stuck them on the walnut serving cart. She turned back to the counter to retrieve the plates and heard a noise behind her.

Whirling around, she yelped. "Henry! You scared me."

"Do you need help?" He stood wearing a sexy, amused smile, with his hands stuffed into his camel-colored trouser pockets.

Heart stuttering, she couldn't think for a second. Why did he have to look so hot?

Chuckling, he stepped forward, and immediately, she woke from her stupor.

"I'm fine, thanks. I was just loading these." She filled the second shelf with the plates, then went to grab the handles. Henry beat her to it, his tantalizing musky scent assaulting her senses. It took major willpower not to close her eyes and breathe it in.

He commandeered the cart. "Let me push that for you."

"Bully," she said with a giant smile.

His lips twitched, but he remained stoic. "I prefer gentleman."

"Whatever you say."

Before they got to the dining room doorway, she gripped his hand. "Thank you," she whispered, her gaze tangling with his. He finally allowed that gorgeous smile free rein. Boy, did it do something crazy to her insides.

"That smells incredible, Emily," Adam said, coming to help them.

Praying her face wouldn't give her away, Emily dropped Henry's hand like a hot potato and smiled. "I hope so. It's one of my mother's favorites, so I had it a lot growing up."

Once everything was on the table, Charlotte told them to help themselves.

Julie plated some crispy, brown-edged potatoes, then looked at Emily. "Did your mom teach you to cook?"

"No. I learned from…" She glanced at Henry.

Sensing her reluctance to finish the sentence, he handed over the water jug and proceeded to plate some chicken for her.

"Don't worry about me, Henry." She gave him a grateful smile but waved him off. "Serve yourself first."

Adam gave thanks as soon as everyone was ready, and they all dug in. When Britt asked Jack about the Jays' latest music, he happily deferred to Julie. She patiently and politely answered the barrage of questions that followed.

As a silent spectator, Emily caught the occasional glance from Henry. At one such time, he nodded in Britt's direction. "I'm sorry," he mouthed.

Stifling a giggle behind her hand, Emily avoided his gaze again until they were done with the meal. She stood to clear the dishes.

"Adam, would you mind helping Emily?" Charlotte threw her fiancé a pleading look.

He pressed a kiss to her cheek. "For you, my darling, anything."

"It's not like Charlotte's got my brother wrapped around her finger or anything," Britt joked. "Am I right?"

A smattering of laughter followed Adam and Emily as they left for the kitchen. Adam was used to helping at his soup kitchens, so it made sense that the clean-up happened in record time.

After a bit, though, Emily became aware of Adam's eyebrows pulled together, his gaze narrowed.

"Hey, I don't mind doing this," she said. "Trust me. Charlotte's super-generous with what she pays me."

"It's not that. It's…" He held the back of his neck. "I must apologize for my sister. Britt's always had a way of claiming the spotlight." He snickered. "Considering Julie's the one used to being there, it's saying something."

She waved away his concern. "Honestly, I admire Britt. She drew out details about the Jays that I don't think Jack or Julie would normally tell anyone."

"You're so right." He laughed, then scratched his chin like he wanted to say more.

"What?"

"Normally, when Britt and Henry are together, one can't get a word in edgewise. Tonight, he's preoccupied." He gave her a pointed look. "Any idea why?"

"You're asking me because…?"

"I wondered if he'd confided in you earlier."

"He hardly said two words."

"But you *are* friends, right?" Adam gave her another quizzical look. "At least that's what he told me."

"Yep. Just friends." Emily spun to the fridge, hoping he'd stop any further interrogation. "Shall we take out the dessert?"

"I think Charlotte wanted a word with everyone first."

"Oh. Okay."

Back in the dining room, Charlotte cleared her throat to get everyone's attention. "Adam and I have made a few wedding decisions." She looked at him, and he nodded for her to continue. "We've finalized the date: April eleventh."

Julie smiled happily at Jack. "If I'm right, we leave for our European Tour at the end of April."

"Yep." Jack grinned. "That's great news, Charlie."

Charlotte's expression turned slightly apprehensive. "Julie, I'd love you to be my Maid of Honor."

"It would be *my* honor, Charlie." Julie blew her a kiss.

"Thank you." She turned to Britt while Emily shifted uncomfortably in her seat. "Will you be a bridesmaid?"

"Of course!" Squealing, Britt rushed from her seat to give Charlotte a sideways hug. "I'd love to be part of your wedding party."

"Henry already knows he's my best man," Adam said matter-of-factly.

"Like you had a choice, bud." Henry grinned at his best friend from college. Adam then sent him a mock glare before reaching over to share their special handshake.

A frisson of jealousy ran through Emily. No one in her life had her back no matter what, unless she counted her aunt. When she'd left New York after graduation, pregnant and alone, she'd purposefully lost contact with all her friends. And although she chatted to other women at college, she hadn't gotten close to anyone in particular either. If Emily were to marry, she had no clue who she'd ask to stand up with her. Other than Henry, Charlotte was probably the only person she considered a friend.

Wouldn't that be weird? One's employee as a bridesmaid? Tears pricked the back of her eyes thinking about it.

"What do you say, Em?"

Pulled back to the conversation by Charlotte's voice, Emily frowned. "Sorry, what?"

"I'd love for you to be one of my bridesmaids too."

Stiffening, Emily's heart thudded in her chest. The wedding would be a reported event. Charlotte had already made the news when she and Adam had announced their Scott Wilson Home project. Given her brother and sister-in-law were famous country artists, this wedding would undoubtedly be splashed across every magazine and television channel.

Henry met her panicked eyes. "I think you took her by surprise."

"Henry's right..." Emily could've kissed him. Uh, maybe not. Swallowing, she shifted her attention from the man who kept swooping in and saving her. Every time. "I'm honored, Charlie, but would you mind if I check my schedule?"

"Sure. I mean, of course. I don't need an answer right this second."

"Thanks. I appreciate that."

"So, Charlotte, have you thought about what bridesmaid dress designs you'd like?" Britt's question broke the awkwardness, and for once Emily didn't mind the inquisitive, talkative woman.

***

Henry chuckled quietly. Britt sure was a force to be reckoned with, launching into question after question about the wedding!

He focused on Emily. Charlotte's proposal had come as a shock. Not that he understood why. Emily's boss was also her friend. If ever there was a time to set the record straight about her identity and financial situation, it was now. If he could get Emily alone, he'd encourage her to do just that.

It wasn't that he wanted her in the wedding party, per se—a terrible idea unless she wanted her name splashed all over the tabloids. Imagine, 'Millionaire Socialite's Bridesmaid Actually Bride's Nanny'—but if Charlotte knew Emily's secret, she'd tell Adam, who'd probably mention it to Britt. With any luck, she'd get off Emily's case. No one else but Henry seemed to notice Britt glaring at Emily after Charlotte's announcement.

Emily pushed back her dining chair. "Shall I get dessert ready?"

"Oh, yes!" Charlotte's expression brightened. Perhaps Britt did need to tone it down a bit.

"I'll give you a hand," Henry said, jumping to his feet.

Julie started to get up too, but he gestured for her to sit. "I've got it."

As they entered the kitchen, Emily spun to him, her eyes narrowed. "You've already been a great help tonight, and you're a guest. You didn't need to do this."

"Helping you is never a chore, Emily." He grasped her elbow and looked her straight in the eye. "I *want* to help you."

While her brown eyes brightened prettily to hazel, pink tinged her cheeks, and she smiled softly. "Well, thank you." She pointed in the direction of the dining room. "And thanks for the save out there. That was the last thing I expected."

"Charlotte considers you a friend, not just an employee. You know that, right?"

She nodded.

"So tell her why you can't be in that wedding party. She'll understand, and"—he winked—"you'll make Britt happy, too."

Her scowl was too cute.

He skimmed the tips of his fingers along her arm to her wrist, loving the goosebumps that arose. "As much as I'd love to have you at all the rehearsal dinners and so on, it's not the way to keep a low profile."

"I know." Her chest rose up and down, yet she kept her eyes on his. Those pretty eyes would be the death of him. All he wanted to do was pull her close and kiss her.

Releasing her arm, he broke eye contact and looked around the kitchen. "So, what's for dessert?"

Later, after finishing some incredible chocolate mousse, Britt's hand found Henry's under the table. He squeezed her fingers. "Everything okay?"

"I don't know." She spoke under her breath. "You tell me. Why do you keep running to Emily's assistance? I thought you were a guest, not a manservant."

"You know she's my friend, Britt." He kept his voice low. "And friends help each other."

She shrugged. "I guess."

Leaning in, he whispered in her ear, "Take a walk with me? Outside?"

A smile swept onto her face, and she nodded.

"Excuse us," Henry said, making a general statement. "Britt and I need to walk off the incredible food."

Adam frowned. "It's cold out. Wouldn't you rather join us in the living room for a hot drink?" He turned to Charlotte. "What do you think, darling?"

"I think Henry should enjoy the fresh air with his girlfriend."

Henry didn't miss the way Emily flinched. A part of him

rejoiced at the reaction; the other—the one reminding him about Luke—didn't.

Once outside the heated house, Henry immediately regretted his decision.

"Ooh, it's freezing." Britt rubbed her gloved hands together while blowing visible puffs of air into the night.

Above them, stars twinkled like they were winking at him. Was it because this was supposedly a romantic walk with his girlfriend? Or because they knew how he really felt about the women in his life?

"Come here." Throwing his arm around Britt's shoulders, Henry pulled her into his side. "Better?"

She shivered. "Much."

He popped a kiss on the side of her head. "Shall we make this a brisk walk with some cuddle stops on the way?"

Britt chuckled humorlessly. "Trust me, it's the only way you'll get me to stay out here for more than a minute."

When they'd walked far enough to have warmed up a little, he slowed. Taking a deep breath, he turned to Britt, who peered up at him with questioning eyes.

"We had an agreement," he said. "I was going to play being your boyfriend to give you a valid excuse to keep the vultures at bay, and you'd pretend to be my girlfriend to get my parents off my case."

"Yes, and it's been working."

"Has anything changed?"

She crossed her arms. "Why? Why would it have?"

"I don't know. You seem extra jealous lately, especially when it comes to Emily."

Her lips twisted. "If this relationship is supposed to appear authentic, it has to feel that way too. So I keep wondering why you chose me instead of Emily since you're such good friends with her." Bitterness laced her words.

"We are good friends. More importantly, though, she already has a boyfriend."

"She does?" Britt's voice rose in pitch, and her expression perked up.

"Luke Bowman."

"Never heard of him."

"He's from New York. Only visits at the weekend."

"Wow, a long-distance relationship. That must be hard." She visibly shuddered, whether from the cold or something else, he wasn't sure.

"Time to share warmth," he said, slipping his hands onto her waist.

Smiling, she wrapped her arms around his neck. "I'm on board with that."

Henry drew her flush against him and hugged her tight. It was amazing how two bodies could generate so much heat. Eventually, Britt pulled back and looked him straight in the eye. "I really like you, Henry. I always have."

"I really like you, too, Britt."

She tilted her head and scrutinized him. He could almost see her brain working hard to figure out how to ask whatever was on her mind. "Do you think we could make a proper go of this fake relationship? Rather than it being a means to an end?"

About to say no, Henry paused.

What did it matter if he agreed? Emily already thought he was in a real relationship, and the point was to show that he could be committed to one woman. Besides, Emily was dating Luke, and considering he was the father of her son, what were the chances she'd decide she wanted Henry instead?

Pretty slim.

Emily thought he was a playboy—one of the reasons she'd turned down his dates—but she was also conscious of keeping her family together for the sake of her son. Although dating Luke hadn't been without conflict—they fit together perfectly, were the same age, and had a child together. Also, anyone could see the chemistry between them.

Yet, when Emily and Henry touched, Henry felt the sparks and saw the desire in Emily's eyes. She felt something for him too. Still fresh in his mind was their one and only kiss. It'd been out of this world. He couldn't imagine ever feeling the same way with another woman. Sure, he hadn't kissed Britt yet, but Emily was taken, and he wasn't getting any younger.

"Yes, I think so, Britt. If you can cope with one thing that won't change for me."

She narrowed her gaze. "What's that?"

"Emily's my friend and will remain my friend."

"I can live with that," she said, nodding. "As long as she's in a relationship too."

"Fair enough."

"We should celebrate." Fluttering her eyelashes, she smiled flirtatiously. "Any ideas?"

His eyes dipped to her full lips. "I think I know just how to do that."

Lowering his head, he kissed her.

Chapter Nineteen

"Charlie? Do you have a minute to talk?"

Emily hoped this was a good time. She'd been rehearsing how this conversation would go for days now. If she didn't get it over with soon, she might never gather the courage again. If only Henry were there to hold her hand and lend his support.

Metaphorically speaking, of course.

Except they hadn't exactly spoken since he and Britt had returned from their walk looking more than a little flushed. From Britt's dancing eyes and tight grip on Henry's hand, Emily guessed they'd been making out. The thought had twisted her stomach into knots and made it difficult to keep her dinner down.

Stupid. She should be happy for Henry finally settling down with a more suitable woman. As his friend, she should be pleased he was showing her that he could stick to dating one person and behaving like a proper boyfriend. Yet she couldn't get excited. Maybe it was because she wasn't a Britt fan.

Maybe it was something else.

"Believe it or not, I do," Charlotte said warmly. "The kids are fast asleep, and Adam's busy tonight. I'm in the mood for a glass of wine. Would you like to join me?"

"I'd love to."

With a glass of Chardonnay each, they strolled to the living room and chose opposite ends of the sectional sofa. Charlotte curled her legs under her while Emily stretched hers out, crossing her ankles. Peace reigned, the only sound from a gentle crackling in the fireplace. The first time Emily saw the fire, she thought it was real until she approached and realized it was artificial.

Charlotte ran her finger around the rim of her wine glass. "How are things going at college?"

"I think I have a handle on things. We're doing placements after Easter."

"Exciting. Where are you planning to do your teacher training?"

"I have a couple of schools in mind, but nothing's concrete yet." Emily had been praying she'd get a position in the same school as Noah; that way, she'd likely see him every day. Of course, she'd need to run it by Noah's parents; they might not be comfortable with her being a daily presence in his life.

"If you need a reference letter from me, you know I'll happily provide one."

"Thanks."

Emily sipped her wine and tried to organize her racing thoughts. Slowly, she raised her eyes to Charlotte's kind ones. "I know you're waiting for me to get back to you about being a bridesmaid," she said.

Charlotte shook her head. "There's no rush."

"The thing is…" Emily bit her bottom lip. "I'd love to, but I can't."

Disappointment flashed across Charlotte's face before a small smile quickly covered it. "That's okay, Em."

"It's not. You need to know why I can't, and I'm not sure how you'll react when you find out why."

Charlotte tensed and sat up straighter. "I don't follow."

"I haven't been entirely honest about who I am."

"That's rather cryptic."

"You've heard of Quinn Packaging?"

A light went on in Charlotte's eyes. "Oh. My. Word! Don't tell me you're *the* Emily Quinn." She shook her head. "Of course you are! It all makes *so* much sense now. Why you have impeccable manners, why you're clearly so educated, and why you and Henry get on so well."

"What? You think that's why Henry and I get on? Because we both come from New York elite families?"

"Well, isn't it?"

"I don't know, maybe a little? I did discover our parents have become good friends over the last few years."

"My question is this, Miss Quinn: what on earth are you doing playing nanny to my children?" Charlotte's gruff tone was somewhat alarming, but she softened the question with a huge smile.

Heart racing, Emily ran a sweaty palm over her jeans. Should she tell her everything?

"Promise me that what I'm about to tell you won't leave this room, and please don't tell anyone my real identity either. When people know who I am, they treat me differently, and I don't want that."

"I appreciate how you feel, Em, but not telling Adam? I'm not sure I want to keep any secrets from him, let alone such a big one." She gestured with her palms up. "I don't think it's a healthy way to start a marriage."

"Fine. You can share what I tell you with Adam if he promises to keep it to himself. Although, Henry knows everything anyway."

"That's a relief." Charlotte's posture relaxed. "I was just thinking how Adam confides in Henry about almost everything. They're like brothers."

"They do share a special bond. They're brothers in Christ, just like we're sisters in Christ."

Lowering her glass to the side table, Charlotte threaded her fingers and eyed Emily. "So what *is* your reason for hiding out in New Haven as my nanny instead of learning how to run your daddy's empire?"

"I have a son."

Charlotte blinked and then blinked again.

Emily wished she'd kept her mouth shut.

"Wow, okay. I never saw that one coming. How old is he? Who's the father?" Grimacing, she covered her mouth. "I'm so sorry, that's none of my business."

"It's fine." Emily gave her a reassuring smile. "Noah's five, and funnily enough, you've met his father already."

"Henry?!"

Snorting, Emily clapped her hands. "Oh, that's priceless. Henry would be horrified that you'd think that of him. Especially since he's so much older than me."

Waving her hands about, Charlotte laughed. "Goodness! I didn't think that one through, did I?"

"No. In any case, Luke's the father."

"Ah, that explains why you two seem so comfortable around each other. I did wonder. What happened, if you don't mind me asking?"

"We dated our senior year and had one night together. Noah was the result."

"But you didn't stay together, get married?"

"No. It's a long story, but suffice it to say, we're together now."

"Well, I'm happy for you, Em."

"Thanks. Anyway, that's why I won't go back to New York. Noah's adoptive parents live here and since the adoption was open, I get to see him. Also, my parents don't know about him."

"You didn't want to cause a scandal for your family."

"You got it."

"And it's why you can't be a bridesmaid. The press will definitely cover the wedding—thanks to Jack and Julie. Your whereabouts might be outed, which would result in more investigating..." Charlotte trailed off.

"Exactly." Emily was impressed by her friend's intuition and deductive skills.

With a gaze full of sympathy, Charlotte laid a hand on Emily's arm. "I completely understand. Consider my request withdrawn. I only hope that you'll still attend as an honored guest."

"Only if you don't treat me any differently to anyone else. And keep me away from the photographer."

"Done. You're my friend. I have no intention of changing the way I treat you."

"Good to know." She squeezed Charlotte's hand.

Leaning back against the sofa, her friend sighed. "This has been quite an enlightening evening."

"I'm so grateful you've taken it all so well."

"Don't tell me you thought I'd fire you on the spot or something?" Charlotte looked horrified.

Emily gave a one-armed shrug. "I didn't know what to expect."

"I couldn't do without you, Em. You're a star, and my kids love you so much."

A grin split her face at the sincere words. "I love them, too."

"You will keep working for me, won't you?"

"I'm not going anywhere. At least, not for the next six- to twelve- months. Unless you and Adam decide you don't need me?" How Emily managed to keep the slight panic out of her voice, she didn't know. Not being a day-to-day part of this family would be strange.

"Can we discuss it all once I'm married and Adam's living here? Knowing you aren't relying on this income is a great relief." When Emily kept quiet, Charlotte frowned. "You don't *need* this job, do you?"

"I don't, but I happen to love it."

"Good, because we love you too."

***

"I did it."

Henry pulled his phone away from his ear and glanced at the time—eleven twenty-five.

Great, he'd been in that in-between state just before falling asleep.

And what did Emily mean she'd done it? Had she quit her job? No, she loved her job. Besides, she sounded way too excited. Maybe she'd told her parents about Noah? Or broken up with Luke? Again, would she be so excited? Probably not. He was the father of her child, after all.

"Uh, you did what?"

"I told Charlotte everything. She knows who I am, she knows about Noah, and she didn't fire me."

He sat up. "Of course she wouldn't fire you."

"I know that *now*."

"Well done. I'm sure it's a weight off your shoulders."

"It is." She sighed, but it sounded happy.

"You told her to keep it quiet, though, didn't you?"

"I'm not stupid, Henry. I said she could tell Adam as long as he keeps the information to himself."

"Makes sense. Those two share everything."

"Almost everything."

He could hear her smirk.

"Emily!"

"Hey, it's not me who has the dirty mind! I was thinking of her kids. They don't share Adam's DNA."

"Whatever you say," he teased.

After a few beats of silence, he heaved a sigh. "This is the first time you've called or texted since Tuesday night. I thought I'd done something wrong."

"A friendship goes both ways, you know." She sounded miffed. "I thought maybe you'd been avoiding me because you and Britt said those three little words, and you were too scared to tell me."

Did he detect a tiny bit of sadness or maybe jealousy in her tone?

Nah. Wishful thinking.

"I'm sorry we haven't spoken," he said. "I promise to be a better friend from now on."

"I accept your apology if you accept mine. I'm sorry too."

"Done." He ran his hand over his face. "So, Luke's meeting Noah tomorrow."

Her smile came through the phone. "He is. Poor guy's so nervous. He keeps asking me a ton of questions. What does Noah like to do? Can he communicate in full sentences? What type of food does he eat? Stuff like that. You'd think Luke was never a five-year-old kid." She gave a nervous chuckle. "I'm worried the meeting will be a complete disaster."

"Hey, stop worrying. It'll be fine. The first few minutes might be a little awkward, but you're great with kids. I've no doubt you'll put them both at ease."

"Thanks." A pause, then, "What about you? Any interesting plans for tomorrow?"

"Britt and I are driving to Boston for the day. We'll take in the historical sights, walk the Freedom Trail, have a seafood lunch at Nautilus, and hopefully have time to visit the bar from Cheers. On the way back, we're going via Hartford for an early dinner with Britt's parents. Adam, Charlotte, and the kids are joining us."

"Jam-packed. Sounds great." Emily sounded decidedly unenthusiastic. Maybe she thought they were boring. Britt's response had been the opposite; she'd clapped her hands while jumping up and down. Henry had laughed, seeing her so excited.

"What are you guys doing with Noah?"

"Luke's agreed to take him to the playground nearby, and we'll have lunch at Pepe's afterward."

"Sounds good. At least you get to see your son. And Luke, of course. I assume you two will go out for dinner?"

"Yes. Apparently, it's a surprise."

"Ah, young love."

"You say it like you're so old, Henry."

"Aren't you always telling me I am?" he teased.

For a few seconds, she was quiet, and he wondered what she was thinking.

"You're not old," she said, her tone suddenly serious, her voice soft. "You're the perfect age."

"For what?" He was curious to know exactly what she meant.

"For everything."

"Except you." The words slipped out, and he wished he could take them back. He was supposed to keep his feelings for her from their friendship. He didn't want her to pull away again. Yet he'd spoken and now it was out there.

"Henry, you can't—"

Clearing his throat loudly, he cut her off. "Listen, I'll pray it goes well for you all tomorrow and that Luke and Noah hit it off. And for God's peace to be with you; that He'll give you wisdom on how to handle the situation."

"Thanks. And I'll be praying for safe travels for you and Britt. Enjoy your adventures in Boston. I guess I'll see you at church on Sunday?"

"Yep."

"Goodnight, Henry."

"Sleep well, Emily."

Ending the call, Henry lay back and folded his arms under his head. A slither of moonlight shone into his room from the gap at the edge of his slated blinds. It wasn't enough to disturb him, but it allowed him to make out the silver frame of the painting on the wall directly ahead of him. He didn't need the light on to know what the picture looked like. The artist had perfectly captured his family and all their different features as they posed for him a few years ago.

His youngest sister, Nicole, her husband, Travis, and their daughter, Isabella, stood together at the front. Mom and Dad were in the middle at the back while he and his middle sister, Lauren, flanked them. Henry remembered being grateful not to be so tied down like Nicole at the time. As much as he loved his niece and liked Travis, he couldn't imagine the responsibilities and lack of independence that would come with having a wife and children. Lauren had felt the same.

Did she still feel like that? He needed to ask her the next time he saw her. He certainly didn't. Emily was right; he was the right age for everything. For the family business, for getting married and having children.

If only he were the right age for her. The fact that she hadn't denied his statement implied he was right. That knowledge caused his chest to tighten. Even taking a deep breath didn't ease the pain. Was he just heartsore? Either way, he had a feeling that falling asleep easily wasn't guaranteed.

Why had Emily called him so late at night? Shouldn't she have been sharing this kind of thing with her boyfriend?

Maybe…

Hope blossomed in his chest. Before long, his breathing became more regular, and he fell asleep picturing beautiful brown eyes.

Chapter Twenty

As she dressed for her day with Luke the next morning, Emily couldn't rid her mind of Henry's despondent *except you*.

Was she focusing on the wrong relationship?

Putting on minimal makeup, she tried to squash the feeling of making a horrible mistake. Henry's age wasn't the problem, though she teased him mercilessly. It was his lack of commitment, and New York being his ultimate destination. And he and Britt appeared to be in a successful relationship. Seemed Britt was willing to take a chance on the former playboy.

Well, Emily wasn't. Not with her son to think of—another reason she didn't date casually.

Phoning Henry late last night, rather than Luke, might've given him false hope.

Why had she done that?

She exhaled a long breath. Likely because she wanted to tell him everything. He'd inadvertently become her confidant. Considering her lack of friends, it probably didn't mean that much.

Was it the smartest move on her part? No. Bringing her family together—her, Noah, and Luke—should be her focus. Not her friendship with Henry.

Thirty minutes later, she and Luke were bundled up in his sports car and on their way to Sean and Lisa's. Luke stayed quiet during the drive, his mouth set in a firm line.

"Hey," she said when she couldn't take the silence any longer. She rested a hand, palm up, on his thigh. "You're overthinking things."

The small smile he sent her way didn't reach his eyes.

"You know me, Em." He rubbed his cheek, his jaw muscles ticking. "I typically find children annoying, often loud, and sometimes rude. Why do you think I wanted—?" He broke off abruptly, forcing his lips together.

"New York wouldn't have worked."

He looked confused for a second, then covered her palm with his and linked their fingers. "Yeah, I realized that was a bad idea."

"Our son is nothing like those children, Luke. Noah's shy and reserved." She smiled softly. "The first time we met, he only spoke when spoken to, and his manners were impeccable. Sean and Lisa have done a wonderful job with him. The more I've gotten to know Noah, the more he's opened up. He has such a sweet sense of humor." She squeezed Luke's fingers. "You'll see, he's kind to other children. He lets others go first, and I've never seen him push or shove anyone."

"He sounds rather unusual."

Frowning at his contrary tone, she pulled her hand from his and crossed her arms. "I trust you mean that in a good way."

"Of course."

She wasn't sure she believed him.

"Noah's a lot like me when I was little," she said. "Being an only child has its advantages, like not having to vie for your parents' attention."

Luke chuckled humorlessly. "I can't relate. My brothers always shoved me out of the way and told me I had to wait my turn. It was tough being the smallest of four. But it helped me learn to stand up for myself and not let others walk all over me. A blessing in the business world."

"And look how far it's gotten you."

He shot her a genuine smile. One that didn't exactly melt her insides but did fill her with joy.

When he pulled up to the curb beside the biggest house in the modest neighborhood, he cut the engine and caught her hand in his. "Thank you for the encouragement and support, Em. I couldn't do this without you. I'm kinda terrified."

Leaning over, she pecked him on the cheek. "There's nothing to worry about. How could a boy not like his father? Especially when that man is kind, wonderful, and as hard-working as you?"

Deep wrinkles formed on his forehead. "Gosh, woman, I know where to go when I need a character reference," he joked.

"You're funny." She tugged his hand. "Let's go meet our boy."

Sean and Lisa opened the front door wearing tight smiles.

"Hello, Emily. How are you?" Sean's extra polite tone was unsettling.

"I'm well, thank you." She checked over their shoulders for Noah but couldn't see him. Strange. He usually came running.

Putting aside her reservations, she gestured to Luke. "This is my boyfriend, Luke." For now, they'd decided against telling Sean and Lisa who Luke was to Noah. No point making the couple nervous about losing their adopted son.

The men shook hands while Lisa nodded her hello, a strained look on her face. Had she changed her mind about allowing them to take Noah out today?

Emily sent up a quick prayer. *Please, Lord, let that not be the case.*

"Come in." Stepping back, Sean waved them inside.

Luke clasped her hand as they entered the warm, neutral-colored home together. Emily loved its light gray walls and weathered oak hardwood flooring. Simple. Classic.

In the living room, Lisa set down a tray of refreshments, including Noah's favorite—chocolate chip cookies.

Emily's shoulders relaxed.

"Do sit." Lisa indicated the olive-colored love seat to her right, then offered them a drink.

"We hope you don't mind," Sean began once he and Lisa were seated in matching cream and brown floral armchairs, "but we wanted to chat with you first." His gaze honed in on Luke. "I'm sure Emily's told you that Noah isn't aware of their real relationship."

"She has."

"We'd like it to stay that way." Sean's tone brooked no argument.

"Yes, sir."

Emily lifted her coffee mug to hide a smile. Luke had every right to kick up a fuss. To contest what she'd done—giving their son up for adoption without him having a say. Even now, he could make life difficult for her by insisting Noah know he's the boy's father.

"Okay, so we've prepped Noah," Sean continued. "You're Aunt Emily's new boyfriend, Mr. Luke." Sean exchanged glances with Lisa. "Noah asked why he couldn't call you Uncle Luke. We told him you wouldn't be his uncle until you two are married."

Emily coughed and spluttered, barely holding onto her mug.

"You okay?" Luke patted her back calmly.

Is that what he was hoping? Marriage?

Her cheeks heated. "Sorry," she said. "I'm fine. Carry on, Sean."

"I'm sure you understand how difficult this is for us, Luke. Introducing Noah to Emily was hard enough. He's the only child we'll ever have, and he means the world to us. We couldn't stand him being hurt. So, you can meet Noah this once. See if you hit it off. But afterward, if there's the slightest chance you're not in this for the long haul, or if you're not serious about investing in your relationship with our son and with Emily, then we'd prefer that you don't come back."

Luke's wide eyes darted to hers with a silent question.

"This is up to you." Emily smiled encouragingly. At least,

she hoped so. "I wouldn't be here if I didn't think this was what you wanted. Am I right?"

A flicker of panic crossed his face, then doubt, and eventually wariness. He gulped. Nodded.

Turning to Sean and Lisa with a weak smile, Luke spoke earnestly. "Trust me, I'm totally committed. I want to meet my…my girlfriend's son."

Emily beamed at him. Being put on the spot wasn't easy. Neither was referring to his son as just another child.

Lisa stood. "I'll go get Noah."

Seconds later, she appeared in the doorway, holding Noah's hand. His face lit up when he saw Emily. "Aunt Emily!"Letting go of Lisa's hand, he rushed forward until his arms wrapped around Emily's legs.

"Hey there, Noah." Smiling, she leaned down to embrace her son. "How're you doing?"

He pulled back, grinning. "I did a drawing for you."

"You did? I'd love to see it."

He spun around to Lisa. "Mommy, can you give Aunt Emily my drawing, please?"

"Of course, sweetheart."

Emily's ribs squeezed tight. Nothing she could do about her son calling Lisa 'Mommy' after giving up her parental rights at his birth. She had to be content with Sean and Lisa allowing her to have a relationship with Noah, on the understanding that they'd tell him the truth when they thought it was time.

Not the other way around. She had to respect that.

Lisa handed her a white paper containing three stick figures—a little boy flanked by a man and a woman, each holding a hand.

"Is this you with your mommy and daddy, Noah?"

He shook his head. "It's me with you and Mr. Luke."

Oh, the irony.

"It's lovely. May I keep it?"

He nodded, then peeked around her and whispered, "Is that Mr. Luke? He doesn't look like Daddy; he looks like me."

"Yes." Perceptive child.

Sean had ginger hair, a matching beard, and blue eyes. Understandable, given his Irish heritage. Luke, the complete opposite, had a mop of dark brown hair, brown eyes, and a distinct lack of facial hair.

"Would you like to meet Mr. Luke, Noah?"

***

Lisa had just finished helping Noah into his warm outdoor gear when he announced, "I need to pee," and it all had to come off. By the time they left the house, Luke's pinched expression told Emily his patience had been tested to the limit.

Boy, did he have a lot to learn about kids.

She tried to imagine what it would've been like if things had been different. If they'd been a family from the beginning.

No matter how hard she tried, she couldn't picture it.

If Noah decided he didn't like Luke or wasn't completely at ease with him, his adoptive parents would find out. They could easily stop or limit Luke's visits. In turn, he could cause waves by running to her parents. If he did, they'd likely use their power and influence and quite possibly have Noah removed from his home. They'd finally have the grandchild they longed for.

So, this outing today had to go well.

Drawing in a lungful of air, she released it slowly.

"Everything okay?" Luke asked as they drove toward the playground in the sensible SUV he'd rented.

"I hope so." She peeked behind Luke at Noah in his booster seat. "You good there, Noah?"

Looking up from his book, he nodded, his cute, lop-sided smile warming her heart. Every time she saw him, he reminded her of Luke. Her little boy was going to be a heartbreaker.

"Are you reading *An Atlas of Imaginary Places*?"

"Yes. It's my favorite." He turned another page reverently, his hand smoothing over the beautiful illustration of a whale with a city on its back, its tail held up by a hot air balloon.

"Maybe I can read it to you later?"

He nodded energetically, his eyes sparkling with delight. "Can Mr. Luke push me on the swing too?"

Smiling, Luke's eyes moved to the rearview mirror. "I'd love to."

Emily took it as a win.

Later, they strolled into the playground, Noah holding Emily's one hand and Luke the other.

"Can I swing first, Aunt Emily?" Noah tugged at her hand, his pace accelerating as they neared the play equipment. "Please?" he added when she didn't immediately answer.

She chuckled. "Of course."

Only one of the four swings was free. Noah hopped onto it and grasped the chains. Emily stood behind him. "No standing, Noah. Okay?"

Lisa had warned her of his latest daredevil antic. Both agreed it was too dangerous at his young age.

"Okay," he shouted. Then, "Ready, steady, go!"

"Em, wait!"

She looked at Luke sharply as he rushed around the swing to join her.

"There are no bars to prevent him from falling off," he muttered. "We can't let him swing on these."

"It's fine." She laughed. "Trust me, he's perfectly capable of holding on tight." Grabbing the iron chains above Noah's small hands, she pulled him toward her. "Ready?"

"Make me fly higher than an eagle!"

She grinned at the delight in his young voice and let go with a swoosh. Luke, still scowling, crossed his arms over his chest. She smiled wider. "Relax. Nothing's going to happen to him."

Shaking his head, he moved in front of Noah. As Emily continued to make him soar higher, the little boy's shouts of glee slowly encouraged Luke to smile.

"Mr. Luke, you said you would push me."

Luke obliged, though he didn't push nearly as high as

Emily had. Thankfully, Noah seemed to have fun.

When some older, more rowdy boys commandeered the other three swings, Noah dragged his feet on the ground. "I've had enough," he declared.

Luke looked relieved as his son wandered toward the massive wooden fort-like structure designed to look like a castle.

"I want to play princes and princesses," Noah said, placing his hands on the edge of an opening into the middle. "Mr. Luke, you can be the king. Aunt Emily and I will be your children."

Oh, again, the irony.

Pulling off his woolly hat, Luke raked his hand through his thick mop of hair. "I'm not sure I know how to be a king."

"Don't be silly, Mr. Luke." Noah had an amused look on his face. "All you need to do to be king is this." Standing up straighter, Noah pretended to place a crown on his own head and made his expression austere. "Now you can say if you want to chop off one of our heads."

Emily laughed at Luke's horrified look.

"He's kidding! We don't chop off heads, do we, Noah?"

With a cheeky smile, he shook his head. "Uh-uh, we knight people. Kneel down, Mr. Luke."

Exchanging a glance with her first, Luke then did as he was told. Noah touched a pretend sword to his shoulder. "I now pronounce you a knight of the Round Table. Knight Luke," he said joyfully.

"I thought I was king?"

"You are. I was just pretending to be you so you'd know what to do." Noah's earnestness was adorable. "Okay. I'm going inside. King Luke, you need to keep watch for dragons. Princess Emily, you must come with me."

Before following their son into the darker fort, Emily blew Luke a kiss. Moving at lightning speed, he captured her waist and drew her to him for a proper kiss.

"Don't leave me out here alone for too long," he said, releasing her and rubbing the back of his neck.

"I won't."

The activity didn't last long. Luke wasn't born to be king, and Noah must've picked up on it because when a group of children he knew from school came over to say hello, Noah quickly abandoned their pretend game.

"Can Noah play tag with us?" one of the boys asked Emily.

"As long as he stays where we can always see him."

Noah bobbed his head up and down. "I will."

After the boys left, Emily pointed to a bench in the far corner. It would give them a sweeping view of the area. "Let's go sit there."

Luke nodded, his gaze tracking his son the whole time. If she didn't know better, she'd think he was on edge about something.

The kids raced around chasing each other, screaming occasionally when they were almost caught.

Eyeing Luke's bouncing knee, Emily gently laid a hand over it. "Hey," she said, "he's having fun. There's no need to worry."

He spared her a glance, his gaze narrowing before he looked back at Noah. "I hope he doesn't trip and fall. He doesn't always watch where he's running."

Did Luke not trust her? Or was his over-protectiveness and unusual agitation because he felt responsible for Noah's safety?

"Luke, I don't know why you're worrying so much. I've brought Noah here many times. I trust God is watching over him and will keep him safe."

"God might be watching, Em, but that doesn't mean he'll stop anything from happening to our son," he said, his voice full of disdain. He glanced back at Noah, then turned hopeless eyes on her. "Bad things happen to good people every day. Where is your God, then?"

Chapter Twenty-One

Luke leaned against Emily's bedroom doorjamb, his eyes skimming her body. "You look incredible, Em."

"Thanks." Flushing, she smoothed her hands down the form-fitting red satin dress and bit her lip.

"I'm going to get my jacket. I'll be back to help you with your jewelry." He spun one-eighty and went into his bedroom.

Luke had booked this five-star hotel accommodation for their Valentine's weekend in New York. When she'd asked if there were two rooms, he'd said yes. Stupidly, she'd assumed two separate rooms with lockable doors.

Not the case.

Glancing around the large room, Emily took in the luxurious ebony and sycamore furnishings, then shifted her gaze to the marble bathroom she'd just vacated. It was a joy to soak in its large clawfoot bathtub with lavender-scented bubbles softening her skin. With soothing music playing on the mini flat-screen TV, she'd almost fallen asleep. The experience had helped her forget those most prevalent on her mind—Luke and Noah.

And Henry.

For the past two weeks, she'd been trying to find the right time to talk to Luke about her faith. Whenever she brought it up, he swiftly changed the subject. After mentioning Luke's reluctance to Henry, he suggested she ask God for wisdom and guidance. She'd been praying ever since.

At least Luke's meeting with his son had gone alright, and Noah seemed okay with a repeat visit in the future.

Luke returned while Emily hovered in front of the mirror, his footsteps masked by the plush cream carpet.

"Necklace," he said, putting out his hand.

Smiling, she handed over the silver and diamond jewelry she'd chosen to wear with her cocktail dress. After securing the clasp, his hands rested on her neck. Their eyes met in the mirror, and he smiled. "Gorgeous," he said huskily.

Emily's heart didn't race, though it did pick up pace, and while her stomach didn't do any flips, it tightened slightly. His hands skimmed her shoulders and arms, eventually moving to her waist. Slowly, he turned her to face him.

"Em." Desire sparked in his cocoa-colored eyes, and she knew exactly what he was thinking. Her eyes closed automatically, and the next second, his lips descended onto hers and moved expertly over her mouth. Her hands circled his neck, and she leaned in as Luke's hand traveled to the small of her back. He pulled her close and deepened the kiss.

A minute later, they were both breathing heavily. Unlike her, Luke had certainly had a lot of practice kissing since high school.

Not a comforting thought at all.

She lowered her gaze to her shiny six-inch heels and worked on regaining control of her breathing.

"Cocktail hour starts at six thirty, so we need to go. But…" Luke's thumb lifted her chin so their eyes met. "How about later we continue where we left things years ago?" he murmured, his eyes hooded as his thumb traced her bottom lip.

Emily stared at him, too shocked to respond. Sure, they'd slept together once before, but still. How could he assume?

Taking her silence as assent, Luke grinned and slipped his hand into hers. "Is your coat at the suite door?"

She nodded, still trying to get her head around his insinuation.

"Your purse?"

"Yes."

"Perfect." He led her toward the door. "I'm looking forward to this, Em. 'Romance Under the Stars' promises to be one of the most romantic nights a couple can enjoy in New York tonight."

While her smile fell flat, she managed to inject some enthusiasm into her voice. "I have no doubt."

The first thing she noticed when they exited the hotel lobby was a horse-drawn carriage waiting at the entrance. She glanced at Luke wide-eyed. "For us?"

"I didn't think you'd appreciate walking through Central Park for twenty minutes." He nodded in the direction of her feet, and she looked down.

"Oh, I hadn't thought. Thank you."

Smirking, he led her to the carriage. After assisting her into it, he climbed in and threw a thick blanket over their legs before wrapping his arm around her shoulders.

Not wanting to spoil their evening, Emily consciously put aside her reservations about later. She would deal with Luke's expectations when the time came.

"This is lovely, Luke." Snuggling closer, she sighed. "Very romantic."

"I'm glad." He pressed a gentle kiss on her forehead.

The ride only lasted ten minutes, but they reached the Museum in time to enter immediately. Memories of childhood visits flooded Emily as they strolled beside other couples along the corridor to the Cullman Hall of the Universe. Inside the hall, an open bar served cocktails, and while waiters handed out hors d'oeuvres, champagne, and chocolate, a live band played a catchy love song in the background.

Grabbing flutes from a tray, they paused to sip their fizz and observe the other guests. Luke's lip curled as he pointed out a few unique dress styles. "In my opinion, those designs are best left in the last century."

An uncontrollable giggle escaped Emily's mouth, and she

managed to spill half her drink down her dress. Wincing, she tried to wipe the liquid away.

"Don't worry, Em," Luke said, ignoring her obvious fretting. "It'll add to your delicious citrus and vanilla scent."

At the Hayden Planetarium, they listened to romantic love stories from the ancient past. Hearing how others fell in love and then had their hearts broken only to have them fully mended again was heart-wrecking and exhilarating. The cherry on the top was enjoying the spectacular view of the starry night sky while being narrated to. It was the most romantic night she'd ever had.

The only damper on the whole evening came when her thoughts went to Henry and Britt celebrating six weeks of dating. Were they having as romantic an evening? Had he taken his girlfriend out to dinner at one of the Michelin-starred restaurants here in New York? Maybe even the one she'd eaten at with him when they attended the Jays' concert last September.

Would he take her dancing afterward and hold her close?

No matter how often she scolded herself and tried to force herself not to compare, she couldn't help thinking that as wonderful as tonight was, she'd happily trade it for a night in front of the TV, cuddling with Henry and sharing popcorn and hot chocolate.

Why, she had no idea. Luke was amazing: handsome, kind, driven, the father of her child. She had no problem being in his arms, kissing him. Was she attracted to him? Yes, but in love with him?

No. No, she wasn't.

**

Henry typically avoided Valentine's Day and all the annoying romantic expectations accompanying it. It meant you were in a committed relationship, which had so not been his thing until now.

This year, he had to make an effort. And bringing Britt to New York for the weekend was not influenced by the knowledge that Luke and Emily were here too.

Nope, it was just a good idea.

Besides, friends of his parents were throwing a party that he and Britt were due to attend tonight. Emily would be there, he hoped. Half-hoped. Her parents had been invited—he'd checked—so the chances were good.

Had she managed to talk to Luke about her relationship with God yet? And what had they done for Valentine's last night while he and Britt ate at another of his parents' restaurants? He hadn't been able to return to the one he and Emily had eaten at last year. It was his favorite, but...

If she were at the party tonight, he might get to ask her the questions he'd been mulling over all day.

"I'm not sure I'm happy with this dress."

Britt's voice cut into his musings, and he looked up at her.

"What time do we need to leave? Do I have time to change?"

"You look beautiful, Britt. Purple is a very regal color. It suits you perfectly."

Frowning, she strolled over, slid her hands around his waist, and drew him to her. Her eyes blazed as her mouth hovered inches from his. "I'm not sure being compared to royalty is quite how I want to be seen. It makes me think of Queen Elizabeth; she was rather old," she said, sounding almost petulant.

"Britt, if you're not comfortable, go change. I'd hate for you to be second-guessing your wardrobe choice all night."

"I'll go on one condition." He raised his eyebrows at her flirty tone. "You promise to dance with only me tonight."

"Impossible." A flicker of irritation shot through her eyes at his answer. He smiled slyly. "I have to at least dance with my mom."

"Funny man. You think you're so clever." She pouted prettily, and he laughed.

Planting a chaste kiss on her lips, he gave her a gentle shove toward her bedroom. When she returned, he wolf-whistled. Uncivilized, but wow! Wearing an electric blue, knee-length, backless dress with cutaway sides, she looked amazing.

"You like?"

"Oh, yeah. Except now you'll have to promise me *you* won't dance with anyone else tonight."

She gave him a mischievous look and crossed her arms sassily. "What? Not even your dad?"

Half an hour later, they walked into the rented venue and what originally appeared to be a warehouse—before the party hosts' event planners had gotten hold of it. Thick metal beams, at least twenty feet above them, supported the arched roof while white-paneled walls surrounded them on three sides. The final side consisted of garage-type, steel roll-up doors. Expecting the concrete floor to be cold, Henry was pleasantly surprised. Most likely they'd incorporated a layer of slab heating mats.

"This place is incredible!" Peering around the huge open space, Britt grinned like a kid at a fairground. "I've never *seen* so many fairy lights." She spun back to him. "Are those real chocolates on those trees? Wait, are the trees real?"

He chuckled at her enthusiasm. "I've no idea. Probably."

She dragged him further in and stared up. "Look at those massive chandeliers, Henry! How do they even clean them?"

Laughing, he scanned the guests' faces within their immediate vicinity. All around, the party buzzed with music and conversation. Arriving late was a smart move.

"Let's go find something to drink," he said to Britt, who nodded while continuing to stare about in awe.

A few men blatantly checked out his girlfriend as they crossed paths. Others gave him envious stares, boosting Henry's ego. Sure, he did have one of the prettiest women on his arm. The prettiest—well, she was nowhere to be seen. Not that he'd been searching for her. Nope, he was looking out for his parents or the hosts, whichever he could spot first.

With a glass of Moët each, he and Britt strolled among the guests. Occasionally, someone called out Henry's name, and they stopped for a short conversation. Everyone wanted to be introduced to Britt and find out when he planned to return to the real world—aka New York—instead of playing in New Haven.

That got old, and Henry started avoiding the kind of people who thought the only place to live was Manhattan until, finally, they bumped into his parents.

"Henry, my boy, I thought we'd never find you!" Mom's relieved smile made him smile too. Her pink cheeks matched her dress, making him wonder if she'd had a few too many glasses.

"This party is pretty big, Mom." After kissing her warm cheek, he shook his father's outstretched hand. "Hey, Dad. You look well."

"Thank you, son."

Henry dragged Britt forward and tucked her into his side. "Mom, Dad, this is my girlfriend, Brittany Wilson. Adam's sister."

"Nice to finally meet you, Brittany," Mom said, giving her air kisses. "Henry's told us a lot about you. I'm so pleased he's finally taken our advice and found a nice woman to settle down with."

"Mom." He shot her a warning look.

"What?" She laughed. "It's true, isn't it?"

Shrugging, he met his father's excited eyes. Oh no. "Don't you get any ideas, Dad. I'm not moving home yet."

"Well, it's a step in the right direction, son," Dad said gruffly. Taking Britt's hand in his, he kissed the back of it. "Miss Wilson, I'm thrilled to meet you. What a vision you are in that dress. You and Henry sure make a striking couple."

"Okay, that's it. We'll see you later." Threading his fingers through Britt's, Henry led her away.

"Save me a dance," Mom called out from behind them. Lifting his hand in acknowledgment, he kept walking.

When they were out of earshot, he turned to Britt. She wore an amused expression. "Sorry about that. One of the reasons I've never had a girlfriend—well, not since college— was because I knew the minute I did, they'd want me engaged and planning my move home."

"I have no problem with that." Reaching out a hand, she cupped his cheek gently. "I'm not a young woman who doesn't know what she wants or hasn't had time to experience life or get her career going like Emily. I'm ready to settle down and start my 'real life,' as your one friend put it. With you."

Over Britt's shoulder, Henry caught sight of a woman in a cherry red dress just before she slipped away. His stomach dropped. He'd know that gorgeous figure anywhere. Mentally rewinding what Britt had just said and how it might have sounded to Emily, he groaned.

Not good.

Chapter Twenty-Two

"Where did you disappear to?" Slipping an arm around Emily's waist, Luke tugged her to his side possessively. "Your parents and I were worried."

Mom and Dad didn't look the slightest bit fazed that she'd gone off on her own, but it was lovely that Luke cared.

"Your dad was just saying we should all have breakfast tomorrow."

"Us?" Emily pointed between them.

Mom nodded. "And the Palmers, of course. I assume you know Henry's here with his girlfriend. It'd be the perfect opportunity for us to get to know her."

Emily felt her peace slipping away. Breakfast with Henry was one thing, but letting Britt in on her secret? No thanks.

"Why would you need to do that, Mom? I'd rather it was just the four of us," she said with a tight-lipped smile.

"You don't like Brittany?"

She huffed. "I didn't say that."

"You didn't have to." Mom gave her a searching look. "I can see it written all over your face. Why? What don't we know?"

"Nothing." She turned to Luke. "Dance with me, please?"

"We haven't finished this conversation, Emily." Her mother's stern voice commanded attention.

"Mom, if you and Dad want to see Luke and me tomorrow, then breakfast would be great. If you insist on inviting the

Palmers, I'm not interested."

Turning on her heels, Emily came face to face with Henry and his girlfriend. The latter was staring at her in shock. Henry's expression, a mixture of confusion and hurt, was quickly masked as his gaze shifted to her right.

"Hello, Henry," Luke said pleasantly. "Nice to see you again."

"You too, Luke." The men shook hands, then Henry turned to Britt. "Britt, this is Luke Bowman, Emily's boyfriend."

"Oh, yes. Henry's mentioned you. Very pleased to meet you, Luke." Britt practically purred in that sugary-sweet voice of hers. The one that grated on Emily's nerves. She should never have agreed to this party. Why hadn't she figured Henry would be invited and actually come?

"Are these your parents, Emily?" Britt asked, looking across at her mom and dad.

"Mom, Dad, Brittany Wilson." Emily's stomach felt like a brick. Could this get any worse?

Further hellos and hand shaking followed, after which she smiled tightly at the group in general. "Luke and I were on our way to dance. See you later." Though not if she could help it. She shot a glance at Henry, but his gaze was averted. Fine.

In Luke's arms on the dance floor, she was finally able to breathe.

His jaw twitched. "What was that all about?"

"Can we just enjoy this dance, please?"

"I would, but I can feel the tension in your body," he said, caressing her bare back.

Ticklish, she giggled involuntarily.

"Hey, that's better," he whispered before softly kissing the skin just below her ear. His lips drifted lower across her jawline until they reached her mouth. The kiss he placed there was tender and inviting. Leaning into him, she let desire take over. When they broke apart, the kiss had done its job. Her stomach was no longer knotted, and her smile felt genuine.

Luke's fingertips brushed her cheek. "You're even more beautiful when your face isn't pinched."

"I'm sorry. I just didn't expect to see Britt in New York. My business is not hers, and I didn't want her knowing who I am."

Luke's eyes grew, then narrowed. "Why wouldn't she know who you are? She's dating Henry. He would've told her."

"I asked him not to."

"And he agreed?"

"He's my friend, Luke, so yes, he did."

"I guess he's relieved he doesn't have to keep your secret any longer," he scoffed.

She hadn't thought about that.

Closing her eyes, she rested her head on Luke's shoulder and let the music calm her now racing heart. Slowly, her mind drifted back to what she'd overheard. Coming across Henry and Britt tonight was the last thing she expected. To discover the woman talking about her as if she knew her? Nightmare.

Letting out a long breath, she bit her lip. That hadn't been the worst part. Hearing Henry basically admit he was dating Britt with the intention of settling down with her, well, that had thrown her. Then, watching the tender moment between the couple had made the relationship so much more real.

The knot in her stomach that had eased during Luke's kiss tightened again. Enough that when the music came to an end, she drew back. "I think I need another drink."

Britt's sudden appearance took her by surprise. "Do you mind if I dance with your boyfriend, Emily?" she asked sweetly.

Luke lifted his hands. "I have no objections, Em. Unless you'd rather I didn't?"

"Go for it."

Not wasting another second, Emily fled toward the drinks area. Unfortunately, an unsmiling Henry was approaching from the other side. Spotting her, his frown deepened, and his pace slowed.

Great, he was mad at her.

Focusing on the bar, she continued until her hands were on the cold counter. Seconds later, she gritted her teeth when Henry's musky scent enveloped her. She ignored him and the warmth his body brought with its proximity. Only her treacherous heart, beating harder and faster, could give her away. And, thankfully, he couldn't hear or feel it.

"I'd like an iced water, please," she told the bartender.

"I'll have the same."

Henry's deep, sexy voice washed over her, but she refused to acknowledge him.

"Have I done something wrong?" he asked in a low voice.

Whirling to face him, she struggled to hide the anger in her voice. "Other than bringing your girlfriend here when you must've known there'd be a mighty big chance I'd be here too?" She shook her head in agitation. "No, you've done nothing wrong."

The bartender returned with her glass. "Here you go, ma'am."

"Thanks." Grabbing her drink from the counter, she strode toward a quieter area.

"Emily?" Henry's hand on her bare shoulder sent an electric zing through her, causing her to spill some water. Luke's touch didn't make her feel like that.

Circling her, Henry stopped to face her. Remorse filled his expression. "I'm sorry. I didn't think."

"You know what? I'm sorry, Henry. I shouldn't have asked you to keep my secret." She shook her head. "I suppose I was fortunate enough to have stayed under the radar as long as I have. Now..." She shrugged.

"You're worried Britt's going to tell everyone back in New Haven who you are."

"Isn't she?"

"I had a quick word and asked her to trust me but not to say anything."

"And she agreed?" Emily couldn't hide the skepticism

from her voice.

He nodded.

"Huh. That surprises me."

The corners of his mouth turned downward. "You really don't think much of her, do you?"

"She's your girlfriend, Henry, and I know I need to love her like Jesus would, but I don't have to like her, do I?"

"Why don't you?"

Mostly because the woman's judgmental and speaks with a condescending tone, and she's with you—that's what Emily wanted to say.

"It doesn't matter if I like her or not," she said instead. "What you think of her is much more important."

***

The myriad of emotions crossing Emily's face before she answered him—without really answering the question—made Henry think she hadn't been telling him the truth.

What *had* he wanted her to say, though? That she didn't like Britt because he was dating her? Because she was jealous of her?

Wishful thinking.

Henry had seen Emily kissing Luke while they danced. That was a kiss between two people who loved each other. His chest had physically pained at the sight, yet he hadn't been able to turn away. He'd endured the torturous experience, all the while wishing she'd been kissing him instead.

"What you think... it's important to me, Emily," Henry said gently, letting his hand settle briefly on her upper arm, though he could never touch her without tingles shooting over his skin.

"As your friend, it's my duty to make sure you're happy. If Britt makes you happy, then who am I to stand in your way?" She patted his shoulder. "I care about you and Adam, so I'll do my best to be civil to her. That's all I can promise."

Lumping him in with Adam made Henry feel *so much* better. He dropped his hand.

"Alright," he said. "Thank you. I appreciate it."

She downed half her water, then gave him a tremulous smile. "Time to hit the dance floor again."

"Does that mean you'll dance with me?"

Her eyes met his and clung, asking him a question he couldn't read. He also couldn't look away. The longer they stayed that way, the stronger the urge to draw her into his arms and kiss her became. His already racing heart accelerated further. He forced himself to lower his gaze, even though she hadn't answered him, and shoved his hands into his trouser pockets.

"Hey, there you are." Luke smiled at Emily, then turned a half-scowl onto him.

Henry raised his hands. "I was just leaving." He gave Emily one last look. Her mouth opened, then closed.

Fine, whatever.

"Enjoy your dance," he said before stalking off.

Probably for the best. Britt wouldn't be charmed if he danced with Emily anyway. Even more so now that she knew Emily was a Quinn. If Britt had been jealous of their friendship before, this new information would skyrocket that feeling. Luke was definitely a buffer as Emily's boyfriend, but Britt didn't seem to think it a strong one. And although Henry tried to hide his feelings, sometimes he wasn't too successful.

Now back from the bathroom, Britt stood peering at the slow-dancing couples. He followed her line of sight and saw her gaze honed in on Emily and Luke. Closing the distance between them, Henry twined their fingers. "Hey."

She looked at him and raised a questioning brow. "I was wondering where you'd gotten to. Can we join them?"

"Of course."

With Emily in his peripheral vision, he led Britt toward the middle of the dance floor. In her arms, he found familiar comfort and closed his eyes. She leaned against his chest with a sigh, and together they swayed in time to the music. Once the song ended, Britt directed him back to the bar.

"I vote we get drinks and find someplace quieter to talk," she said.

He didn't argue.

Drinks in hand, they found a free table and sat opposite each other.

"So, Emily Quinn. Why didn't you tell me?" Britt's voice held a hint of accusation and hurt.

"She asked me not to."

Britt's chin dipped. "Oh. I feel like such a fool."

"Why?"

She met his eyes, hers glassy. "The things I said to her. The way I said them."

"You're not a fool, Britt." He gave her a soft smile. "I'm sure she won't hold them against you."

"I can't believe she's working as a nanny, Henry. A nanny! I can't imagine she ever needs to work a day in her life."

"She loves her job, Britt, and she's studying to be a teacher. It suits her, living below the radar. Having a normal life."

Britt's eyes narrowed. "She sounds just like you."

"You make it sound like a bad thing."

Her hand touched his. "It's not." That occasional sexy smile of hers made an appearance. "It's one of the things I love about you."

Alarm flew through him.

"Don't panic." She winked. "I'm not expecting us to say those three little words to each other."

Trying to calm his racing heart, he swallowed. "Good to know."

"So... Who else in New Haven knows about the real Emily?"

"Only you, me, Adam, and Charlotte. That's it, as far as I know. And that's the way it needs to stay, Britt. Unless Emily decides to tell other people, her secret is exactly that: hers. Okay?"

She reached over the table and pressed her lips to his. Pulling back, her eyes sparkled. "Okay."

"Thank you. I know she'll be relieved to hear that you're

not about to rat her out."

Britt huffed and wiggled back against her chair. Glaring, she folded her arms. "Is that what you thought I'd be itching to do? Rat out your friend?"

"No." He shook his head slowly. "But I didn't want to take a chance."

"Because she's a very important friend, right?"

Their gazes tangled, and Henry refused to look away first. "Yes. She is important to me, Britt. Her friendship is important to me."

After a few beats of silence, he felt the need to add, "Our parents are also friends, which means when we come to New York, the chances of us bumping into each other are extremely high."

Tilting her head, Britt regarded him. "You never used to come to the city much. Why has that suddenly changed?"

Interesting question. How to answer without incriminating himself?

He cleared his throat and ran a hand over his head to the back of his neck. "I guess because I finally have a girlfriend who my parents approve of, and it means I can visit without them being on my case or attempting to set me up with this or that businessman's daughter." He chuckled. "They once tried to entice me to stick around by bringing over a princess from Europe."

Britt snorted, then quickly regained her composure. "You're kidding?"

"She was already thirty years old and unmarried. Does that tell you anything?"

"I can only imagine."

Sipping her wine, Britt's eyes swept the room.

Who was she seeking out? When Henry followed suit, his gaze snagged on Emily and Luke a few tables down. Luke had his arm around Emily's shoulders and was leaning in as though kissing her. Henry couldn't see their faces, so he was assuming, but it certainly seemed that way.

Ugh. He didn't need to witness that. Again.

He redirected his attention to Britt, who slowly brought her eyes back to his. "So does that mean we're going to be coming here more often?" she asked, nothing in her expression revealing how she felt.

Did he really want to spend weekends here when Emily was in New Haven?

"Is that what you want, Britt?"

He held his breath.

"Yes. Yes, I do."

Fantastic. He'd walked right into that one.

Chapter Twenty-Three

A month later…

"Isn't that Emily?" Adam asked.

Glancing up at the viewing area's balcony on the far side of the massive hall, Henry did a double take. A woman was waving down at them with a hesitant smile.

"Yep," he said, waving back at her.

What were the chances they'd end up at the same venue, at the same time? He pursed his lips, trying to recall what she'd told him about this weekend, and grinned. Of course! Noah's birthday party was today; he just hadn't asked for details.

"Why don't we join her and get those coffees Holly suggested?" Adam said, moving in that direction.

Grasping his arm, Henry stopped him. "I don't think she's alone, bud. Luke's around here somewhere, guaranteed."

Adam frowned. "You don't have a problem with him, do you?"

"Nope." His laughter was strained. "But I'm not sure they're gonna want us interrupting their date."

"Date?" Adam motioned to their surroundings and chuckled. "At an indoor adventure park for kids?"

Henry's gaze swept over the trampolines, the obstacle courses, and the climbing wall. They had basketball somewhere, too. Throw in the squealing kids and the not-so-pleasant smells? Yeah, it was a strange place to have a romantic rendezvous.

"Hard to believe anyone would choose a kids' party venue for a date. Emily won't mind if I ask," Adam said.

Great. How would she explain being at some random kid's party?

While Henry refused to rush, knowing things could get awkward, Adam bounded up the winding staircase.

"Fancy meeting you guys here." Emily greeted them from the top of the stairs, then peered over Adam's shoulder. Concern filled her expression. "Where's Charlotte?"

"She and Amy are getting their nails done and lunching at Pepe's." Adam's focus shifted back to the trampoline where Charlotte's son, Daniel, was still bouncing, then back to Emily. "Peter's here for Joe's party, and Danny's keeping his younger brother, Caleb, company."

"Of course, that's today!" Emily smacked her head. "Well, it's nice of you to bring the boys." She gestured to Henry. "I assume you're Adam's company."

"Yep. Two hours here instead of watching the football." He smiled cheekily. "I'm a good friend, aren't I?"

"Hey!" Adam gave him the side-eye. "You told me you were happy to skip the game."

Henry playfully shoved his friend's shoulder. "Kidding, bud. Watching Danny doing front flips on the trampoline has made my day."

"Not seeing me?" Emily smiled coyly.

He chuckled. "That too."

"So, what brings you here, Emily?" Adam asked, crossing his arms.

"My friends."

Distracted by a shout, Adam's gaze darted to the trampolines, where Daniel was stepping off the bouncy surface with a broad grin. The boy guzzled down some water, then jumped back on.

"Danny's sure having fun," Henry commented. He watched the youngster for a moment, then looked back at Emily. Peering into her pretty brown eyes, his heart beat erratically. He blinked.

"Sorry, Emily. You said your friends?" Adam prompted, just when Henry thought she'd gotten away with it.

"Sean and Lisa. Their son, Noah, turns six tomorrow. They invited Luke and I."

"Ah. I see."

"Where's Luke?" Henry blurted.

Emily's forehead wrinkled in annoyance. "He left to take a call."

Fantastic, so the boyfriend was here.

Pulling a hand down his face, he then glanced at Adam. "Okay, well, I'm gonna go get us drinks."

Waiting in line, he tried to figure out which kid was Emily's. He spotted a gorgeous little boy with a dark mop of hair and a sweet smile—a miniature version of his father—waving at Emily. Bingo. He couldn't imagine how hard it must've been for Emily, seeing the result of their one night together and knowing Luke hadn't wanted him. Good thing Luke had changed his tune. Otherwise that could've been a huge conflict in her life.

Luke's arm was slung over Emily's shoulders when Henry returned with the coffees, and while Adam spoke with Luke about the new Scott Wilson Home, Emily was totally focused on her son.

Trying not to scowl at a certain man's presence, Henry grabbed a seat.

"Hey, Henry. I was just hearing about your latest charitable endeavor." Luke half-rose, his hand outstretched toward him.

Gripping his hand, Henry gave it a firm shake. "Not so much mine as Adam and his fiancée, Charlotte's. I'm more involved with Adam in Daily Bread."

"Yeah, Em told me about that. All super impressive. I must admit, though, this charity work you guys do?" He sniffed. "It's not for me. I'm way more of a city guy. Prefer the corporate life, you know." He squeezed Emily's shoulder. She glanced back at him, and they shared an intimate look.

Forcing down a crazy surge of jealousy, Henry looked

away, knowing he had no right.

"Em's dad's great to work with," Luke continued, as if anyone had asked. "Actually, I'm surprised you're not working with your dad, Henry."

That made him resume eye contact. Why did this guy think it was any of his business?

"I'd have thought you needed to be learning the ropes already. Unless one of your sisters is earmarked to take over Palmer Enterprises?" Luke smirked.

"Nope. It's me." In his peripheral, Emily stiffened. His eyes drifted to hers as he added in a softer tone, "But I don't plan on leaving New Haven for a long while yet."

"Aunt Emily!" The same little boy came running to her side. "Did you see me on the trampoline?" He jumped on the spot, resembling a little jack-in-a-box.

Grinning, her eyes shone with pride. "You did an amazing job, Noah. Just like a bouncing bean." Patting his shoulder, she encouraged him to stand still. "What's next?"

"Climbing. Will you and Mr. Luke come watch?"

"Of course we will," Luke answered, his smile not quite reaching his eyes.

What was his reservation? Did it have something to do with his son's safety, or wasn't he as enamored with the kid as Emily was?

Smoothing a hand over Noah's head, Emily glanced hesitantly at Henry. "Noah," she said, "would you like to say hello to some friends of mine?"

Suddenly aware of others at the table, Noah ducked his head and shifted closer to her. Emily's arm immediately came around his tiny shoulders. She leaned in, pointing at Adam first. "Remember I told you about Miss Charlotte?" He nodded shyly. "Well, this is Mr. Adam. He's marrying her."

"Hello, Mr. Adam."

"Nice to meet you, Noah. I believe you're turning six tomorrow."

Again, he nodded. "Mommy says I'm gonna be a big boy."

Henry stifled a chuckle. The kid was absolutely adorable.

"And this is Mr. Henry," Emily said in a breathy voice.

Unless he was imagining it?

"You're Aunt Emily's best friend!" Noah's eyes lit up just as Luke visibly tensed beside Emily. "She talks about you a lot."

"Oh, she does, does she?" Henry's eyes shot to her face, revealing pink-filled cheeks.

"Don't let it go to your head," she admonished sternly, a smile tugging at her lips.

"Okay." Henry let out a loud guffaw. "Whatever you say." He stuck out his hand to the youngster. "I'm honored to meet you, Noah," he said, shaking his small hand. "Happy sixth birthday. I hope you're having a fantastically fun party."

"Thanks! I am." Noah's smile was the biggest he'd seen on the boy since he came upstairs. He shook Henry's hand but then peered nervously over his shoulder. "I gotta go. Mommy said I had to be super quick."

"We'll be there soon." Emily pulled him in for a tight hug, then released him.

After giving them a cute wave, Noah disappeared toward the steps.

Scratching his temple, Adam eyed Emily. "I thought you said his parents were friends. Why is he calling you Aunt Emily? Aren't you an only child?"

"I am. Sean and Lisa are super close friends, and because I'm listed as Noah's guardian in his parents' absence, they figured he should call me Aunt."

News to Henry. Smart move, considering.

"I see." Adam nodded, seemingly satisfied with her response.

"We'd better go, Em." Luke pushed to his feet and helped her up. His challenging gaze connected with Henry's for a millisecond before it shifted to Adam. "I'm sure we'll bump into you guys down there."

Adam stood, too. "Sure. Have fun."

As the couple passed Henry, Emily's sweet scent filled his nostrils. When her hand brushed against his, his pulse accelerated. "Talk to you later," she murmured, her eyes meeting his for a long second.

After a slight nod, he watched her leave. The woman was beautiful, captivating, and kind. If only—

"Mind if I go check on Danny?"

Adam's question tore Henry out of his Emily-induced fog. He stood abruptly. "Wait, I'm coming too."

A ringside view might be great, but he'd rather be closer to the action. And Emily.

***

"Why didn't you tell me Henry would be here?" Accusation laced Luke's voice, his expression sullen.

"Hey." Emily touched his cheek and forced him to meet her eyes. "I didn't know. Adam probably asked him at the last minute. Besides, I didn't tell Henry *where* Noah was having his party."

"But you did tell him about it."

"Yes." She stroked his face, loving the feel of his smooth skin.

Clenching his jaw, Luke studied the climbing wall, where Noah waited patiently at the bottom.

"Luke?" Slowly, he faced her. "You know Henry's my friend and that I talk to him often. You also know he has a girlfriend, and I have a boyfriend who I'm pretty serious about, so why—"

"You're serious about me?"

A smile lifted the corners of her lips. "I am."

Leaning forward, he cupped her chin and kissed her softly, drawing back before she could really respond. She pouted.

He placed a firm finger on her lips, his smile roguish. "I'll kiss you properly later. I promise."

"I'll hold you to that." She caught his hand and threaded their fingers. Thank goodness she could trust that he *would* only kiss her. Nothing more.

When they'd gotten back to the hotel after their romantic Valentine's Day evening, Luke tried continuing where he'd left off. Emily had stood her ground and said no.

"I admire your conviction, Em," Luke had said once he realized she wouldn't back down. "I promise I won't push you to do anything that makes you uncomfortable. Ever."

"You might want to watch your son." Henry's murmured comment from right beside Emily brought her crashing into the present.

She glared at him. "You scared me!"

Ignoring the tingling awareness traveling across her body, she swung her gaze to the wall. Noah had lifted one foot onto a foothold while one hand held onto an outcrop a little higher up. Her heart dropped into her stomach.

Lord, please keep him safe, she prayed, one eye on her son.

When she looked again, he'd moved on and was making steady progress. Amazing. Thankfully, she didn't have to worry about taking pictures. Sean and Lisa's professional photographer was snapping photos left, right, and center. They'd promised copies and even organized a photo of her, Luke, and Noah when they arrived.

She spared Luke a glance. "Look how good he is at climbing."

"Yep." He wore a smug expression. "He takes after his father."

"Funny, I seem to recall someone struggling to make it halfway up the wall in the school gym." She bumped his shoulder with hers. "I rather think he takes after me. I got the fastest time in my year."

Next to her, Henry snickered. She'd almost forgotten he was still there.

Almost.

Huffing, she twisted to see him better. "Got something to say?"

"Nope. Nothing." He hid a smile behind his hand. "I just can't picture you climbing up that wall."

"Is that a challenge?"

Henry looked past her to Luke. "What do you think, Luke? Would you like to place a bet on Emily getting to the top of that wall before me?"

Luke laughed. "Absolutely not. I'd have thought, no matter how quick Em is, she can't compete with a man who probably has at least ten years' experience on her."

"Oh, look," Henry teased, lifting his brows suggestively. "Another one who thinks I'm an old man."

She laughed, then shot a mock glare at her boyfriend. "Thanks for the support, traitor. I accept Henry's challenge. But not today." She motioned to the short skirt she wore. "I'm not appropriately dressed."

When her eyes lifted, they landed on Henry. The desire flashing in his eyes left her momentarily breathless.

"Raincheck then," he said. "As pretty as your dress is, you're right, it's not suitable climbing attire."

"Gee, thanks." She spun to concentrate on Noah, who, rather incredibly, was almost to the top of the wall. Within seconds, he was grinning down at them, ringing the bell. On the sidelines, his friends cheered.

"Well done, Noah!" Luke shouted. "I knew you could do it!"

Emily's smile matched her son's. "Fantastic job, Noah!"

Standing not too far away, Sean and Lisa looked as proud as she felt. Lisa raised a thumb at the same time Emily did, and they laughed.

"Clearly, as talented as his mom." Henry's soft breath at her side gave her goosebumps. "He's a wonderful little boy, Emily."

She raised her eyes to his earnest ones, happiness flooding her at his high praise. "Thanks," she murmured.

A few beats passed until Henry averted his gaze. "Okay, well, I'm off to find Adam. He mentioned something about basketball."

"I'm glad you've met him, Henry."

He chuckled, stuffing his hands in his pockets. "Yeah, I was beginning to think you made him up."

"Ha ha." She swatted his arm—a far safer bet than asking for a hug. "Off with you."

"See you at church?"

"Definitely."

Luke slipped his arm around her waist and nudged her closer, blocking her view as Henry sauntered away. Probably for the best. The longer the man stood next to her, the faster her heart had raced. Though her mind might say she loved Luke, her heart absolutely begged to differ.

The real traitor in all this?

Her heart.

Chapter Twenty-Four

Silencing an early alarm, Emily rose reluctantly to dress in black leggings and a striped, long-sleeved T-shirt. Yesterday, disappointed that Luke had bailed on his weekend visit, she'd messaged Henry: *Want to go bouldering tomorrow?*

He'd replied with a grinning face emoji.

Now, desperately needing a strong coffee after a restless night, Emily headed to the kitchen. A short while later, she pulled into the venue's parking lot and her heart rate rose. Henry waited outside the entrance looking cool, calm, and collected.

And hot!

First fanning her heated cheeks, she then went to meet him.

Inside the building, Emily faced Henry, where he'd challenged her at Noah's party. She stuck out her hand. "So, you ready to lose to a young woman?"

Grinning, he shook her hand. "Bring it on."

After a short countdown, they began.

Emily navigated the holds, relying primarily on muscle memory. Henry easily kept up until they hit the halfway mark, then he slowed. When she couldn't see him in her peripheral vision, she peered over her left shoulder. "You okay?"

"Yep." He winked. "Just working out strategy."

"Alright, then." She chuckled before continuing as fast as

her limbs would allow.

The next time she checked, he was seconds behind. Urging tired muscles to work harder, she reached the top hold in record time. Henry arrived a split second later, smirking. Though she strongly suspected he'd let her win, she couldn't prove it.

"So much for more experience," she teased when they landed on solid ground. "I guess you *are* an old man. Maybe I *should* get you a walking stick."

Smiling broadly, Henry grabbed her around the waist and growled, "That's enough!" before tickling her mercilessly.

"Fine!" Breathless, she raised her hands. "You're a young man with plenty of energy and experience. I don't know how I beat you."

Henry's fingers stilled, yet mischief remained in his dark green eyes. Her heart rate skyrocketed. All she could think about was kissing him. Desire blazed across his face, and his gaze slid to her mouth.

Stepping back with a tiny gasp, she forced him to release her. No good would come of exploring what would happen if she remained near the man who'd kept her up last night. Nope. Temptation like that was best avoided.

Another week passed, and again, work commitments prevented Luke from visiting their son. Hearing Noah's father had let him down once more, Henry offered to meet Noah and Emily at the park on Saturday.

"Sean and Lisa can't stop me from turning up at a public playground now, can they?" he argued.

Within minutes of Henry's arrival, Noah—his eyes sparkling with undisguised joy and hope—snagged the man's hand. "Push me on the swing, please, Mr. Henry?"

"Of course."

Soon tiring of that activity, Noah requested the ball Emily had brought with them. She handed it over, and he immediately turned to Henry. "Will you kick the ball with me, please?"

"I'd love to, Noah."

Emily marveled at her changed son. With Luke, Noah behaved differently—less relaxed and more cautious. With Henry, he was confident and happy all the time.

Afterward, they sipped hot chocolates in a small café until Noah wandered over to a bookcase. He chose a book, then read it cross-legged on a rainbow-colored rug.

"He seems happy." Emily smiled at her son, then looked back at Henry. His soft smile and intense gaze made her stomach flip. "What?" She wiped a hand over her mouth. "Do I have something on—?"

Shaking his head, he leaned closer. Emily's breath hitched, and her heart thudded in her chest. Gently, he tucked some hair behind her ear, his eyes dropping to her lips.

"Don't even think about it," she warned, easing back from the infuriating man. If he wanted to kiss her while dating Britt, his playboy ways were not over.

She crossed her arms. How could she contemplate dating Henry if he couldn't commit to his current, stunning girlfriend? Besides, she had a boyfriend. One committed to her and their son. One who wasn't avoiding marriage.

For the past month, Luke had flown to New Haven in the company helicopter once a week to take her to dinner—a sure sign her parents were on board with their relationship. Stunning bouquets arrived regularly at the house, and little love notes came in the mail, too. Luke's thoughtfulness and attentiveness were a testament to how much he loved her. When they were together, he often said those three little words.

Yet rather than elation at his declarations, Emily felt… Well, that was it; she wasn't sure how she felt exactly. Though she hadn't echoed his words, she was beginning to think it was time.

So why did her heart ache when she looked at Henry? Why did she picture Noah and her with him and not Luke?

***

Emily frowned. The understated yet elegant shift dress— pale blue and edged with lace—wasn't exactly what she'd usually wear to a wedding. But, hey, she needed to blend in, so it would do.

She heaved a heavy sigh. Turning down the bridesmaid opportunity meant spending less time with Henry today. If only she didn't care so much whether or not the press dug up her secret, even if her parents discovered it as a result.

But, no.

Emily pushed those unsettling thoughts aside. Luke was accompanying her to the church, and she expected his knock any second.

After a passionate kiss hello, Luke drove her to the church. There, they sat on the bride's side. White roses, mixed with baby's breath, punctuated the pew ends, while two huge floral arrangements decorated the front corners of the church. The florist had cleverly included Charlotte's accent color by wrapping the vases in emerald tulle.

Adam and his groomsmen, Henry and Jack, faced the congregation. They looked entirely too handsome in their traditional attire. Well, one man in particular did. When Henry's eyes searched the seats and stopped at her, Emily glanced away, but not before catching his slow, heart-tugging smile. Blushing, she ducked her head to fiddle with her phone.

Luke nudged her. "I thought you silenced it," he whispered.

"I was checking to see if Noah sent a message."

"He knows we're at a wedding, right?"

"Yes, but Lisa's allowing him texts since we couldn't visit today."

"That's sweet. I've missed him." Luke leaned in, his gaze suddenly hooded. "Almost as much as I miss you every time I have to leave." Caressing her lower arm, he murmured, "I want you so much, Em. When are you going to stay the night?"

Ever since their weekend in New York, where he'd made his intentions clear, Emily had avoided the topic. Now, memories from their long-ago night together—her first and only time—flooded her mind. As did Luke's admission of subsequent relationships.

An uncomfortable lump formed in her throat. She'd vowed never to repeat that experience with someone who wasn't her husband.

"This isn't the time or place, Luke," she quietly urged.

"I know, but I love you, Em. I think we're ready to move our relationship forward. You know my greatest desire is for us to be a family."

"I want that too. It's just, I can't see how with you in New York and me here. And I refuse to move away from our son. I'm sure you understand."

He nodded, but she could see his brain ticking away in overdrive.

Everyone stood when the bridal march started. Julie and Britt strolled down the aisle, their green chiffon dresses dancing at their feet. A pang of envy hit Emily. She could've been with them if only—

No point finishing that thought. She focused on the groomsmen. Of course, Jack's eyes were riveted on his wife, while Britt claimed Henry's appreciative smile.

Emily firmed her lips. No surprise there.

Seconds later, Henry's gaze landed on her and subtly changed to tender admiration. Her heart skipped a beat. Jerking her eyes back to Luke, she found him watching her, confusion and concern on his face. She squeezed his fingers, giving him what she hoped was a reassuring smile.

Next came Amy in her miniature bridesmaid dress and the boys in black-and-white suits. Adorable. Emily stifled a laugh when Daniel gave her a little wave which almost caused him to miss a step.

Eventually, the radiant bride appeared in a gorgeous 'ball gown' style white dress with layers of chiffon skirt. Adam couldn't take his eyes off Charlotte as she swept down the aisle. Before she'd even reached him, he stepped forward.

Emily giggled, then quickly covered her mouth. A glance at Henry revealed dancing eyes and a knowing smile. She inhaled a long, calming breath, then did her best not to look at him because every time she did, she wanted to laugh. He kept checking on her, making funny faces until the vows were said. Then he became serious and concentrated on handing over the rings.

The ceremony went without a hitch.

Once the bridal party left the church, Emily turned to Luke. "Okay, so photos are planned for around thirty minutes. We have time for a walk before heading to the reception venue."

"Walking's good." Wearing a saucy grin, he slipped his hand around her waist and pulled her closer. "I'll be even happier if we also find somewhere private."

"Why?"

"Em," he drawled, frowning like she was a belligerent child.

Feigning innocence, she gave a one-armed shrug. "I don't get it."

"My girlfriend's hot," he said in an extra low voice, "and I want to kiss her senseless."

"Luke!" Covering her burning cheeks, she shook her head. "I swear, there's only one thing on your mind."

"Do you blame me?" he said as they followed everyone out of the church. Pausing at the bottom of the steps, he looked around. "You're the most stunning woman here, Em."

Tucking hair behind her ear, she chuckled. "I think you're a little biased."

"Nope." Luke smirked. "And I wasn't the only guy who thought so." She raised an eyebrow at the certainty in his voice. "So did Henry."

"He didn't."

"Em," Luke half-growled, "that man might have a super-attractive girlfriend, but his eyes were stuck on you. Way more than on Britt."

"Rubbish." Waving him off, she shook her head. "Henry only wanted to make me laugh. I had a case of the giggles, so he made it his mission to try to embarrass me. That's all."

He huffed. "Whatever you say."

Skillfully avoiding the photographer, Luke led her behind the church and gathered her in his arms. His ardent kisses affected her body, leaving her breathless.

She pulled back, staring at him while working hard to get her breathing under control. "You know what you're doing isn't fair."

"Come on, Em," he whined. "You're driving me crazy. Holding you close—kissing you—and not being able to take it all the way is torture. Just a smile or a flick of your hair turns me on. I need you."

Pressing her mouth to his, she kissed him slowly and deliberately before breaking the contact. "That, Luke," she said, pointing between their lips, "is as far as I'm prepared to go. I gave in to my desires one time. Now, I'm waiting for my wedding night."

He gawked at her. "You're not serious!"

Taking a half-step back, she crossed her arms. "Oh, I absolutely am."

***

Henry scowled. His jaw hurt, and he desperately wanted to escape the blustery wind. If he had to smile one more time, either voluntarily or on command…

He glanced at Charlotte, who positively glowed like she was happy being photographed. How? Perhaps the blushing bride had only one thing on her mind—her husband.

Not the weather conditions, obviously.

Emily should count her blessings. She at least had a valid excuse to not be in the wedding party. He wished he could say the same.

"You look like you're being forced to endure the most painful experience of your life, Henry." Britt bit her lip to hide a smile. "Is it really *that* hard to pose and smile for the camera?"

Running his fingers through tangled hair, he released an exasperated puff of air. "If I'd wanted to be a model as a *child*, Britt, my parents would've gladly arranged it."

Laughing, she wrapped her arms around his waist. "Just a few more. Then we can go inside and collect a well-deserved drink."

"Can't we go *now*?" Returning her embrace, he gave his best impression of puppy dog eyes.

She planted a firm kiss on his mouth, then drew back. "Patience. One or two more group photos and we're done."

He sighed. "Fine."

Later, after downing a glass of champagne, devouring the scrumptious five-course meal, and giving his best man speech, Henry finally relaxed.

The Jays then took to the stage, accompanied by a live band. They sang a touching love song written by Julie for the occasion. Not a female eye remained dry in the venue, and a few men discreetly wiped their eyes too.

Naturally, Henry's gaze lingered on Emily's beautiful, tear-stained face. He couldn't help it. As if feeling the weight of his stare, she turned. The seemingly special, only-for-him soft smile that lifted her pink lips completely undid him. Time stood still, his heart flip-flopping in his chest. In the background, Jack and Julie continued serenading Adam and Charlotte.

Henry forced his eyes closed, breaking contact with the bewitching woman. He took a deep breath and clasped his girlfriend's hand. "I think this will be their next big hit, especially for weddings," he murmured in her ear.

"Yes." Britt swiped at her eyes. "Julie has the most amazing voice, and Jack's complements hers perfectly." She fanned herself. "He's so handsome."

"Hey!" He yanked his hand out hers.

Giggling, she cupped his face. "Luckily, he's not nearly as handsome as you." She kissed him briefly. "I can't believe he's indirectly my brother-in-law now."

"Huh." Henry tapped his chin, then grinned. "I hadn't thought about that. My girlfriend has connections."

"And don't you forget it." Britt smirked.

Halfway through the bride and groom's first dance, Henry

and Britt joined them, along with Jack and Julie, who'd relinquished their microphones to members of the live band. Dancing with Britt was easy, but Emily's half-hearted promise to dance with him as long as it was an upbeat song was never far from his mind. Between Luke, and various other men who monopolized Emily's company all evening, Henry wasn't certain he'd even get a chance.

"These are killing me." Britt glared at her impractical, sling-back heels. "I'm going to sit the next few out."

"I'll join you in a bit. Emily promised me a dance."

Britt eyed him for a moment, then nodded. "Good luck. She's avoiding you."

"What?"

"Every time we head anywhere near her, she slips away."

"You've been watching her?"

She shrugged, her expression closed. "I expected your best friend to at least come talk to you—"

"Britt," he warned.

"It's fine." She shot him an unconvincing smile. "Have you seen the way she and Luke look at each other? I'm not worried."

Without waiting for his response, she limped off toward their seats.

Clenching his fists, Henry spun to take in the room. While low lights added to the romantic atmosphere, it made it trickier to spot a specific person. An elusive beauty.

Maybe a drink would help.

As he approached the bar and spotted a familiar figure, his heartbeat quickened in time to his footsteps.

"Hey, stranger," he said, bumping Emily's shoulder with his.

Jerking her head his way, her eyes widened for a split second. "Hey, Henry. You here for a drink?"

"Actually, I came to collect on a promise."

Lines dotted her pretty brow.

"Dance with me?"

"Nope," she replied, and his heart dropped. "This isn't

upbeat." She glanced over at the pink-haired bartender. "I'll have an iced lemon water, please."

"And you, sir?" the young woman purred, her eyes skimming him appreciatively.

Squirming, Henry thought quickly. If he had a beer, he'd be stuck having to take it to the table, allowing Emily to disappear again.

"Tap water, please."

A small smile hovered on Emily's lips. "You must be really thirsty."

He nodded and stuck his hands in his pockets. Better than reaching out and tucking that loose strand of hair behind her ear. Unfortunately, the longer they waited, the stronger the urge to touch her became. On the other hand, Emily appeared totally unaffected by his company.

Maybe Britt was right. Maybe Emily was in love with Luke.

"You look stunning," he blurted.

Pink immediately tinged her cheeks. She smoothed down her simple yet elegant dress. "Thanks. I…"

"You what?" he asked tenderly, shoving his itchy hands deeper into his pockets.

The bartender set two glasses in front of them. "Here you go."

Emily grabbed her drink and gulped it down. Henry did the same as an upbeat song came on through the speakers.

Stretching out his hand, he smiled tentatively. "Now, will you dance with me?"

She stared at his hand for a long second, sighed deeply, and finally slipped her hand into his. "Okay."

Loud music made talking impossible. Instead, they moved to the beat, each throwing out an occasional awkward smile. When the music slowed right down, and before Emily could leave, he grasped her hands and held firm.

"Henry." She scowled, attempting a half-hearted tug.

"Come on, Emily," he coaxed, using his most persuasive, charming voice. The one that usually convinced donors to open their purses much wider than they'd originally planned. "You know you want to."

Though her eyes shone brightly, she pursed her lips. "I told Luke I'd be back five minutes ago."

"He can come looking for you."

Dropping one hand, Henry slipped his arm around her waist and brought her close. Emily immediately sucked in a breath, her eyes shooting to his. As they swayed to the music, their heads inches apart, neither looked away. The longer they stared into each other's eyes, the more the air between them felt charged. If he wasn't careful, he'd completely lose himself in her tender gaze. Already, she was reeling him in like a fisherman hauling in his catch. This woman would be the death of him. Even so, a question burned in his gut.

"Are you in love with him?"

Her soft expression shuttered. "Why?"

Swallowing hard, he tried to read her emotions. She hadn't immediately confirmed that she did.

Could that mean…? Hope fluttered in his chest.

"Because if you aren't—"

"Luke's family, Henry," Emily said, her tone emphatic. "Of course I love him."

Chapter Twenty-Five

"Something you want to tell me, bud?"

Shielding his eyes from the rising June sunshine, Henry gave his running buddy a sideways glance. "Like what?"

"Oh, I don't know," Adam said nonchalantly. "Like maybe you proposed?"

Stumbling over a small rock in his path, Henry caught his breath. Somehow, he managed to right himself before face-planting in the dirt.

Adam's hand stretched out to steady him. "You okay?"

"Yeah, I'm good, thanks."

They covered a few more yards before Adam cleared his throat. "So, are you and my sister…?"

Was six months of dating someone long enough to be considering asking them to marry you? Adam had with Charlotte, so obviously he didn't think it was too soon. Honestly, the thought hadn't even crossed his mind until now.

"Sorry, bud, I'm not about to propose." Henry shot him a sly look. "Even if I were, you think I'd tell you?"

A pained look shot across Adam's face. "I thought we were best friends."

"We are, but I'm dating *your* sister. No way would I tell you what I'm thinking before I talked to her first."

"Fair enough."

Another mile, possibly two, passed in silence as they

concentrated on climbing the hill. Although fit enough to converse while running, they tended to save their breath for the top. There, they'd cross the level ground before going back down, talking a little while taking in the view of New Haven.

As he put one foot in front of the other, Henry reflected on the past two months. Running Daily Bread had kept him busy. Adam had gone on a two-week honeymoon after his wedding, returning to become more involved in the Scott Wilson Home renovations.

He and Adam still ran together most mornings, using the time to catch up on Daily Bread business, but the dynamics of their friendship had changed. They no longer spoke of personal struggles. It seemed Adam now confided in Charlotte more and Henry less. As a result, Henry had gotten better at praying, bringing his cares before the Lord, and asking for His direction.

He and Britt had grown closer, celebrating their six-month anniversary a few weeks back. She'd finally settled into her new job, allowing them much more time together. Henry's friendship with Emily suffered as a result. At least, that's what he told himself, rather than admit it was because Emily had pulled away. He seldom saw her at church. When he did, she was never alone. Adam and Charlotte were always with her. Or she was with them. Whichever.

Henry had suggested a catch-up coffee, but Emily named one excuse after another. It took him a while to figure out that Luke had likely put his foot down about their friendship. Henry couldn't blame him. If Emily were his girlfriend, he'd have done the same thing.

As time passed, Henry just assumed his feelings for her had faded away. Looking at Britt, he saw a woman he could grow to love, hopefully deeply, and ultimately marry one day.

Except, he'd woken this morning feeling something big was about to happen. With his heart racing for no apparent reason, he prayed for the people he cared deeply about: Britt, Adam, and his family.

And Emily.

In that moment, he realized he couldn't dismiss his feelings for her. Truth was, he missed Emily. A lot.

So, he'd texted: *Hey, just thinking about you. Hope you're well. How are things with Noah and Luke? If you ever feel like talking, I'm here for you. Henry*

Within minutes, she'd replied: *Thanks, that means a lot. We're all good. Excited about staying over at Noah's tonight. Sean and Lisa have a wedding in Boston. Hope you're well? Emily*

His response had been short: *Wow, enjoy! Take care xx*

Picturing Emily and Noah in their pajamas had brought a smile to his face. Obviously, it hadn't left.

"You never did tell me why you had that goofy grin on your face when you arrived." Adam's voice drew Henry back to the present.

"Believe it or not, I wasn't thinking of Britt."

"Not *Emily*." Adam sounded disappointed, or was it annoyed?

"Why do you say it like that?"

"I thought you'd gotten over your obsession with her."

"She's my *friend*," he ground out, slightly irritated. "We haven't been in contact much the past couple of months but texted briefly this morning." He glowered. "It made me smile. So sue me."

"Sorry, bud." Holding up his hands, Adam shook his head. "Just looking out for my little sister. I warned you to be careful about breaking her heart." Henry opened his mouth to object, but Adam kept talking. "And for a while, I thought that was exactly what you would do."

A measure of alarm flowed through Henry. "What are you talking about?"

"I might've had eyes for only my wife the day of our wedding, but I wasn't completely blind to stuff happening around me. The way you and Emily kept looking at each other had me worried. Charlotte thought I was being overly dramatic, but I couldn't shake the feeling that something was happening between you."

Needing to nip this in the bud, Henry halted. He laid a hand on Adam's shoulder. "Listen, whatever you think you saw, there was—and is—nothing going on between Emily and me. That ship sailed a long time ago. She's in love with Luke, and I love your sister."

Adam's eyes brightened. "Have you told Britt that?"

"Not yet."

"What's stopping you?" Adam half-growled, his gaze intensifying again.

Expelling a long breath, Henry turned back to the path and resumed running. Adam joined him, but Henry could feel his friend waiting for an answer.

"Timing," he said. "It hasn't felt right. Saying those words —it's not something I take lightly either."

"I respect that, bud, I do, but I think she'd love to hear how you feel."

Henry shot Adam a concerned look. "Has Britt said something?"

Adam shrugged. "She might have mentioned feeling a little unsure about where you two stand."

He huffed. "It's not like she's said those three little words."

"Honestly, I think she's too scared. Face it, this is the longest relationship you've ever had. Britt's nervous that if she says something, you'll end it and go back to dating multiple women."

"Wow." Pulling up his T-shirt, Henry wiped the sweat from his brow. "That's really what she thinks?"

Adam gave a slow nod.

"I guess Britt and I need to have a serious conversation."

"Probably a good idea." His friend narrowed his eyes. "But maybe pray first. Don't say you love her unless you know in your heart that she's the one you want to spend the rest of your life with. Britt isn't the kind of woman you toy with. She's a keeper, understand?"

He gulped, then nodded.

"The minute you tell her you love her, you'd better be

prepared to follow through with a ring." From Adam's serious tone, Henry knew he meant every word.

"I promise, I will."

***

Answering her phone, Emily frowned at Luke's face on the screen. "Hey, I thought you'd be here already."

"I'm so sorry, Em, but I won't make it today." Luke released a long breath, the rings under his eyes visible even over video. "Your dad insists I fix the issues stalling this deal, which means staying in New York and speaking directly with the clients. I can't say no."

"Of course not. That would be career suicide." Emily kept her tone neutral. Luke was under enough pressure as it was. He didn't need her adding to it.

"I'll fly there first thing in the morning. We can have breakfast together."

"That'll be lovely." Not that she would hold her breath. If he made it to New Haven for even half a day tomorrow, she'd consider herself lucky. "I hope your deal gets sorted. See you in the morning."

Ending the call, she counted to ten slowly, trying to contain her irritation. Luke had been as excited as her to spend two whole days alone with their son. Once again, he'd let her down.

Shaking her head, Emily chided herself. Noah didn't need her putting a damper on his spirits. He likely wouldn't be upset anyway. He mentioned missing Mr. Henry way more than Mr. Luke.

Hearing Henry's name so often? That was hard.

Pretending he was just another person in her life hadn't exactly worked out. She missed him so much.

After seeing them dance at the wedding, Luke had issued an ultimatum. "Either you step back from your 'friendship' with Henry, or I will seriously consider telling Sean and Lisa that I'm Noah's biological father. I may just have to sue them for custody. You wouldn't like that, would you?"

Emily had been livid until she'd prayed about the situation

and realized Luke was only protecting his family. He may have been going about it all wrong, but his intentions were good. In the end, she apologized and agreed to Luke's demands by breaking off almost all contact with Henry.

Church had been trickier. Coming late and leaving early helped, along with ensuring she was never alone. She declined Charlotte's meal invitations when she knew Henry would be in attendance. Her list of inventive excuses had lengthened, and she hated every single one.

The ache in her heart from thinking about him, hadn't lessened with time. It had grown. She missed his friendship enormously. His text that morning had filled her with joy. Knowing he still cared meant a great deal.

Luke's news had burst her happy bubble, though. She could've throttled her father—the reason her boyfriend had to work on a Saturday! Calling to demand he release Luke for the weekend had crossed her mind until she realized she'd have to explain why.

So, she let it go.

During the twenty-minute drive to Sean and Lisa's, Emily forced herself to relax. Having looked forward to this night since Charlotte's wedding, she couldn't afford for anything to go wrong.

She rang the doorbell with an overnight bag in her hand and a smile plastered on her face. A subdued-looking Lisa ushered her inside.

"Aunt Emily!" Noah's little legs pumped hard as he barreled down the hallway toward them.

Emily laughed, catching him in her arms and kissing his head. "Noah, you almost bowled me over!"

"Sorry!" He grinned, looking anything but sorry. "I missed you. Mommy said you're sleeping in my bedroom tonight!"

"Hey!" Lisa stood with her arms crossed over her chest. "I'm feeling a little left out here."

"Aw, Mommy." Noah's earnest little face was adorable. "You know I love you, and I'll miss you, but I see you *every* day."

Lisa smiled, though not as wide as usual. Something was definitely up. Emily's stomach clenched.

"Everything okay?" she asked Lisa after Noah carried her bag to his bedroom.

Lisa nodded, her lips pursed. "Fine. Everything's fine. Sean's just packing last-minute toiletries, but we'll leave soon."

In the kitchen, Lisa showed Emily the food she'd cooked, as well as the hotel's contact details. "We'll both have our cellphones on silent. But I'll check mine as regularly as I can."

Laying a hand on Lisa's arm, Emily smiled reassuringly. "Don't worry about a thing. Noah and I aren't going anywhere we haven't been before, and you know I'll look after him like my own son."

"Funny." Lisa smiled tightly.

Emily took it as a win.

"Thank you, Emily. If there's anyone I trust with Noah, it's you."

Sean strode into the kitchen, an overnight suitcase rolling behind him. "Hey, Emily," he said. After running a jerky hand through his hair, his eyes flitted around the kitchen, then landed back on her. "I take it Lisa's briefed you on the food she's left for an army?"

Emily laughed. "She has." She waved them off. "Go. Have a great time in Boston and drive safe."

Noah entered the kitchen at a run and skidded to a halt beside her. Emily ruffled his hair, then focused on Sean and Lisa. "When you get back tomorrow, your son will be exhausted from playing with his Aunt Emily."

"I will?" Noah piped up.

"Yes, but you'll also be thrilled to see Mommy and Daddy. Am I right?"

"Yep. I'm gonna miss you, Mommy." He hugged her, then moved to his dad to do the same. "And you, Daddy. Come home soon. I love you."

"We love you, too, Noah."

With that, they left.

Noah turned to Emily and grinned. The kind of smile that told her he was about to get his own way. "Aunt Emily, could we ask Mr. Henry to come play with us at the park?"

Her immediate reaction was no, and she opened her mouth to say just that.

"Please," Noah pleaded, putting his little hands together and wearing the cutest, most hopeful expression.

Boy, Noah sure knew how to pull at her heartstrings when it came to Henry. The more she thought about it, the more she wanted to see Henry too. Wouldn't he already have plans with Britt, though? Probably. No harm in asking, she supposed.

Luke wouldn't be happy.

Too bad.

"He might already have plans. We'll have to see, okay?"

"Okay." Brown eyes, so like his dad's, shone up at her expectantly.

Dragging her phone from her jeans' back pocket, she pressed call on Henry's name. The phone rang for ages. About to give up, she pulled the phone from her ear but heard her name. "Emily?"

Henry's familiar deep voice washed over her.

"Sorry. I didn't think you were going to answer."

"I just got out the shower."

"Let me guess, you went running with Adam."

He chuckled. "You remembered."

She laughed too. "Just because I haven't seen you in so long doesn't mean I've forgotten your routine."

"Glad to know you still think about me."

"All the time."

Great, she shouldn't have said that! Silence on the other end had her heart rate increasing wildly.

"Emily, you're the one who—"

"I know, and I'm sorry." She cut him off. "I'm hoping you won't hold it against me."

Noah squeezed her hand, reminding her why she'd called. "I have a little boy here who wants to know if you're free to join us in the park?"

"Isn't Luke there?" Henry sounded confused.

She tried to keep the annoyance out of her voice but failed. "He's working."

"I see…"

When Henry didn't say anything further, Emily's stomach dropped. He was trying to figure out how to let her and Noah down gently.

Not wanting to prolong the agony, she sighed. "It's okay. I told Noah you already had plans. I'm sorry I asked."

"No. No, it's not that. I just…" There was another long pause and what sounded like keys tapping on a keyboard. "Would Noah maybe want to do some go-karting instead?"

"Um, that sounds awesome, but isn't he a little young?"

"I checked," Henry said. "According to the Adventure Park website, even if he's too short, he can ride in tandem with you or me."

"Are you sure you're not busy? I wouldn't want to impose."

"Emily, you could never be an imposition. Besides, I've missed Noah. And you."

"I've missed you, too." She smiled at Noah and gave him a thumbs up. He immediately did a little jig, making her laugh.

"Why are you laughing?" Henry sounded amused rather than concerned.

"Noah's so happy, he's dancing."

After a snort of amusement, Henry's tone turned somber. "What about you? Are you dancing too?"

Ignoring his insinuation, she changed the subject. "How soon can you pick us up?"

Chapter Twenty-Six

The next morning, Emily rubbed her eyes and stared at Luke's post-midnight text.

Bad news, Em. My meeting ran so late yesterday that your dad suggested we meet first thing. Gonna do my best to get to you for lunch. I'll let you know when I leave. Love you x

What did she say to that—no problem? It's fine? See you later?

Throwing the phone onto the bed with a frustrated groan, she lay back down and stretched her arms above her head. Linking her fingers underneath, she exhaled deeply. Thank goodness Noah knew nothing about breakfast with Luke.

Soon after she'd called yesterday, Henry had arrived on Sean and Lisa's doorstep. Dressed in tan cargo shorts and a black T-shirt, which hugged his broad shoulders and muscular biceps, the man had caused her heart to skip a few beats. He'd come bearing gifts—hot chocolate with marshmallows for Noah and an iced caramel latte for her.

In a rush to wrap his little arms around Henry's legs, Noah had almost bowled him over. Still, Henry laughed at her son's exuberance.

Mouthing 'sorry,' she quickly rescued the drinks and waited for Noah to stop fawning over him. Not that she minded. It gave her a chance to do some fawning of her own.

"I'm *so* glad you came, Mr. Henry. I missed you *so* much! Aunt Emily said you were busy, and we shouldn't disturb you."

Henry lifted twinkling eyes to her. "Is that so?"

"Yes. She said you had a girlfriend." Noah's disappointed tone and matching frown were adorable, if not slightly embarrassing. "Is that true, Mr. Henry? Do you have a girlfriend?"

With the child still hugging him, Henry crouched down to his level. "I do. Her name's Britt."

"Is she pretty, like Aunt Emily?" Noah asked, releasing Henry and glancing at her.

"Noah," she admonished, her face heating, "that's what we call a personal question."

Chuckling, Henry raised tender-filled eyes to her. When his smile grew and softened, her knees threatened to give way. Leaning a hand on the wall steadied her body but not her beating heart. Nope, once Henry spoke again, that was in serious trouble.

"It's okay, Noah," he said, "Britt is pretty. But no one's as pretty as your aunt Emily."

"Except my mommy." Noah's innocent comment made them both laugh, easing the moment.

The go-karting activity was a hit. Noah insisted Henry join him in the kart, so Emily got to watch all the bumps and near misses. A few times, Henry allowed Noah to steer—the boy's favorite part—and Emily almost forgot to breathe. Thankfully, they left with all their bones intact and her heart beating near enough normally.

If she concentrated hard enough, Emily could still feel Henry's warm embrace—the one he'd given her after taking them home. "I had fun today. Don't be a stranger, Emily," had been his parting words.

"Morning, Aunt Emily." Noah's groggy voice greeted her from his bed across the room.

"Morning, sweetheart." She smiled gently at him. "Did you sleep well?"

He nodded, yawning. "What's for breakfast?"

And so, the day began.

Though Luke wasn't there to share the planned experience, Emily and Noah still ate bacon, eggs, and waffles in their pajamas while watching kids' television—usually a definite no-no, according to Lisa.

Later, they headed to the park, the gorgeous sunny day only slightly marred by the absence of Luke and knowing, that in a few hours, Sean and Lisa would return home.

She considered calling Henry again, but he was sure to be at church. Though she could've taken Noah, it was too risky. A Bible story at bedtime and singing kids' praise songs while she cooked breakfast had to suffice. Thankfully, one thing she had insisted on when choosing adoptive parents was that they were believers.

A couple of hours later, she'd just cleared away the lunch dishes when the doorbell rang.

"The small hand's pointing to one, Aunt Emily, not four," Noah declared, his brow furrowed. "It can't be Mommy and Daddy."

"I'll go check."

Marching to the entrance, she yanked open the door and grinned. "You made it!"

Luke immediately wrapped his arms around her waist and kissed her like his life depended on it.

"Wow. I think you missed me," she teased, breaking off the kiss.

"Maybe." A flicker of irritation passed over his face before he shrugged and peered over her shoulder. "Now," he said, his tone falsely bright, "where's that special little boy I've also missed?"

"Hello, Mr. Luke." Noah came into sight, briefly allowing Luke's embrace before quickly edging away.

A knot formed in Emily's stomach when she compared Noah's different reactions to the men in her life. What was it her son sensed that made him treat them differently?

"I brought you something, Noah." Reaching into a backpack beside him on the porch, Luke dragged out a Lego Super Robot toy.

"Awesome! Thanks, Mr. Luke." Noah bounced from foot to foot. "Can I go play with it?"

"Of course. I need to talk to your aunt anyway."

Noah hurried down the hall to the living room.

Emily narrowed her eyes at her boyfriend. "I thought you came to spend time with your son."

"I did." He slipped his arms around her waist and dragged her against him, a roguish twinkle in his eyes. "But I also came to see you," he said huskily right before his mouth descended to meet hers. Another kiss left her breathless, and she took a step backward to put some necessary distance between them.

"Why don't you come in? I'm sure you'd like some coffee."

"Aww, I *was* kind of enjoying myself." His eyebrows jumped suggestively, and as he reached for her again, he lowered his voice, "It's a pity we're not alone. I want you, Em."

"Luke," she warned, gently pushing him away. "We've spoken about this."

"Fine." With a huff, he stuffed his hands in his pockets and brushed past her. "Okay. Then let's have coffee."

***

Emily watched Luke pace the living room floor, his phone clutched to his chest. Ever since he'd stepped outside for an important call a little over an hour ago, he'd been on edge.

"The pilot's on standby. I can't make him wait much longer, Em. When will they be back?"

She peered at the mantelpiece clock for what felt like the hundredth time. According to Lisa's last text, Emily had expected them home over an hour ago. Traffic must be terrible.

She met Luke's agitated gaze. "Why don't you go? I'm supposed to be babysitting at Charlotte's tonight anyway."

He walked over and cupped her face, his eyes searching hers. "Are you sure? I hate leaving you in the lurch."

"Thanks for coming," she said, forcing a smile. "Even if it wasn't for the whole weekend."

"I promise I will another time. When there isn't a huge deal hanging over me." The strain in his voice made her feel bad. She shouldn't be guilt-tripping him.

Leaning forward, she touched her lips to his. Luke responded by taking control and deepening the kiss. Giving in, she slipped her fingers behind his neck and into his silky soft hair.

"Aunt Emily?"

They sprung apart. Goodness, she'd forgotten Noah had gone to the bathroom!

"When's Mommy coming? I'm hungry."

"I'm not sure, sweetheart. Did you wash your hands?"

He nodded, holding them up for inspection.

"Good boy." She turned him to face Luke. "Mr. Luke's got to go now. How does mac and cheese sound?"

"Yay! It's my favorite. Are you going home in the helicopter, Mr. Luke?"

He nodded.

"Can I go with you and Aunt Emily one day?"

Looking over at her, Luke raised a questioning brow. She shrugged. It wasn't exactly up to her.

"If your parents say it's okay, we can arrange it."

"Awesome!" Noah ducked his head and curled his hands around Emily's arm. He waved shyly at Luke.

"Bye, Noah." Luke glanced at her, then smiled tightly at his son. "Look after Aunt Emily for me, okay?"

"Okay." Noah skipped off to the TV room to play with his new toy.

The way Luke kissed her in the entryway? Let's just say the man was determined to remind her of the one night that had resulted in their son. He ended the kiss with a heavy sigh, and her eyes popped open.

"Is everything alright?" she asked, brushing her fingertips over his clenched jaw.

"It will be soon."

Her brow furrowed. "I don't understand."

"I have to go. We'll talk later, okay?" Hoisting his backpack over his shoulder, he turned, his hand on the doorknob. "I miss you already, Em."

"Then stay," she implored. "Tell the pilot to go, and you can get a cab home. I'll even pay."

His gaze dropped to his hands. "I can't."

Disappointed, she strode over to him. "Okay. Be safe," she said after one last lingering kiss.

"Don't ever forget that I love you," he whispered fiercely as his tortured gaze met hers.

She sucked in a breath. What was going on? Something about that phone call earlier had led his mind elsewhere and darkened his mood.

Emily stayed rooted in the entryway, even when the door closed behind Luke. Why had it sounded like he was saying goodbye for more than the next few days?

Since she had no clue, she went to find her son. He was sprawled out on the carpet, totally preoccupied with his new Lego. She chuckled.

"Noah?" He turned his head slightly to look at her. "Would you like to help in the kitchen?"

"Can I grate the cheese?"

"Oh, I insist."

At that, he jumped up with a gigantic smile.

Though the activity distracted Noah, Emily's heart beat more quickly. Where were Sean and Lisa?

Seconds later, the doorbell rang for the second time that day.

"Mommy doesn't ring the doorbell." Noah's bottom lip wobbled. "She has a key."

Emily rose to her feet and smoothed down her skirt. "I know, sweetheart. Stay here. I need to check who it is."

As she rushed to the door, dread pooled in the pit of her stomach. Luke had texted when he was in the air, so—

She pulled open the door and froze.

"Miss Emily Quinn?" the older of the two state troopers asked.

Gulping back the bile rising in her throat, she nodded.

There was only one way they could know her name—from Lisa and Sean's 'in case of emergency' contacts on their phones.

"I'm Officer Norton." He waved toward the younger, female trooper. "This is Officer Smith. May we come in?"

"Yes. Yes, of course." She swept to the side, allowing them entrance, then shut the door.

"Where's Noah?" Officer Norton asked in a low voice, his brow knitted in concern.

"In the kitchen diner." Emily pointed to the end of the passage. Officer Smith's eyes darted in that direction, her face full of compassion.

"I'm afraid there's been an accident," Officer Norton said. "Noah's parents were involved in a head-on collision on the I-95 about two hours ago." Gasping, Emily threw a hand over her mouth. "I'm very sorry, but they didn't make it."

Suddenly, her legs felt like jelly. Silent tears fell as she thrust out a hand to steady herself. Noah would be devastated. How would she tell him?

Officer Smith touched her arm. "Would you like to sit down, Miss Quinn?"

Emily shook her head, then took a few deep breaths. In. Out. The lump in her throat grew. She needed to be strong for Noah. He had no one else now—only her and Luke.

Dear Lord, please give me strength. Help me find the right words for Noah.

"Is there anyone we can call? Someone who can come give you support?" Officer Norton asked.

"I-I need to call my boyfriend, Luke Bowman."

"May I?" Officer Norton held out his hand, nodding toward the phone in her hands. Unlocking it, she passed it over, but the call went unanswered.

Officer Smith gave her a sympathetic look. "Is there someone else?"

"Um, Henry Palmer."

The phone call was quick—Henry said he'd be right over.

Officer Smith suggested Emily keep Noah's routine as

normal as possible, so she did. But when she heard the officers talking to Henry, she left Noah engrossed in a book in his bedroom and strode back to the living room.

"I'm so sorry, Emily." Henry immediately rushed over to hug her. Tears she'd managed to keep at bay while with Noah escaped in seconds. As she wept, Henry rubbed circles on her back while murmuring words of comfort.

Eventually, she lifted blurry eyes to his and gave him a tremulous smile. "Thanks for coming," she said, extracting herself from his arms. She turned to the officers watching them. "Thank you for staying. I'll be fine now."

"No problem, Miss Quinn." Officer Norton nodded. "I can see you're in good hands. Again, we're sorry for your loss, and since you're Noah's next of kin, we're happy to leave him with you."

"If you need help sharing this tragic news with Noah, call this number." Officer Smith handed over a card.

"Thank you."

Once they were alone, Henry touched her lower arm. "Where's Noah?"

"In bed. Waiting for me to read him a story."

"Let me do that for you," he said, capturing her hand. He gazed at her warmly, his thumb rubbing circles on her knuckles. His soft touch sent tingles up her arms, and she struggled to concentrate. "Unless you'd prefer I make you some coffee?"

Lost in his kind, gorgeous eyes, it took her a few seconds to comprehend his words. "Yes," she finally responded, her voice breathy. "You read. I'll make coffee."

"Okay." He squeezed her hand and dropped it. "What have you told Noah about his parents?"

She gave a humorless laugh. "All he knows is Sean and Lisa aren't coming home tonight, but that they love him. Nothing about his real parents."

"Wow. Of course." Henry blinked and swallowed. "You and Luke..."

His attention shifted toward the bedrooms, an emotion she

couldn't identify passing over his face. When he looked back at her, his expression was shuttered, the tenderness from earlier replaced by a stoicism she didn't like.

"Where is Luke?" he asked, his tone clipped. "I thought he'd be here."

"He flew back to New York a couple hours ago. They couldn't get hold of him."

Henry frowned. "They?"

"The officers."

"I see." A muscle in his jaw twitched. "Would you... Would you like me to try him again on your phone?"

"No." Reaching out, she rested her hand on his arm. "It's you I want here. Please?"

"Okay."

The smile that lit his face warmed her to the core despite her gnawing guilt. She really should be urgently trying to get hold of Luke. Yet, if anyone could support her in this difficult time with Noah, it would be Henry. Noah may be Luke's flesh and blood, but somehow the bond between Henry and Noah was much stronger.

She didn't stop to unravel why that was. Going there was too scary.

Chapter Twenty-Seven

After a gruff "Okay, fine," Emily ended the call and slipped the phone into her jeans' back pocket. She crossed her arms and faced Henry, waiting in Sean and Lisa's kitchen for her to finish her conversation. "Luke's not coming."

"I'm sorry. What?" The only parents Noah had ever known had suddenly died, and Luke wasn't willing to drop everything and rush to Emily's side.

Surely he'd want to comfort his son when he got told the news?

Burying his indignation, Henry strode toward Emily. He stopped a few steps away, his fists clenched at his side. "Did he say why?"

"They're on the verge of closing this major deal he's been working on for ages. If he leaves now, it would be career suicide—Luke's words. My father's a shrewd businessman, but even he has feelings. If Luke explained…" She trailed off, her lips twisting.

"He can't though, can he? Without giving away your secret?"

"No. But it won't be a secret for much longer, will it? Officially, Noah's my son again." She hugged herself, a faraway look in her eyes. "I have to tell Charlotte. My parents."

Henry's heart beat erratically. All he wanted to do was wrap Emily in his arms and tell her everything would be alright. But it wasn't his place. Luke was her boyfriend and the boy's father. Henry was just a stand-in for the real deal—Emily's friend, nothing more. The truth punched him squarely in the gut. No matter how much he wanted Emily and Noah, someone else had all the rights.

Even if that man didn't seem to want them.

They hadn't been able to get hold of Luke last night. As a result, Henry, being the 'good friend' he was, had slept in the guest bedroom and taken the day off work. Adam and Charlotte were amazingly supportive and told Emily to take as long as needed.

Henry glanced at his watch. "What time does Noah's summer program finish at school?"

"Twelve-thirty."

"Plenty of time to visit Charlotte beforehand and pack a bag of clothes."

Emily nodded, her teeth biting a trembling bottom lip.

"Would you like me to go with you?" he asked gently, trying not to focus on her mouth.

"Please." Relief flooded her features briefly. "Unless there's somewhere you need to be?"

He smiled softly. "I'm exactly where I need to be."

For what felt like ages, she peered at him. He, in turn, met her searching gaze head-on, refusing to flinch. He wouldn't take back his words, whatever she was thinking. It was the truth. Her wellbeing was the most important thing to him.

Did that mean he loved…? His heartbeat sped up at the thought.

"Thank you," she murmured, her hair hiding pink cheeks as she dipped her head.

Charlotte took one look at Emily when they arrived and dragged her into a hug. "I'm so sorry to hear about your friends, Em. That poor little boy."

"T-thanks, Charlie."

A few seconds later, Charlotte broke the embrace and mouthed "Thank you" to Henry before showing them into the living room. A tray of drinks and mini pastries sat on the glass coffee table.

"Take a seat wherever you're comfortable." Charlotte's gaze moved from Emily to him. "Iced tea?"

"That'd be great."

Plopping down onto the smaller couch, Emily motioned for Henry to join her. When his thigh brushed against hers, and his body buzzed with awareness, he second-guessed his decision.

To heck with it! He'd enjoy being close to her for as long as possible.

Other than the ticking clock on the mantelpiece and an occasional rumble from a lawnmower outside, the house was quiet.

"Are your kids here?" he asked Charlotte.

Shaking her head, she poured their drinks. "They're at summer camp this week." She glanced at Emily. "It's during vacation times that I realize what a blessing you are, Em."

"Actually, that's one of the reasons I needed to talk to you."

"Oh?"

"The thing is,"—Emily accepted a glass from Charlotte and took a quick sip—"Sean and Lisa don't have any other family."

"Noah's an orphan?"

"Yes, and they made me his guardian in the event of their absence."

"Oh, wow." Charlotte schooled her shocked expression. "That complicates things."

"I feel awful," Emily said, looking anything but happy, "but considering the circumstances, I'm afraid I have to resign with immediate effect."

Smiling sympathetically, Charlotte patted her hand. "Don't worry, Em. God's timing is perfect. The kids are sorted for this week and the next. Adam and I will be able to juggle our schedules after that. Also, I'm sure that if we call his parents, they'd be thrilled that they get to spend more time with their grandchildren."

Emily sighed with relief. "I appreciate your understanding,

Charlie."

"Of course. Besides, I knew you wouldn't be our nanny for much longer anyway."

Henry raised a brow at Emily, who appeared as confused as he felt.

Charlotte shrugged. "I figured Luke would eventually whisk you away to New York."

"Luke?" Emily sounded surprised, as if she hadn't considered the possibility.

Hating the idea, Henry stifled a groan.

"Yes, although…" Charlotte trailed off, red creeping up her neck. "How does he feel about parenting a six-year-old?"

"Oh, there's no issue there." The corners of her lips curled up marginally. "Luke loves Noah," she said confidently. "But I'm staying here. I can't take Noah away from the only place he's ever known. His school, his friends, his church. I need to stay in New Haven for now."

The pesky knot in Henry's stomach loosened somewhat, and a look of relief filled Charlotte's face. "Oh, good," she said. "I'd hate to see you leave. Would Luke move here?"

Emily scratched her forehead. "Uh, no. I don't think he can. Working for my father… well, it's not something he wants to give up, and I'm not sure my dad would let him."

"So where does that leave you two? Your future?" Charlotte's blunt questioning had Henry shifting sideways, his knee knocking into Emily's.

She shot him a conflicted glance, then let out a big breath. "Honestly, Charlie, Noah is all I can think about right now."

A phone buzzed—Emily's. She skimmed the message. "Luke's on his way."

"Do you need to pick him up from the airport?" Charlotte asked.

"No, he's renting a car and meeting me at Noah's school." She laid a hand on Henry's thigh. "Would you mind driving me there after I've packed?"

"I'm here for you. Whatever you need." Squeezing her hand caused a spark of heat to travel along his skin. He ignored it.

"Thank you." She stood. "I won't take long."

The minute Emily was out of earshot, Charlotte gave him a pointed look. "Is there something you want to tell me?"

"What do you mean?" Casually crossing his arms, he leaned back.

"I see the way you look at her. I know you're friends, but I think it's more than that."

He swallowed and forced a neutral tone. "Did you forget I'm dating Britt or that Emily's not single?"

Charlotte's knowing smile as she scrutinized him almost made him cave. "I would never judge you, Henry. We don't choose who we fall in love with. Love chooses us. I just wouldn't want you to be settling, even if it's with my husband's amazing sister. Especially if your true love isn't the one you're dating."

He chuckled nervously. "Who said anything about true love? I think you're reading too much into my concern for Emily."

"Am I?" She shook her head, her smile widening. "Okay. Whatever helps you sleep at night. I know Adam's fiercely protective of his sister—if that's what you're worried about—but Britt can look after herself. It's your life, at the end of the day."

With a tight smile, Henry pushed to his feet. "I'll go see if Emily needs a hand."

***

Emily scanned her bedroom. She'd have to come back when there was more time. If they hurried now, they'd get to school with enough time for Henry to drop her off and be gone before Luke arrived and kicked up a fuss.

"Why the frown?"

Startling at the deep voice, she turned to see Henry leaning against the doorjamb.

"Just hoping I'm not forgetting something silly, like my toothbrush." She smiled tentatively while Henry reached for the larger of her suitcases.

"Alright." He looked skeptical but let it go.

During the short journey, Emily silently reviewed what she needed to organize: food for tonight, where Luke would sleep if he stayed the night, how she would break the news of Noah to her parents, and whether or not they'd insist she and Luke got married.

She felt a little breathless at the thought. Was she really ready to be married and become a family all in one go?

"You okay?" Henry glanced at her before focusing back on the road. "You've gone pale all of a sudden."

Lifting her hair into a temporary ponytail, she took deep breaths, then dropped it. "Just thinking about the enormity of the situation. Luke and I haven't been dating all that long. Certainly not long enough to be contemplating a future with our son already. I never imagined the possibility of a ring before Christmas, let alone being married by then."

No response.

Surprised, she cast a sideways glance at Henry. His fingers gripped the steering wheel, and he wore a stony expression. Whatever was going through his mind, they weren't happy thoughts. She knew he wasn't exactly fond of Luke, but if he wanted to be her friend, he'd have to deal with her boyfriend and the father of her child.

Henry cleared his throat. "Is that what you think will happen now?"

"What?"

"Luke proposing."

"Well, we've spoken about getting married—"

"You have?" he interrupted brusquely.

"Henry, we have a child together. It makes sense, don't you think?"

He muttered something she didn't quite catch.

"I don't think that's a good reason to have to spend your life with someone," he said gruffly.

Did he *seriously* think she'd marry Luke just because of Noah?

"I don't *have* to spend my life with anyone, Henry," she

said more forcefully than she intended. A flicker of hurt crossed his face, so she softened her tone. "Luke loves me. It's my choice."

He pulled into the school grounds and eased into a parking spot. Half-turning in his seat, he gave her a long, assessing look. "Do you love him?"

Luke climbed out of an SUV a short distance away, his expression cloudy. Distracted, Emily reached for the seatbelt release button. "Sorry, Henry, I'd better go. Thanks for everything."

As she opened the passenger-side door, Henry popped the trunk open. But when she went to retrieve her luggage, Henry was already there. Leaving it to him, she strode toward Luke and was immediately caught up in his embrace.

"Hey, beautiful." Seemingly oblivious to their audience, he kissed her like he hadn't seen her for weeks.

When they broke apart, her face felt hot.

"Shall I put these in your car, Luke?" Henry's tone bordered on unfriendly.

"That's not necessary. I'll take care of Em from here on out, thank you very much."

"Fine." Henry dropped the bags and strode away, his long legs eating up the distance to his vehicle.

"Henry, wait!" Emily called out a little too late.

Without any acknowledgment, Henry slipped into his car and slammed the door. Backing out quickly, his wheels spun as he drove away.

Luke closed the trunk, and Emily glowered at him. "Why did you treat him like that?"

"Like what?"

"A porter at a hotel."

Working his jaw, Luke walked over to her. His hands settled on her hips, and she stiffened.

"Sorry, Em. I just didn't expect to see him here when we're about to collect our son."

His smooth voice usually consoled her. Not this time. Instead, she bit back a retort at his lame excuse.

His gaze narrowed. "What *was* he doing with you anyway?"

"I know you find this hard to understand, but Henry's my friend," she said, keeping her tone even. "I needed support when I went to Charlotte's to resign. You weren't here and—" Emily stopped before she said something she'd regret.

Irritation flamed in Luke's eyes. "Well, I'm here now, and we could've done that together."

"I asked for your help first, Luke, but your job was more important." She rubbed her brow. "I had no clue you were coming."

"Hey." He tugged her closer. "I really am sorry. I spoke to your father and booked the helicopter as soon as I realized my mistake."

The school bell rang.

"Fine." She huffed out a breath. "Let's go get Noah."

As they strolled toward the line of parents, Luke scooped up her hand. "Em?"

She spared him a glance. "What?"

"Maybe don't mention who I am just yet. Noah's gonna have enough to adjust to. Let's wait until you and I make our relationship more permanent. Until we're able to adopt him as our son officially."

"I suppose that makes sense."

Noah suddenly appeared, running toward her with a bright smile and wide open arms. Mentally, she captured the photograph of her precious son looking so happy. Because once he knew about his parents' death, it'd be a while before she'd likely see it again.

Later that evening, the only thing that helped Noah get to sleep were the tablets the doctor prescribed. She and Luke watched him for a bit until Emily's cell buzzed, then she mouthed 'sorry' to Luke and wandered into the living room.

"Emily Quinn here."

"Miss Quinn, it's Officer Norton."

"Oh, hello."

"I have some new information regarding the accident. I

assumed you'd want to know."

Her heart thudded in her chest. "I do."

He cleared his throat. "It turns out Sean suffered a heart attack right after receiving a phone call from a Mr. Luke Bowman."

Emily gasped. "Luke's my boyfriend!"

"I thought so. We managed to retrieve a recording of the conversation from Lisa's phone. But I must warn you, it wasn't without conflict, and you may find it upsetting. Would you like me to play it back?"

"Please."

Emily listened intently.

"Sean, it's Luke."

"I told you, Luke, the discussion is over. Our son's too precious to us." Sean's voice sounded strained. "Right, Lisa?"

"Yes," Lisa responded firmly.

"I know," Luke said, "but Mr. Quinn insisted I try one last time. He's offering you one hundred million dollars to give up your rights as Noah's parents."

Emily was shocked to hear Luke's cold voice. It was like he was simply negotiating a business transaction, not his son's future.

"Unbelievable!" Lisa shouted. "Does Mr. Quinn *really* think he can put a price on our love? We'll never give Noah up, no matter how much money he throws at us." She sounded disgusted at the mere suggestion.

"Go back to your boss, Luke," Sean said, barely controlling his anger. "Tell him the answer is no and always will be."

Luke swore. "I didn't want it to come to this," he said, "but since you won't accept Mr. Quinn's very generous offer, he has no choice but to get his lawyers involved. Trust me, you won't win this battle."

"We'll see about that," Sean ground out. "Emily willingly signed Noah over to us."

"She may have done that, but she didn't consult Noah's father. And guess what, that's me. So when we get married and apply for custody, you'll not only lose your son, you'll also not get a cent from Mr. Quinn."

A high-pitched scream came next, followed by the squeal of rubber and the crunch of metal. Emily's breath caught in her throat, and her eyes slammed shut.

"Miss Quinn?"

Officer Norton's voice broke into the darkness, and her eyes flew open. "I-I'm here."

"Would you like me to send someone over?"

"N-no." She sank to the sofa, tears leaking like a broken faucet. "No, thank you. I'll be okay."

"Alright, but if you change your mind, please call."

"Okay."

Feeling numb all over, she dropped her phone into her lap. How could Luke have gone behind her back?

Then reality suddenly hit—her secret was no more. Her parents already knew all about Noah. How long had they known?

They'd been using Luke to get to their grandson, via her. She'd been a pawn in their game.

Did they know Luke was Noah's father?

They must have. Otherwise, why had they given up on the idea of Henry and her as a couple? They'd always wanted a strategic match. But what better way to cover their daughter's indiscretion than by getting her to marry her son's biological father?

Like an urn coming to temperature, heat flooded through Emily.

No doubt a considerable incentive was involved in this for Luke. Did he even want Noah? Or her? He'd never completely warmed up to Noah; intuitively, their son had known.

"Em, what's wrong?" Luke stood in the doorway, his hair ruffled, his eyes tired.

"How *could* you?" she spat, miraculously remembering to keep her voice low.

Pushing to her feet, she strode over to him and poked him in the chest. "You're the reason Sean crashed his car. You're the reason Noah no longer has parents."

Shock ricocheted across Luke's face. Stepping back, he held up his hands. "I don't know what you're talking about. It was an accident. We're Noah's parents."

"No," she hissed. "I'm his legal guardian now. The only thing you are is his biological father. Whatever deal my father made with you, forget it. It's never going to happen. You can stop pretending."

"Em, please—"

"What did my father promise you?" she asked, needing to know what had motivated Luke to get close to her and Noah.

"He didn't, it's not…" A curse escaped Luke's mouth, and he ran a hand over his mouth.

"Tell me," she said, her tone stern, unrelenting.

He hung his head and muttered, "CFO."

Steeling her expression, she growled, "I want you out of here."

When he didn't move, she pointed to the door. "Call Dad's pilot *now*, Luke. You two seem tight."

"Can we at least talk about this? Please?"

"No." She shook her head emphatically. "As far as I'm concerned, you and I are over."

Chapter Twenty-Eight

Well, that was unexpected. Henry stared at his cell phone.

"Hey, bud." Adam crossed their small office space to Henry's desk, his brow furrowed. "Something wrong with Emily?"

"She broke up with Luke last night."

He still couldn't believe it. When he'd answered Emily's call, her explanation about the accident and the events leading up to it made everything clearer. Yet he'd secretly imagined a different ending to that relationship. One where Emily realized she was in love with him. Not Luke turning out to be an underhanded spy for her parents while having his own agenda—one with job promotion as the motivating factor.

"I didn't see that coming," Adam said, folding his arms. His eyebrows bunched together and a muscle worked in his jaw. "Unless…"

"Unless, what?"

"How are things with Britt?"

Huh? What did *she* have to do with this?

"Good, actually." He nodded. Their relationship had been ticking over nicely. "Why do you ask, and what does that have to do with Emily?"

"Nothing, I was just…" Adam scratched the back of his neck. "Did she say why they broke up?"

Henry chuckled, still finding the whole situation rather

unbelievable. "It appears Luke was working for Emily's father in more ways than one."

"Seriously?"

"Yep. Dating her involved a plan to effectively buy Noah from his adoptive parents and force Emily and Noah to move to New York."

He flinched. "Ouch."

"Yeah, well, obviously that didn't work out."

"The lack of trust explains the breakup."

"Exactly."

Eager to release some pent-up frustration, Henry shot to his feet and paced. If Luke hadn't betrayed Emily, she'd still be dating him. Not Henry. Never him. Unreasonable as it sounded, that hurt. His insides twisted and ached with longing; longing to be the one she wanted to be with.

"There's Noah to think about now too," Adam said, stuffing his hands in his pockets. "I assume the last thing Emily wants to do is to relocate him while he's grieving the loss of his parents. What she needs right now is support from a good friend."

Stopping mid-stride, Henry stared at his friend.

Adam rubbed his temple. "You should take some time off, bud," he said, his tone earnest. "Go be that support. You've already secured plenty new donors for us. I can hold down the fort."

"I'm not sure—"

"If you're concerned about Britt, don't be." He gave an encouraging smile. "She'll understand. She trusts you. Just fill her in."

Shoulders slumping, Henry expelled a deep breath, grateful that Adam knew him so well. "Thanks, bud."

Adam patted his back. "Hey, remember, Emily's part of our family. I'd hate for her to feel isolated. Especially not after what Luke and her parents pulled."

Henry shut down his computer, snagged his keys and cell, and left. He called Britt on the way to his car, but it went straight to voicemail, so he left a message.

Next, he dialed Emily.

"Hey," she said almost immediately, "I didn't expect to talk to you again so soon."

"I can call tomorrow if you'd rather I spaced out our communications."

"No. No, I—"

"I'm just kidding. I told Adam about Luke, and he suggested I take some time off and help out a friend. I thought I'd come over and keep you company."

"That's really kind, but you don't need to disrupt your life for me. Besides, I'm not sure Britt would appreciate your spending time with me, even given the circumstances."

"Emily, you're my friend," he said, using his not-negotiable tone, "and friends are there for each other."

There was a long silence on the other end of the line, then, "Okay."

He grinned, even though she couldn't see him. "Great. See you in fifteen minutes."

"I'll fire up the coffee machine."

When Emily opened Sean and Lisa's front door, her smile seemed forced, and her eyes shone with unshed tears. Henry pulled her into a hug without a second's hesitation. As she held on tight, her slim body shuddered slightly.

If this was what she needed, he could stay here all day.

Eventually, she drew back, her hands resting on his chest. Sad-looking eyes lifted to his. "Thanks for coming." Her quiet voice wobbled.

"For you, anytime," he murmured, smiling softly.

Emily stepped back, dropping her hands, along with her gaze. "Um, I need caffeine."

A minute later, she handed him a steaming mug of freshly brewed coffee. "Here you go." Her fingers skimmed his, causing a spark.

He jerked his hand away, then sipped the coffee to cover his reaction, only to almost burn his tongue. Meanwhile, Emily spun back to the counter to finish fixing her drink.

She pointed to the far corner of the open living space.

"Shall we sit?"

"Sure."

While he chose the cozy loveseat, she sank into a single wingback opposite. He couldn't help feeling disappointed. He gently reminded himself that no matter how he felt about her, *he* had a girlfriend, and this woman had just ended a serious relationship.

"How is Noah?" he asked.

"Acting strong, mostly. Occasionally something reminds him of his mom or dad, then he breaks down and gets angry with himself. He keeps saying he's a wimp for crying." She screwed up her face. "*I* keep telling him he's not. That it's perfectly normal to be sad and upset when you lose someone you love. I've tried reassuring him, telling him they're in heaven, which is a much better place. You know, where there are no more tears, only laughter, joy, and love."

"He's so young. It's gotta be hard. At least he's not all alone. If Sean and Lisa hadn't made you his guardian…"

"I know. I'm so grateful they agreed," she said softly before her expression hardened. "Thank goodness I never told them Luke was Noah's dad. Can you imagine if I was stuck in a shared custody situation right now?"

Henry frowned. "Won't Luke be able to take legal action?"

"He could." She briefly pressed a finger under each eye. "But I have a feeling he won't." Drawing in a deep breath, she squared her shoulders. "He never wanted children in the first place. Although he may have grown fond of Noah, I'm convinced it was never his intention to be a family."

Heat built in Henry's chest as his protective instincts kicked in. He could barely reign in his anger. "You think he was just using you? For what? To get ahead in your parents' company?"

She nodded slowly. "He loved me, I believe that. But ambition has always been more important to him. Noah was definitely much further down his list than he should be," she said bitterly, anger blazing in her eyes.

Leaning forward, Henry placed a hand on her knee and

lowered his head to make eye contact. "I'm sorry he misled you, Emily. You don't deserve to be treated like that. Luke doesn't know what he's given up by being deceitful." He squeezed her leg, his voice dropping almost to a whisper. "I would never do that to you." The second the words were out, his chest constricted in pain.

Swallowing hard, he hauled his hand away and scrubbed it over his face. He was no better than Luke. His whole relationship with Britt was based on deception.

"Henry? What's wrong?"

Shifting back on the cushioned seat, his eyes darted to the open window. Tall, majestic, red maple trees swayed in the breezy backyard, reminding him of their Creator and of his Majestic Savior.

God would want him to be honest.

Taking a fortifying breath, he faced Emily, who stared at him confused. Though he yearned to smooth out the worry wrinkles on her forehead, he kept his physical distance. If he didn't, he'd end up kissing her.

"I need to tell you something." His voice came out strained.

"What?" she whispered.

Clearing his throat, he leaned forward. "You considered me a playboy when we met, right? Someone who didn't date a woman more than a couple times before breaking it off."

She started to shake her head. "I don't—"

He waved his hand to stop her. "No, you were right. I wasn't ready to settle down, so I purposefully acted like a man incapable of being in a committed relationship." He half-smiled, half-grimaced. "Until I met you."

"Henry."

"Let me finish," he said roughly. "You wouldn't date me, so I decided on a game plan. Britt agreed to go out with me so you'd see I *could* commit to someone for more than two seconds."

Scowling at him, she crossed her arms. "So you've been using Britt this whole time? I don't see how that's any better."

"No, that's not the way—" He rubbed his hand over his jaw. "Britt needed my protection. It was a mutually beneficial arrangement." Emily's eyebrows almost hit her hairline. "A couple of male co-workers in Hartford—rather unsavory characters, according to Britt—made some unwelcome advances. She struggled to ward them off, so a pretend boyfriend was the obvious solution."

"Was it now?" An unsmiling Emily rose to her feet, her expression impossible to read. Searching eyes snagged his, and he wished he could read her mind.

He stood too, his heart thumping in his chest, praying he hadn't made a complete mess and ruined any hope of more than friendship with the only woman he'd ever wanted.

"I suppose now that I'm free," Emily said, her voice suddenly catching, "you're planning on breaking things off with her."

***

Henry, his gaze sparking with intent, moved to close the distance between them. In turn, Emily's pulse increased alarmingly, and her eyes dipped to his mouth. Instantly, she wanted to be back in his arms, his lips on hers, feeling like she was home again.

How could she feel this way? She'd literally just broken up with Luke—the man she thought she loved. Disgusted with herself, she dragged her eyes from Henry's enticing mouth and stepped back. His tender gaze followed her, flooding her body with warm tingles. Though she shook her hands to rid herself of them, it did nothing.

Why hadn't she gotten over Henry by now? Trying to convince herself that what she felt for the man was just affection was useless. She may have loved Luke, but she was head over heels in love with Henry. Knowing Henry was a believer and could love her differently than Luke made all the difference. Because of their shared faith, Henry's love would come with a deeper connection. And that mattered. If she had married Luke, their marriage would've been superficial, based on physical intimacy and their child.

Of course, Henry wasn't perfect—his ruse with Britt demonstrated that.

Emily didn't particularly like that he felt the need to fake a relationship to prove something to her. But it meant he was serious about his intentions, didn't it?

As Henry edged closer to her, his eyes darkened. "I think you know what I want, Emily." His husky voice sent shivers over her skin. "What I've always wanted."

The moment his eyes sank to her mouth, a magnetic force she had no control over pushed her in his direction. All she could think about was kissing him. Strong hands slipped around her waist, drawing her flush against a firm chest. Her hands, of their own accord, slid up Henry's muscular arms to his shoulders. A musky scent invaded her nostrils, and her heart raced like crazy. With her eyes stuck on his, she couldn't look away even if she'd wanted to.

"Emily, I..." Henry murmured.

Not daring to move, Emily could barely breathe.

Lifting one hand off her waist, Henry's gentle fingers then reached up to stroke her cheek before trailing a path to the back of her neck. He leaned in, and her eyes closed. Warm, firm lips moved over hers, soft yet demanding, tender but firm. While she'd imagined a repeat of their first kiss a million times over, never in her wildest dreams had it even come close to being like this—utter perfection.

A soft moan escaped her lips, and she wrapped her arms around his neck. With a groan, Henry tightened his hold. Emily lost herself in his thorough kiss, which he eventually broke to plant tantalizingly brief kisses across her jawline.

"This is where I want to be," he whispered in her ear, his warm breath touching her skin. "*You* are exactly who I want to be with."

Goosebumps erupted everywhere, and she struggled to focus on anything but the man melting her insides, reaching to her very core.

"Henry," she murmured.

Before she could say more, his mouth was back on hers, the

kiss deepening fast. Sensations she'd never experienced in her life filled her, and she worried she'd have no self-control if this continued any longer.

Lord, please give us the strength not to take this too far.

As if in immediate answer to her prayer, Henry's cell rang with a unique ringtone. He pulled away, and she immediately felt the loss. Like a part of her was missing.

"I have to take this," he said, his expression regretful as he brought the phone to his ear. "Hi, Mom."

Hauling in a deep breath to steady herself, Emily collected their mugs and wandered to the sink to rinse them before sticking them in the dishwasher.

"What? No." Henry's strangled cry and grief-stricken face sent a fission of alarm through her.

Her eyes flew to his. What on earth had happened? Should she leave the room? Or stay to lend him support?

Henry beckoned her over, taking the decision out of her hands. When she reached him, he wrapped an arm around her waist and pressed a kiss on top of her head.

"Please don't worry, Mom. I'll be there as soon as I can." He nodded at something she said. "Yes, he's in good hands. The best." He went quiet for a few seconds. "I love you, too."

Sliding his cell into his pocket, he turned to face her.

"Your dad?"

He nodded solemnly. "They think he's had a stroke, but they aren't ruling out a brain tumor. They're sending him for an MRI right now."

"I'm so sorry, Henry. That's so scary."

"I have to go." His gaze bore into hers, his fingertips reaching out to stroke her lips, her cheek.

Covering his hand with hers, she put a stop to the delicious torture. Sure, they needed to talk. They weren't a done deal just because she'd kissed him back. He had a girlfriend. Guilt wracked through her, and she slowly shifted out of his embrace.

"Go, Henry. I completely understand."

A muscle twitched in his jaw. "I don't know when or if I'll

be back. My family needs me. Mom needs me." He croaked out the last few words, his eyes glistening with unshed tears. "But you…"

Oh, this man! He was trying to figure out how to be in two places at once. Her heart went out to him.

"Hey, don't worry about me." She brushed her fingers over his upper arm. "I'll be fine. All I have to do is call Charlotte; she'll be over in a heartbeat. In fact, Noah and I might just crash at hers until we get ourselves settled. It's a long summer. Once his summer camp is finished, I may even take him abroad for the holidays to get his mind off everything."

"Would…would you consider coming to New York instead? With Noah, obviously." She heard the hope in his voice, saw the light that had gone from his eyes after the phone call, return.

Shaking her head, she again put distance between them. "I can't do that, Henry. I won't. Not right now, and maybe not ever."

An emotion she couldn't identify flashed across his face.

"There's an excellent chance I'll have to step in for my dad for a few weeks, maybe even permanently. What if I can't come back to New Haven?"

She kept her tone even though the rip in her heart had begun. "Then you'll be in New York, and I'll be here."

"As simple as that?"

"Yes."

"I see," he ground out, his eyes narrowing. "You're not prepared to compromise even a little bit?"

"No. This isn't a sudden decision, Henry. You've known how I felt about New York from the beginning of our friendship."

Hurt shot across his features as he pointed between them. "That's all this is to you, a friendship?"

They hadn't made any declarations or promised each other anything. Their kisses had been intense and wonderful. More than wonderful, incredible, but kisses did not make a relationship.

"Yes." Saying the word tore a hole in her chest. But she needed to release him. "Unless there's something I don't know, Britt's still your girlfriend."

That was the truth, no matter the reason Henry and Britt's relationship had originally begun.

Emily tilted her head. "You should be asking her to go to New York with you."

He opened his mouth and closed it. Then, with a tiny shake of his head, he raised his hands and muttered, "Okay. Fine."

Spinning on his heel, he left without another word.

Chapter Twenty-Nine

Over the next two months, Henry's father's health was never far from his mind. Nor was the blonde-haired woman with the mesmerizing brown eyes he'd left behind in New Haven. Emily's admission that they were nothing more than friends —their kisses notwithstanding—hurt more than he cared to admit.

After a long day in the office, he'd collapse into bed—the same one he'd slept in before leaving for college over fourteen years ago—and his thoughts would wander to Emily and their incredible kisses. Stealing his breath away, they'd ignited intense feelings of rightness in him and of home. And she'd convinced him she felt the same by responding with equal amounts of passion and tenderness.

Obviously, he'd been wrong.

Emily had been right about one thing—he did have a girlfriend, even if his heart hadn't ever truly been in the relationship.

Rather than ask Britt to accompany him to New York, he'd used his long days and huge responsibilities as an excuse not to see her. Then, when her daily texts slowed and eventually stopped, he'd been too busy to worry why.

Three weeks later, she surprised him by reaching out.

They exchanged awkward greetings before she declared, "I've fallen in love."

"Really?" He wasn't shocked; more like grateful.

"It's true, I had a major crush on you, Henry, but it wasn't love. With Jeff and I, the chemistry is off the charts. We go together like pumpkin and spice. Like ketchup and cheese."

He chuckled at her crazy comparisons. "Jeff, huh?"

"Please don't be mad. I wasn't looking for love, honest."

Relieved, he wished Britt the best and released her from their relationship.

A week later, she called in tears.

"Jeff doesn't feel the same! All that flirting? Apparently, it's just because he's a friendly guy. I must've imagined the chemistry between us." She sniffed. "Who leads someone on then rejects them?" She paused to blow her nose. "Thank goodness my work contract ended today. Please let me come to New York and work in one of your hotels. I'll do anything: reception cover, server in a restaurant, even cleaning if I must," she begged, sounding desperately unhappy.

Agreeing, he'd set her up in an apartment near his parents' Fifth Avenue penthouse and organized her an administrative job at Head Office. Since they hadn't told anyone of their breakup, he and Britt resumed their fake relationship, which kept Henry's mother off his back and helped Britt in her attempt to get over a broken heart.

If he thought Britt's presence would numb his rejected and aching heart, he was sadly mistaken. Instead, it made him crave stability more.

Finally ready to settle down and live the life he'd been born for, the only woman he could picture beside him, wearing his grandmother's ring, wasn't the brunette, blue-eyed bombshell he was supposedly dating. Nope. Emily's bright smile, soft heart, and beautiful laugh were what he craved.

Last weekend, he'd casually asked after Emily during a flying visit to see Adam and Charlotte with Britt. The couple had shared a strange look—one Henry decided not to try and interpret.

"Oh, I thought you knew," Charlotte had answered with false brightness. "Emily took Noah to Europe for the summer.

They'll be back when school re-opens in September."

Like the final curtain of a play, it signaled their friendship was well and truly over. Emily hadn't even bothered to text him her plans.

In his quiet time that morning, Henry poured out his heart to God. "Lord, this perpetual daily loop is making me feel despondent. I need your wisdom and direction in my life. Please help me to trust your perfect plans. Amen."

With peace flowing over him, Henry decided breakfast before work would make a nice change.

"Morning, son." Robert Palmer sat at the family dining table, a poached egg on his plate and a glass of orange juice in his hand.

Grinning, Henry crossed the marble floor to stop beside his father's chair. "You're up!" he said, squeezing his bony shoulder.

"It's about time, don't you think?" Blue-gray eyes sparkled as a slow smile spread over his mildly wrinkled face.

"Uh, yeah. I guess." Henry dropped into a seat opposite his father.

How long had it been since Dad looked so healthy? Certainly not since the surgery eight weeks ago. Had it really been that long living with his parents again? Henry shook his head in amazement. He supposed running a multi-billion-dollar company while worrying about his sixty-four-year-old father, recovering from a benign brain tumor, *had* been a full-time challenge.

Despite a successful operation, the recovery process hadn't been a walk in the park. For way too long, his salt-and-pepper-haired father had lain under gray satin sheets, his ashen face blending perfectly with his surroundings. Each morning on his way into the office, Henry had checked in on him. Seeing his lifeless body on the king-sized bed? Not comforting at all.

"You've done a good job of holding down the fort, son, but it's time I resumed control."

Dad's commanding voice brought Henry back to the

present. "Has doc given his approval?"

"Yep. I'm good to go."

Wow, that was good news for the family. But as acting CEO of his father's company, Henry had enjoyed putting his Harvard degrees into practice. He'd learned a lot while managing the company, and his significant involvement in important decisions had been both exhilarating and terrifying.

His face must've fallen because Dad gave him a sympathetic look and held up his hand. "Don't think you get to leave, son. I've been hearing nothing but good things from the board of directors. From all they've said, you're well on your way to the position I've had in mind for the past few years." Rubbing his hands together, Dad chuckled. "I can finally see myself retiring in the not-too-distant future."

Henry frowned. "I thought you wanted me to be settled here with a wife and family before you even considered such a thing?"

"Wife?" Mom waltzed into the room, her hair perfectly styled and wearing a freshly pressed suit.

If he remembered correctly, she was going out to meet friends for brunch.

"You finally asked Britt to marry you!" The hopeful, excited look on her face instantly made him feel guilty. "I take it she said yes?"

"I—"

"Actually, Denise, we were talking about him taking over some of my responsibilities at the office." Dad's eagle eyes shot to Henry. "*Are* you marrying Britt, son?"

"I—"

Mom cut off his reply by hauling him into a firm embrace. "I can't tell you how happy I am you're getting married," she whispered in his ear. "Britt will make a lovely wife."

Easing back, she cupped his cheeks and scrutinized his face. "I had thought, no wished that you and Em…" She shook her head, her smile drooping momentarily. "Never mind." Her smile resurfaced. "Britt's wonderful."

Henry blinked rapidly, an all too familiar ache spreading through his chest. A throbbing pain, not too dissimilar to when he'd fallen out a tree and onto his arm as a kid, took hold. Ultimately, his broken humerus had healed—but he wasn't sure this pain would ever leave.

Swiftly masking those feelings, he narrowed his eyes at his mother. He didn't need her getting her hopes up on either count. "Mom."

She cleared her throat. "Don't have a long engagement," she said in a hushed tone. "The sooner you take over from your father, the less worried I'll be about his health."

"Mom," he repeated more firmly. "I haven't asked Britt to marry me."

"Oh, I thought..."

He shook his head. "Not yet."

"Oh, okay." She chuckled nervously. "Sorry I jumped the gun."

"It's alright." Ready for this conversation to end, he glanced at his watch. "Don't you need to leave?"

"Oh, yes! Yes, I do." She rushed to kiss her husband's cheek, then called out, "See you later," on her way out the door.

Dad stood. "Wait here, son. I'll be right back."

"O-kay."

His appetite gone, Henry poured himself a cup of coffee. A minute later, Dad returned carrying a small black box.

Henry's brow raised. "Is that what I think it is?"

"Your mom wanted you to have this. For when you do decide..." Snapping open the lid, he revealed a stunning antique ring that had Henry's heart speeding up. His sisters had once begged Mom to let them have it, but she'd waved them off, declaring the ring was for her firstborn's wife and no one else. Afterward, Henry had taken Mom aside and asked her to reconsider giving it to Lauren, his eldest sister.

Obviously, that had never happened, and besides, Lauren wasn't even in a relationship.

Henry gazed at the two-carat diamond solitaire, flanked by

eight tiny round diamonds. It was an elegant ring and deserved to adorn his beloved's finger.

His gaze slid to his father's. He swallowed. "Thanks, Dad."

"Make sure you do it justice, son. I look forward to congratulating your fiancée." His expression turned solemn. "Sooner rather than later."

Henry nodded despite the tightness in his stomach and throat. Slipping the box into his jacket pocket, he forced a smile. "I'd better get to the office."

"You do that." Dad retook his seat. "And I'll join you on Monday."

The town car ride to Palmer Enterprises went by in a blur. Henry spent it considering what his father's imminent return to the office meant for him. Dad needed to be confident that his son was ready before he'd contemplate retiring.

How long did that leave him? Six months, maybe a year, to get his life in order?

The last thing Henry wanted was to be officially taking the reins at the same time as planning a wedding or even being newly married—because that was what was expected of him, to be married when he became CEO of Palmer Enterprises.

He groaned in frustration. He was in serious trouble.

***

Emily stared at her reflection in the mirror and sighed.

Just one more week in New York. One more week of this knot in her stomach and the constant looking over her shoulder. Running into Henry and his girlfriend? The last thing she wanted.

She couldn't wait to establish a routine for her and Noah back in New Haven.

Pushing back from the mahogany dressing table, she walked over to the matching nightstand and grabbed her phone. With a smile, she tucked it into her fuchsia pink Birkin purse. The generous gift from her mother—and likely a peace offering—had been a total surprise.

Emily had been livid when her parents tracked her and Noah down at their hotel in Prague. After organizing a nanny to watch Noah, she'd sat them down and had it all out with them. They had begged her forgiveness for their interference, for manipulating Luke, and for invading her privacy. In return, she had apologized for keeping her pregnancy a secret. Countless tears were shed, followed by warm embraces.

Later, Mom and Dad met their grandson.

"Oh, Em, he's the cutest, most handsome boy I've ever seen!" Mom declared.

Thrusting out his chest, Dad beamed as he shook Noah's little hand. Clearly, he agreed with his wife's assessment.

"We'd love to stay and get to know Noah. If you'll let us?"

Emily relented, and the week flew by. Especially once Noah overheard his nana say they were in the golden city of a hundred spires. Then the youngster insisted they visit all of them.

As her parents were leaving the Prague hotel, Noah had nudged Emily's arm to get her attention and then clasped his hands like he was praying. "Please can we go to New York with Nana and Papa? They promised they'd show me all the cool places."

She'd eyed her parents' innocent faces and guilty smiles, then her son's adorable, pleading expression and relented. Fortunately, returning to the States a week earlier than planned wasn't an issue. It gave her a chance to see how Noah would cope with being in a big city.

Amazingly, he loved it.

All the cookies, milkshakes, and candy he consumed? That made her second guess her decision. Preventing her parents from showering their grandchild with anything and everything, including their undivided attention, was useless. They were totally besotted, and honestly, the admiration went both ways. Seeing her family so happy together filled her with joy. The gaping hole left by a certain dark-haired Casanova? Stubbornly, that remained.

Although the adoption process had officially begun, she hadn't insisted on Noah calling her Mom. He had enough to deal with, so she tried to keep things as normal as possible. Part of that would mean living in Sean and Lisa's house on their return to New Haven. It suited their needs and was within walking distance of Noah's school. When she mentioned it to her parents yesterday, they made no qualms about how they felt.

"You owe it to Noah to find him a school here." Mom's eyes had begged for understanding, her tone half desperate. "We're his grandparents, and he needs his family around him. We want a relationship with our grandson. Doesn't he deserve that, at least?"

Noah had formed a special bond with her parents in Europe, and it did worry her how it would affect him if they went home and couldn't visit every weekend.

"I know you and Luke aren't together anymore, and we're to blame for that—"

"It's not entirely your fault, Mom," Emily had interrupted.

"Even so. Noah still needs his father, and Luke is here."

Emily didn't want to see Luke. His betrayal still hurt too much. Still, she knew that, in time, she'd have to for Noah's sake, if nothing else. Luke still worked for her father, so there was that too.

Funny enough, Noah hadn't mentioned Luke much over the summer. On the other hand, Henry had been brought up on too many occasions. According to Mom, Henry had remained in New York, and Britt was with him. It was hard to be annoyed. After all, he'd done exactly as she suggested.

Sometimes, Emily fell into a daydream where she and Henry were together, Noah their son. Touching her lips, she'd relive their kisses and remember Henry's whispered words, "This is where I want to be. *You* are exactly who I want to be with," and she'd melt all over again.

If only she'd said yes and agreed to go anywhere with him, even New York. Her heart ached terribly, knowing she'd chosen New Haven over being with the man she loved. But she had to learn to live without him in her life.

As hard as it was.

What didn't help were the rumors running rampant in New York's elite circles. Apparently, Henry, the most eligible bachelor in the city, was on the brink of proposing. It made sense. He needed to marry to take over Palmer Enterprises.

Swallowing down a sob, Emily shook her head and squared her shoulders. After pressing beneath her eyes, she left her bedroom suite.

"There you are!" Mom set her hands on her hips and smirked at Emily as she entered the kitchen. "Noah and I were about to come and tickle you out of bed, weren't we, Noah?"

"Yes, Nana."

Noah turned to Emily and pouted. "Mommy, you slept so long! Now the sun will be too hot for us to go to the zoo."

Her heart quickened at registering his words and tears sprung to her eyes. Stepping over to her son, she pulled him to her and held on tight. "You called me Mommy," she said, her voice cracking.

Noah wriggled in her arms. "Hey! You're squishing me. I can't breathe."

Laughing, she released him. "Sorry."

His brow furrowed. "You said I could call you Mommy because you're adopting me."

"I did and I am." Touching his cheek, she met her mother's glistening gaze and smiled.

"Can we still go to the zoo?" Noah's voice rose a notch, his big brown eyes brightening as his smile grew. "Maybe Mr. Henry could come! Nana said he's in New York, like us."

Emily's heart stuttered, and she shook her head. "I'm so sorry, Noah. He's not on vacation, sweetheart. He's working."

"He can't work *all* day," he whined. Emily shot him a sharp look, and he immediately adjusted his tone. "I miss him. If you call him, I know he'll want to come."

Emily closed her eyes for a brief second. Oh, the innocence of a child. If only it were that easy.

She offered a compromise. "Why don't we see if we can ride in a carriage around the park before we visit the zoo?"

Crossing his arms, Noah pursed his lips. "I don't want to go if Mr. Henry can't come."

"Will you go if Papa and I join you, Noah?" Mom coaxed, her arm on his shoulder.

With an exaggerated sigh, Noah lifted his shoulders, then dropped them. A mischievous look entered his eyes as a slow grin lifted his lips. "Yes, if I can get an ice cream cone too."

"Deal," Mom quickly responded with a wink at Emily.

Noah ran off to brush his teeth while Mom went to get Dad. In the meantime, Emily ate a few strawberries and a pancake. Her gaze drifted to the floor-to-ceiling glass windows on the far side of the vast open-plan kitchen, where the Manhattan skyline was a sight to behold. Her vision blurred slowly, and her throat felt scratchy.

Was Henry enjoying running his father's company? Did he miss her at all?

Rubbing a fist against her chest, she drew in a deep breath.

Then again, with the stunning Britt at his side, why would he give her a second thought? The woman was exactly what he needed in a wife: beautiful, single, and most of all, childless.

Chapter Thirty

"It's your last night here; go enjoy yourself," Mom said, practically pushing Emily out of the apartment. "Noah and I have a popcorn-and-movie date."

Laughing, Emily made her way to the trendy bar and restaurant where she'd agreed to meet some old school friends. Once there, she soaked in the familiar decor of her old hangout. Her last time there, she hadn't been old enough to drink, and Luke had been her boyfriend.

Crazy.

Luke's betrayal still caused a fleeting pain in her chest. Forgiving him hadn't been easy. But, after traveling Europe with Noah, she'd finally let it go and handed the hurt over to God.

Minutes later, the four women clinked glasses.

"So, tell us about your life in New Haven, Em," Jenna, senior year cheer captain, instructed. Raven curls still framed her pixie face all these years later. "Are there lots of hot guys? Are you dating anyone?"

Fellow squad members Stacy and Kimberly leaned in, their eyes glued to Emily.

Heat rushed to her face at the memories of Henry's handsome face and kind smile. Ducking her head, she swiftly banished them.

When Emily could be certain she wore a neutral expression, she raised her eyes. "Nope. I'm single." She sighed theatrically. "All the great guys I've met are either in relationships or married."

"Pity. I was thinking we could all crash at yours for a weekend." Jenna glanced at the others. "Wouldn't that be fun?"

They nodded enthusiastically.

"It'd be like old times, right?" Jenna continued. "Except, if you're serious about no available hotties, Em, we could hit the nightclubs and drown our sorrows instead."

Emily's stomach muscles knotted. She wasn't ready to mention Noah. Besides, revealing her secret would put a damper on this evening—the last thing she wanted.

"You'd be bored, Jenna. New Haven's mostly full of families and Yale students. Besides, my place is tiny," she hedged, hoping to put them off.

"Ooh, but I bet lots of them are getting Master's or Ph.D.'s." Toying with a lock of copper-colored hair, Kimberly's gaze turned dreamy. "And what about all those hunky professors?"

Emily frowned. "I guess…"

Stacy flipped bleached hair over bare shoulders, her dark blue eyes sparkling. "I heard New Haven's got an amazing music scene," she said in a know-it-all voice. "I'd love to experience the small-town atmosphere. Go to a couple of concerts."

"Me too!" Grinning, Kimberly clapped her hands.

"Your table's ready, ladies." A slim, middle-aged woman with a foreign accent Emily couldn't quite place beckoned them forward. Relieved at the interruption, she grabbed her purse and Coke.

Once everyone was seated, the conversation moved to what food to order, and Emily breathed a sigh of relief. She was off the hook. For now.

Throughout the meal, she stuck to soda while wine flowed freely among her friends. Other customers occasionally gave them the side-eye. Even so, hearing about their antics and failed relationships was entertaining.

Dessert dishes had just been cleared when Jenna's eyes bugged out. "Is that?" She fanned flushed cheeks. "Oh. My. Gosh. That's one GQ specimen!"

"You can say that again, Jen." Stacy's voice was low and sultry. "Doesn't he look super-hot in an Armani suit?"

Curious, Emily half turned in her seat and stilled. Henry stood just inside the door, his eyes searching the large room. When his gaze snagged on hers, his eyes widened. A slow, tentative smile touched his lips, and he strode directly to her.

"He's coming this way!"

Startled by Kimberly's shrill voice, Emily spun back, her heart jumping erratically.

What were the chances?

"Quick, Stace! How do I look?" Jenna whisper-shouted, fingers fiddling with her hair. A second later, her pointed gaze spun toward Emily. "Why was Henry Palmer staring at you? Do you know him?"

She could only nod.

"Hey, Emily." Henry's deep voice caused goosebumps to break out all over her skin. Though his eyes remained solely on her, his gorgeous smile slipped. "I didn't expect to see you here," he said softly.

"I-I'm visiting my parents," she stuttered.

What was wrong with her? Acting like a love-struck teenager!

Henry ran a hand through his already ruffled hair. "Not what I meant."

Snapping her lips together, Emily took a fortifying breath and squared her shoulders. "What are *you* doing here?" she asked.

His gaze skittered from her momentarily before returning. "I'm meeting—"

"Em?" Jenna grasped her wrist. "Aren't you going to introduce us?"

"Yes, Em. Great idea." Stacy hopped to her feet with a flirtatious smile.

"Fine." Standing, she motioned to the three women.

"Henry, these are friends from high school. Jenna, Stacy, and Kimberly."

Henry, being a gentleman—one of the things she loved about him—shook their hands and allowed them to introduce themselves fully. After entertaining small talk, he touched Emily's shoulder and leaned in. "Can we go someplace private to talk?"

"Sure. I was about to leave anyway."

Casting her eyes over her friends, Emily smiled. "It was great catching up. I'll be in touch."

They exchanged hugs, each with a comment: "You're so lucky," "You'd better tell us everything next time," and "How could you have held out on us, Em?"

Chuckling, she trailed Henry out of the bar.

The minute they were outside, he turned to face her, leaving hardly any distance between them.

"I thought you didn't want to be in New York," he accused, his expression guarded. "I thought you'd still be mad at your parents."

She crossed her arms. "A lot has happened in the past couple months."

Sadness settled in his features and his voice softened. "Charlotte said you went to Europe. Why didn't you tell me?"

"You knew it was a possibility. I mentioned it before..." Emily trailed off and pursed her lips. "I needed Noah to feel completely comfortable with me. To give him a chance to deal with his grief."

"And did it work out?"

"Mostly." She nodded. "My parents tracked us down, and, to cut a long story short, I've forgiven them. They deserve to know their grandchild."

"What about Luke?"

Tilting her head, she blinked. "What about him?"

"Have you forgiven him?" Henry's whole body appeared tense as if holding his breath.

"Yes."

Swallowing hard, his posture sagged.

Unable to bear his defeated expression, Emily gripped his upper arms, the solid muscles beneath her fingers sending shivers of awareness through her. She looked him straight in the eye. "Henry, Luke and I are never ever getting back together. Not for Noah or anyone."

His body relaxed, and she sighed, dropping her hands.

"How's your dad?" she asked, smiling softly.

"Going back to work on Monday."

"Wow, that's great!"

Except, why the furrowed brow?

"Isn't that what you want? For him to release you so you can go home?"

Shifting away slightly, Henry folded his arms. "I'm not going back to New Haven."

"Oh. I thought..." She gave a small shake of her head. "Never mind."

Did she really think that now his dad was better, Henry would return to his life in New Haven? To her?

How easily she'd forgotten about Britt, his *actual* girlfriend.

Tears pricked her eyes.

"It was good to see you, Henry. I don't want to keep you from your date." Hopefully he hadn't noticed her scratchy-sounding voice.

"It's not—" Distracted, he pulled out his phone and held up a finger. "Wait. This conversation isn't over." He scanned the screen and typed a rapid reply. Then, after rubbing the middle of his forehead, his conflicted gaze met hers. "She's canceled."

"Oh, okay."

So now what?

"Emily, listen," he said, his eyes imploring and his hands clutched together. "I know a quiet place we can get a drink. Come with me, please? There's more I want to say."

***

Henry placed a steaming cappuccino on the table in front of Emily.

"Thanks." Her tight smile didn't bode well, but he wasn't about to let that deter him. No matter what was happening in his personal life, this was more important. She was more important.

He dropped his jacket onto the chair opposite before checking out the sparsely occupied restaurant. A few couples remained after rush hour, talking quietly over dessert and coffee.

"You didn't want a coffee?"

Bringing his gaze back to Emily, he took a seat. "I changed my mind." More like his churning stomach decided for him.

Emily gripped her mug, refusing to meet his eyes. If she held it much longer, she'd have burn marks.

Was he making her nervous or tense?

He ducked his head, made eye contact. "Are you okay?"

"I'm fine."

Any man with half a brain cell knew *that* answer meant a woman was *not* fine.

Prying her hot hands away from the mug, he blew on them gently.

"Emily," he said gruffly. Her head lifted, exposing a wide-eyed stare and reddish cheeks. Ignoring an ineffectual tug from her hands, he swept his thumb over her knuckles instead.

"To clarify," he said, "I'm staying because my father's job is what I was born to do, and I've loved every minute." She raised a questioning brow, and he chuckled. "Well not everything, but certainly the majority. I'm finally putting my degrees to good use and I'm ready to start the rest of my life. Here in the city."

"I'm glad you've had an epiphany, Henry." She slid her hands out of his and into her lap. For a fleeting moment, she stared down at them. "I pray everything goes well for you."

After one sip of coffee, she set her mug down and rose to her feet.

"Wait!" Henry jumped up, his heart thundering.

A small object clattered onto the wooden floor. As he

crouched to pick it up, his stomach clenched uncomfortably. Of all the times!

"Is that what I think it is?" Emily spoke so quietly that he almost didn't hear her.

Grimacing, he hid it in his inside jacket pocket and nodded.

"Show me." Emily's tone was hard, her voice more confident.

He blinked.

"Henry."

He gave her a pleading look. "Please don't make me do this."

Steely eyes bore into him. Great, she wasn't going to budge.

Rounding the table, he stopped close enough to see the honey flecks in her beautiful brown eyes. With a heavy sigh, he dragged out the tiny black box—the one he'd been carrying around for the past week, hoping he'd bump into her.

At their brunch last week, Emily's mom had mentioned to Henry's that Emily and Noah were staying with them. Knowing she was in New York but not in contact had been torture. Still, he reckoned if he could just have five minutes with her, he might be able to win her heart and convince her to stay. And God willing, make a life with him.

In light of his decision, Britt had graciously agreed to 'break off' their fake relationship. Henry figured he'd deal with the fallout if his plan didn't work.

"Open it," Emily demanded, bringing him back to the present.

He frowned. This was so not the way he wanted her to find out.

"Fine." Slowly, he lifted the lid to reveal the antique engagement ring.

Emily's hand flew to her mouth. "Oh, it's…"

"Wow. You're speechless." A smile tugged at the corner of his mouth. "That's a first."

Eyes on the verge of tears met his. Ridiculous. Why?

"It's the most stunning ring I've ever seen." A soft voice matched her tender expression. Seconds later, all trace of warmth disappeared. "So, when are you planning on proposing?"

"I'm not sure."

"Why not?" She sounded huffy. "I assume you've been thinking about it for a while."

"I have, but the timing may not be right." He wished he knew what she was thinking. "I'm in two minds."

Confusion flashed in her eyes. "That's never a good thing. If a man's going to propose to the woman he loves, he should be one hundred percent sure it's what he wants." Her gaze drifted to his open hand as if the piece of jewelry contained some sort of magical pull.

He stifled a maniacal laugh. Now he was definitely projecting.

"Don't you want to get married, Henry?"

"I do. It's time I settled down and became the man my father expects me to be." He twisted his lips. "But I was hoping to do that with the right woman."

"The right woman? You mean Britt?"

Huh? Henry's mind raced while his heart rate doubled as if to catch up. Why would she say that? Maybe she just wanted to be certain?

Glancing away, he wondered if he was making the wrong assumptions.

"You don't seem sure of yourself." Emily's words forced his attention back to her. "If I were Britt, I'd be extremely concerned." Setting her hands on her hips, her eyes sparked with annoyance. "I think you need to explain yourself, Mr. Palmer."

He stuffed the ring box back into its hiding place, then ran his hand over his hair and held the back of his neck. Peering at her intently, he shrugged. "Well, the right woman turned me down, so now…"

Her eyes widened the second she clocked his meaning, and

her mouth formed a cute *O*.

Henry almost groaned aloud at the strong urge to pull her into his arms and taste those adorable lips. But to risk rejection? Nope, he couldn't do it. Even if it meant experiencing torture of the worst kind.

"But you brought Britt to New York. Don't you love her?"

"Actually, Britt begged to come. And I do love her. Just not like I love—"

A finger shot out and covered his lips. "Don't," Emily whispered, her expression softening while her eyes suddenly danced.

Hope swelled in his chest, and he clutched her hand. Ever so gingerly, he pressed his lips to each fingertip in turn. She let out a soft moan, her eyes filled with longing.

"Henry." The tenderness in her voice was the last straw.

With one hand, he brought her flush against him, her soft body fitting perfectly against his hard muscles. While his eyes drank in every beautiful curve, his fingers feathered the outline of her face.

Man, he *had* to kiss her.

Powerless to resist, he pressed his lips to hers and drew back. Their eyes locked, and Emily hesitantly wrapped her arms around his neck. When she kissed him back, he was a goner. Like thirsty travelers coming across a water fountain, they drank each other in. Fast and furious at first, then deliciously slow as they found their rhythm. Her lips were a mix of sweet and salty.

Angling her head for better access, he deepened the kiss and felt her crumple in his arms. As amazing as kissing her was, though, he needed to stop.

Dragging his lips off hers, he peppered her jaw and nose with soft kisses before meeting her eyes. Unmistakable love shone back at him.

Would she deny it?

Emily's fingertips brushed his waist, her thumbs settling on his stomach. Her electric touch made his senses go on high alert.

"Emily," he murmured, undeterred, "I love you. I know you love me too."

She blinked. "How do you know that?" Her voice was breathy and low. "What makes you so sure?"

"Because I see it in the smile you reserve only for me. I can tell from the way your eyes light up when I look at you." He brushed his thumb over her bottom lip, loving how it trembled at his touch. He focused on her mouth. "I hear it in your voice and feel it when our lips meet."

She shook her head, silky hair wrapping around her cheeks. Flattening her hands against his chest, she forced some distance. "It would never work."

"Because I'm an old man?" He chuckled nervously.

"No."

"Then why not? You've forgiven your parents. They know about Noah, so staying away from New York's a moot point. We can make a life here, Emily. Please say you will."

"I can't." A shadow crossed her face. "Noah."

"Noah's adorable, wonderful, and amazing. I love him as much as I love—"

"Your parents," she inserted, and he frowned.

"I was going to say—"

"I know. Noah loves you, too. He missed you so much while we were away." Her eyes shut for a second. She sighed. "Your parents would have a fit if they knew the truth. A woman with an illegitimate child? Imagine how that would go down in our circles."

Gathering both her hands in his, he squeezed them reassuringly. "Emily, my parents love you. They'd be thrilled if I brought you home as my fiancée. Do you know my sister got pregnant at sixteen? Were they disappointed? Sure, but they never ever judged her. Instead, they gave her and my niece all their love and support. Why would they treat you and Noah any differently?"

Skepticism showed in her expression. "She's their daughter."

"And they'd kill to have you as their daughter-in-law.

Trust me."

A myriad of emotions reflected in her eyes—doubt, fear, and anxiety appeared briefly until faith, love, and trust won out.

"I do," she whispered.

Releasing her hands and the breath he'd been holding, he backed up half a step and reached inside his jacket pocket. Dropping to one knee, he snapped the box lid open and held it out to her. "On that note—"

"Henry!" Emily's hands flew to her mouth. "What are you doing?"

"I love you, Emily Quinn. With all of my heart." He paused to clear his throat. "I think I fell in love with you the first second I laid eyes on you. I gave Adam such a hard time for saying he believed in love at first sight, but it happened to me too. I desperately want to be with you. Forever. I believe you're the woman God has for me."

Another beat and a deep breath. "I know it's fast, but will you marry me?"

When she didn't immediately respond, his heart sped up from a canter to a gallop. "I promise to spend the rest of my life loving you and Noah. And, if you let me, I want to adopt Noah as my son."

"Yes." Brushing away escaping tears, she nodded. "Yes, I will."

As he slipped the ring onto her third finger, tears pricked his eyes. Never could he have predicted this result when Britt arranged to meet him tonight.

He rose to embrace Emily, reveling in the warmth and joy of holding the woman he loved in his arms.

"I can't believe you said yes," he whispered in her ear. Drawing back, he gave her a teasing look. "Especially since you wouldn't even date me."

Her radiant smile fled. "Do you really want to remind me how spontaneous I've just been? Maybe I should—"

"Don't," he said in alarm. Then more gently, "Please, my darling. Please don't take it back. We can take it as slow as you like." Though, he wasn't so sure their mothers would agree.

"Maybe I should tell you…" she began again, this time with a flirty smile.

Keeping him in suspense, her fingers stroked his jaw, brushing over his rough skin until she leaned in close. As her mouth hovered over his, their breaths mingled, and his pulse skyrocketed. Finally, she planted a soft, tantalizing kiss on his lips. Though she eventually broke the kiss, he couldn't complain. Not when she gazed at him like he was her world.

The feeling was mutual.

"I love you, too, Henry Palmer." She punctuated each word with a kiss. "And I can't wait to be your wife."

Acknowledgments

I can't believe the New Haven series is complete! Each of these five books have been a labor of love, and I'm sad to say goodbye to the characters who've been part of my life for literally years.

As with any writing endeavor, there are others who have helped shape this story. Tamlyn—my friend and alpha reader—your constant encouragement, helpful suggestions, and honest critique were invaluable. Thank you for talking over plot points and helping me find solutions to those pesky plot holes. I'm so grateful for you!

Caitlin Miller—my brilliant editor—your edits are what made this story better. Thank you for your kind words and gentleness in steering me in the right direction. I couldn't do this without your wisdom and encouragement.

Krista Noorman—my fellow sweet romance author—your willingness to read my manuscript and point out non-American words and phrases is so appreciated. As is your friendship.

To my wonderful husband, thank you for giving me the freedom and space to write—I love you.

My ARC team and readers, thank you so much for giving up your valuable time on Her Secret! I hope you enjoyed reading it as much as I did writing it. I appreciate every one of you.

To my Heavenly Father, who has blessed me with every good gift in my life, I am forever grateful.

About the Author

Samantha J. Ball grew up in South Africa and moved to London, England as a young wife with a toddler. An accountant by qualification, she never thought she'd be a writer. Watching romcoms set in New York, listening to many a love song, and reading countless romances growing up inspired her to write her own stories. She has two beautiful grown-up daughters, and a gorgeous Tibetan Terrier. Other than writing, she loves long walks with her husband, curling up with a good romance book, watching movies, and serving in her local church.

You can learn more about Samantha and her books at www.samanthajball.com or by following her on Instagram or Facebook @authorsamanthajball.

Printed in Great Britain
by Amazon